LIKE CLOCKWORK

novelist, award-winning journalist, film director
hor, Margie Orford was born in London and
p in Namibia and South Africa. She lives in Cape
Like Clockwork is her first novel.

D1146423

LIKE
CLOCKWORK

Margie Orford

Atlantic Books
LONDON

First published in 2006 by Oshun Books, an imprint of Struik
Publishers (a division of New Holland Publishing (South Africa)
Pty Ltd).New Holland Publishing is a member of Johnnic
Communications Ltd.

This revised edition first published in hardback and export and
airside trade paperback in Great Britain in 2009 by Atlantic Books,
an imprint of Grove Atlantic Ltd.

This paperback edition published in Great Britain by
Atlantic Books in 2010.

1 3 5 7 9 10 8 6 4 2

A CIP catalogue record for this book is available from the
British Library.

ISBN: 978 1 84354 943 7

Typeset in Meridien by Ellipsis Books Limited, Glasgow

Printed in Great Britain by Clays Ltd, St Ives plc

Atlantic Books
An imprint of Grove Atlantic Ltd
Ormond House
26–27 Boswell Street
London WC1N 3JZ

www.atlantic-books.co.uk

For Andrew

PROLOGUE

The man watches the cigarette burning between the fingers of his right hand. The cuff of his silk shirt strains against his lean wrist, the cuff link glinting in the artificial light. Although the room is hidden at the centre of the house – a warren of rooms and passages – he hears the thud-thud of slammed car doors in the garage. He raises his head, close-cropped and scarred in places, and listens. He waits. He knows how long it will take. Then he uncoils himself from the leather chair. He walks to the door that slides open at a touch. This room and its records are not visible from anywhere. No one ever enters it.

Two strides take him to the room where they have brought the new consignment. She looks at him, terrified. He finds this provocative. He holds out his hand to the girl. Conditioned to politeness, confused, she gives him hers. He looks at it. Then he turns the palm – secret, pink – upwards. He looks into her eyes and smiles. He stubs the cigarette out in her hand.

'Welcome,' he says.

The girl watches her heart line, curving round the plump mound of her thumb, burn away. Her sharp, shocked intake of breath breaks the silence.

'What's your name?' he murmurs, smoothing her long hair behind her ear.

'I want to go home,' she whispers. 'Please.'

The man strokes the rounded chin, her soft throat. Then he turns and walks back to his office. He is used to power, there is no need to swagger. He knows that the girl will not take her eyes off him. He punches a number into his phone. The call is picked up at once.

'I have a little something for you. Fresh delivery. No, no other takers as yet.' He laughs, turning to watch as the girl is led out, before ending the call.

Many hours later, the girl sits huddled in the corner of a room, unaware of the unblinking eye of the camera watching her. She is alone, knees pulled tight into her body. A blanket, rough and filthy, is wrapped around her. Her clothes are gone. She shivers, cradling her hand in her lap, the fingers trying to find a way to lie that will not hurt the burnt pulp at the heart of her palm. Her skin is tattooed with the sensation of clawing hands, bruised from her brief resistance. She hugs her knees. The effort makes her whimper. She cringes at the sound, dropping her head, unable to think of a way of surviving this. And she is too filled with hatred to find a way to die. After a long time, she lifts her head.

Something that the camera does not see: to survive, she thinks of ways of killing.

The door opens. 'Dinner, sir,' announces the maid, transfixed by the image on the screen.

A finger on the remote and the bruised girl vanishes.

'Thank you,' says the host. He turns to his guests. 'This way, gentlemen.'

The maid gathers glasses and ashtrays after they have left the room. She switches off the lights and closes the door and goes downstairs to help serve the meal.

1

It was old Harry Rabinowitz, out for an early morning walk, who found the first body. Her throat had been precisely, meticulously sliced through. But that was not the first thing he noticed. She lay spreadeagled on the promenade in full view of anyone who cared to look. Her face was child-like in death, dark hair rippling in the breeze. Blood, pooled and dried in the corners of her eyes, streaked her right cheek like tears. Her exposed breasts gestured towards womanhood. One slender arm was lifted straight above her head; the fingers of the left hand were extended, like a supplicant's. The right hand – its fingers clenched – had been bound with blue rope, and rested on her hip.

A bouquet, just like a bride's, had been placed next to her. Later on, in the ensuing jostle of people approaching, then recoiling, the flowers were trampled, becoming part of the gutter debris.

He had stopped in shock next to the dead girl. The pounding of his heart deafened him. Darkness gathered in the periphery of his vision. He turned away from her and leant on the solid mass of the sea wall, gulping in the cold morning fog. He watched as a group of old women approached. He lifted his arm in a feeble effort to summon help. The women waved back. It was only when they were close to him that he could get them to stop waving and look at the dead girl. They flocked around the body.

Ruby Cohen had recognised Harry and scurried over to take his arm. 'You look terrible, Harry. Come and sit down.' She led him to an orange bench. He sat down, waiting for his heart to quieten, grateful to her. Ruby made sure that he was settled before returning to her friends.

'You call the ambulance,' Ruby ordered. 'I'm going to ask Dr Hart for help. There's her flat, next to the lighthouse.' Harry watched her stride off officiously.

More people arrived. Some, he noticed, gagged at the sight of the dead girl. Harry pulled his coat closed. When I'm not so cold, when I regain my strength, he thought to himself, I'll cover her.

2

Last night's chill seeped from the floor into Clare's bare feet despite the sunlight filtering through the window. But she was too lazy to go and fetch her slippers. The muted rush and retreat of the waves against the sea wall was comforting after the chaos of the storm that had spent itself an hour before dawn. As Fritz wound herself around Clare's legs, she tipped a heap of crumbles into the purring cat's bowl. The morning routine anchored her. She waited, watching the steam snaking up, her hand braced on the coffee plunger. The grounds formed a satisfying resistance to her hand as she pressed down firmly.

Clare poured the coffee and sat down at the table. Fritz leapt into her lap and purred, kneading her thighs rhythmically. The pain was pleasant. Clare stroked her and straightened the newspaper. She read the surfing report. She drank more coffee and read the weather forecast. It would be fine weather for the next few days.

It wasn't working, but Clare had learnt not to panic if she failed to keep herself in the present. She tried a different tack.

Shopping. She would go shopping. There was nothing to eat in her flat and she needed new towels. Clare picked up a pencil and started to make a list.

Sugar.

More coffee.

Loo paper.
Whiskey.
Fruit.
Soap.
Cat food.
Stockings.

Clare leaned forward so that the sun warmed her back. Surely she needed other things. She had been living out of a suitcase for so long that she had forgotten what was needed to run an orderly home. Milk, she added after a while. She couldn't think of anything else, so it was a relief when the phone rang. Clare picked it up, spilling the cat.

'Hi, Julie.'

'How do you always know it's me?' asked her sister.

'You're the only person who phones me so early.' Julie's voice filled the silence, its warmth chasing Clare's shadows back into their corners.

'What are you doing?'

'I'm making a shopping list.'

'You *are* being domestic,' said Julie.

'I'm trying,' said Clare. 'I felt so out of whack from being away from home for such a long time. Fritz is only just starting to speak to me again.'

'We saw your documentary last night,' Julie remarked. 'Have you seen the review in this morning's paper?'

'I haven't,' Clare replied, turning to the arts pages. '"Clare Hart",' she read aloud, '"award-winning journalist, investigates the implosion of the eastern Congo." Blah, blah.'

'Come on, Clare, don't be like that. At least you got it out there.'

Clare scanned the article. 'Look at it, Julie. It doesn't even mention that the peacekeepers there are exchanging food aid for sex. That is not even a blip on the scandal radar.'

'I know, but at least you're putting the war into the public eye again.'

'I don't think people can tell the difference between a documentary and reality television any more,' said Clare. 'What makes me ashamed is how intense the pleasure to be had from power is. And when you have a camera you have power, pure and simple.'

'It's your work, Clare, it's what you do,' said Julie. 'I'm not going to try and persuade you that you're the best again. So tell me something else. How was your surfing lesson?'

'Brilliant,' said Clare. 'Absolutely terrifying, but brilliant. I stood up for at least ten seconds. I've booked again for this weekend. You must let me take Imogen with me. How is she, by the way?'

'She's fine, I think. Quiet, but fine. Hard to tell with sixteen-year-olds,' said Julie. Clare was close to her niece, but Julie did not always think that she was the best chaperone.

'How's Beatrice doing?' Clare heard an enraged bellow. 'Right on cue,' she laughed. Beatrice was four, and steadfastly refused to compromise.

'Oh, God, here we go,' said Julie. 'She'll only wear purple at the moment and everything purple is wet. Poor Marcus is trying to persuade her that pink is as good as purple.'

'Judging by the noise, he's failing miserably,' Clare laughed.

'Utterly,' said Julie. She closed her kitchen door and the noise was suddenly muffled. 'Tell me about this new project of yours.'

'The story about human trafficking?' asked Clare.

'That's the one,' said Julie. 'Did you get the go-ahead?'

'Not yet. I did get a scrap of research money so I'm ferreting anyway,' said Clare.

'Be careful, Clare,' Julie warned. 'Investigating those guys is like poking a wasp's nest.'

'I am careful,' said Clare. There was a crash and Beatrice was shouting at her mother. She sounded apoplectic. 'Jules, I can hardly hear you.'

'That's because I didn't say anything,' said Julie. 'What you heard was a disbelieving silence.'

'I'm going for a run now, Julie. Can I call you later?'

'*Ja*, I want to see you,' said Julie. 'I want to hear more.'

The phone was dead before Clare could say goodbye. Clare stepped out onto her balcony to stretch. It was cold despite the sunshine so she pulled on her sweatshirt. A decade of running had earned her a lean, supple fitness that still surprised her.

The summons of her doorbell was intrusive. She went inside. 'Yes?' she asked, irritated. The intercom stuttered. Clare could not make out what was being said. 'Hold on,' she said. 'I'm on my way out.' She picked up her keys and cellphone and locked up. Two leaps took her to the bottom of her stairs but there was no longer anyone outside her door. It must have been an early-morning beggar. She was about to break into an easy lope when an old woman called to her from an eddy of people on the promenade along Beach Road.

'Over here, Dr Hart. Help!' It was Ruby Cohen. Clare's heart sank. Clare's single status offended Ruby's sense of order, as did her refusal to join the Neighbourhood Watch.

'Morning, Ruby,' she said. 'What is it?'

'Dr Hart. It's terrible. Come see. That poor girl is dead.'

Clare saw the body lying on the promenade. A dead body was not that unusual in Cape Town. Ports discard human flotsam, and last night had certainly been cold enough to take a vagrant off before receding with the morning sun. The crowd pressed together, as if to reassure each other that they were alive. Clare went over, wondering if it was one of the homeless who sheltered nearby.

8

The dead girl froze the blood in Clare's veins. A lock of the girl's black hair lifted briefly in the wind, then settled onto a thin brown shoulder. Clare was slipping back into her nightmare. It took an immense exercise of will to bring herself back to the present. To this body. Here. Today. Then her mind made the switch to trained observer, and all emotion was gone. She scanned the placement of the body, logging each detail with forensic precision.

She noted the faint marks on the bare arms, bruises that had not had time to bloom. The girl's right hand was bound, transformed into a bizarre fetish. It had been placed coquettishly on her hip. Something protruded from the girl's hand, glinting in the low-angled sunlight. Her boots were so high that she would have struggled to walk. But she was not going anywhere: not with her slender throat severed.

Clare instinctively switched on the camera of her cellphone and snapped a rapid series of pictures, ignoring the indignant whispers around her. She zoomed in on the girl's hands, but an old man stepped forward and covered the girl before Clare could stop him, separating the whispering living from the dead. The message encrypted in the broken, displayed body was obscured.

Clare stepped away, flicked open her cellphone and dialled. She willed him to answer. 'Riedwaan,' she said, 'you've heard about the body found in Sea Point?'

'We just had the call,' he answered, his voice neutral. 'There is a patrol car coming with the ambulance.'

'You should come, Riedwaan.' She could sense his reluctance. She hadn't called him since she had been back and here she was phoning him because someone had been murdered. 'There is nothing straightforward here.'

'What?' he asked. Clare looked back at the small coat-covered mound. The sight of the slim, lifeless legs made her voice catch in her throat. 'It's too neat, Riedwaan, too arranged. And there's no blood. It doesn't look to me like an argument over price that went wrong.'

'Okay, I'll be there,' said Riedwaan. He trusted Clare's instincts. Her work as a profiler was hard to fault, despite her unorthodox methods. His voice softened. 'How are you, Clare? We've missed you.'

Clare heard, but she did not reply. She snuffed the emotion that flared in her heart and snapped her phone closed. The morning felt even colder.

There was nothing more she could do. Clare forced herself to run. She had no need to hover and see what would happen to the girl's body. She already knew. Clare ran for three kilometres before the rhythm of her feet on the paving dislodged the image of the dead girl from her mind.

She tried to lose herself in the noise of the pounding surf. Clare didn't want to think of the dead girl on her pavement, but her thoughts returned to her, like a tongue probing an aching tooth. Half an hour later she looped back home along the promenade. Riedwaan's car was parked next to the taped-off area around the girl's body. The body was in good hands now.

Inspector Riedwaan Faizal's taste for vengeance had given him a nose for the killers of young girls. Clare resisted the pull to go up to Riedwaan. And he had not seen her on the edge of the crowd, so she went home. Once inside her flat, Clare showered then grabbed a top, trousers, a jacket and scarf with the swift certainty of a woman who owns good clothes and knows how to dress. The local radio station was already carrying the first reports of this morning's gruesome offering. By this afternoon, headlines about the murder would be plastered all over the city's lamp posts.

Clare switched off the newsreader's voice and sat down at

her desk. She looked out of the window. The view of the sea restored her equilibrium, and after a while she was able to turn her attention to her own work. Clare pulled a bulging file towards herself. She had scrawled 'Human Trafficking in Cape Town' in gold down its spine. She had found that women lured from South Africa's troubled northern neighbours were being pimped along Main Road, Cape Town's endless red light district bisecting the affluent suburbs huddled at the base of the Table Mountain. The women also stocked the brothels and the plethora of gentlemen's clubs. The trade was increasingly organised. Clare was preparing herself for an interview that had required delicate negotiation to arrange. Natalie Mwanga had been trafficked from the Congo and she was risking a great deal by speaking to Clare.

Clare's investigation was not making her any new friends. She had had to persuade her producer far away in safe London to let her 'feature' a trafficker in the documentary. It was a risky proposition and she needed more time. Clare had put out feelers before she had gone to the Congo two months earlier. On her return she had heard that Kelvin Landman might talk to her. He had been pimping since he was fifteen. Clare could not verify the rumour that it had started with his ten-year-old sister. Landman, one of her police sources had told her, had moved rapidly up the ranks of a street gang. He was a man with vision, though, and the porousness of South Africa's post-democracy borders had been a licence for Landman to print money. His name had become synonymous with trafficking for the sex industry. And Landman ruthlessly punished any transgression of his rules.

Clare had once asked a young street prostitute how Landman worked. The girl pointed to two long, light scars across her soft belly. Punishment for a careless pregnancy. She then told Clare that the baby had been aborted and she had been working again the next day. She'd laughed when Clare asked for an interview, and then wandered away. Clare had not seen her again.

She looked out at the sea again. Mist was rolling in, blotting out the morning's early promise.

Trafficking was risk free for the trafficker, that was clear enough, and it generated a lot of cash. Lately, Landman had become notorious for insinuating himself into the highest echelons of business and politics. He had even been profiled as a 'man about town' by a respectable Sunday paper. Clare pulled out a clean sheet of notepaper and jotted down her questions.

Where did the cash go?

How was it made legitimate?

If Landman was selling, who was buying?

What were they buying?

She would find out. But the dead girl on the promenade surfaced unbidden in her thoughts. Clare stood up abruptly. She needed to get out, to be with people. She picked up her shopping list and headed for the Waterfront. As she drove, she thought she might add a few things to the list she'd made earlier.

Smoked salmon.

Wine.

Maybe some washing-up liquid.

3

Riedwaan Faizal had stared straight ahead of him after Clare's call, his phone open in his hand. He could picture her as clearly as if she were in front of him. She was brilliant and obsessive, but difficult to work with. She didn't like teams, she didn't trust anybody. Her relationship with the law was flexible, although right and wrong for Clare were absolutes. These were not things that bothered Riedwaan. It was Clare herself who got under his skin. He needed her, like a man needed water. He put his phone back in his pocket and stood up. Being with her was like being thirsty all the time and never knowing if you would get a drink. The minute you thought you had her, she slipped away. The one time she had reached out for him he had turned away. Nothing could change that, so he shrugged the thought away.

Riedwaan turned his attention to the dead girl instead. She had not been ID'd yet, but he was sure it was the girl who had been reported missing since Friday. Today was Tuesday. He did not want to think about what had happened to her in the intervening four days. But he was going to have to. He finished his coffee and picked up his keys. This was going to be awkward. The case officer was Frikkie Bester simply because he had answered the call. He had already opened a docket and he was not going to be pleased to have Riedwaan

Faizal on his turf. But the station commander, who was generally pissed off at having been landed with Riedwaan, had been very happy to assign him to the case. Riedwaan knew Phiri well enough by now: by giving Riedwaan the case there was at least a hope in hell that it would be solved. And if it wasn't, then there was his record of insubordination and alcohol and violence to wheel out. At least Phiri had volunteered to call Bester himself.

Riedwaan's battered Mazda coughed into life long enough to drive the three blocks to where Harry Rabinowitz had found the dead girl. There was a press of people around the taped-off area where the body lay. He could see Bester on his phone, bull neck distended with rage. That would be Phiri, thought Riedwaan, telling Bester that Riedwaan was in charge. Bester stalked over to Riedwaan, flinging his folder at him.

'Good luck, Faizal. I hope you stay sober long enough to work out which bastard did this.' Riedwaan straightened the papers in the file and said nothing. A *klap* from Bester was not something you wanted to provoke.

'Thanks, Frikkie.' He saw the man twitch at the use of his first name. Riedwaan suppressed a smile. Words could be powerful sometimes. He opened the docket to check it was in order. 'Looks perfect. Thanks.' He ducked under the tape, and did not flinch at the sight of the splayed girl discarded on the pavement. He bent down next to her.

'Who covered her?' he asked.

'The old guy who found her,' a young constable answered. Her name tag stretched across her breast pocket: Rita Mkhize.

'Shit!' muttered Riedwaan. He removed the coat and handed it to the constable. 'Bag that.' Then he snapped his phone open and made the calls he needed to. The photography unit was on their way. He looked at the knife wound to her throat. The force of it had all but decapitated her. He put a call through to ballistics. They would work out what knife had been used if there were grooves in the bones. And if they found the weapon to match the wound then he would be one step closer to catching the killer.

Riedwaan looked around. He could predict within seconds who had killed a victim. With female victims it was usually the husband or a boyfriend. He was willing to bet that this was a stranger killing. The body had been arranged. There was a message here, but it was written in a language he had yet to decipher. Riedwaan guessed she had been killed elsewhere and dumped here. He would wait for the forensic pathologist to tell him that: he was a cautious man despite his reputation. He called Piet Mouton.

'Howzit, Doc. Riedwaan here. Are you on your way?' He heard Mouton's low laugh.

'Jeez, no wonder they call you Super-cop. You must catch these guys all the time. Turn around.'

Riedwaan turned to find the shabby, plump figure of the forensic pathologist right behind him. Riedwaan laughed. 'Doctor Death and his bag of tricks. I'm glad it's you.'

'What have we got here?' asked Mouton. He looked down at the dead girl. 'Where is that idiot Riaan?' he asked, looking around for the police photographer who was smoking and trying to flirt with Constable Mkhize. 'Come and do your job and leave that poor girl alone. You're so ugly you'll frighten her!' called Mouton.

Riaan Nelson sauntered over with his camera. 'What you want for your necrophilia collection this time, Doc?' Mouton told him what to photograph. He was meticulous, and he knew his photographs were essential to Mouton and to Riedwaan. And to this dead girl, in the end. Piet Mouton sketched the girl while Riaan worked. A defence lawyer would pounce on one imprecise line on his autopsy report if it ever came to trial.

Mouton checked all around the body. There were two Marlboros very close to her; one was smoked down to the filter, the other had been stubbed out when it was half smoked. He bagged them.

'Hard to tell with these, but we can give it a try. If there is other DNA on the body, then maybe we can do a match.'

Riedwaan stood close by, listening to Mouton. He was a fussy, shy man and he muttered away to himself while he worked a crime scene. Riedwaan had long since learned to stick close and glean everything he could.

'Look here.' Mouton swabbed a streak on her stomach, 'Could be semen.' There was some of the same substance on the skirt too. He collected and labelled it.

Mouton was satisfied that he had enough photographs now. He told Riaan, and the photographer packed his bags and was circling Rita Mkhize before Mouton could close his clipboard.

'She wasn't killed here, Riedwaan. I'll check during the post-mortem but I would say she was killed somewhere else and dumped here.'

'How long has she been dead, Doc?'

Mouton put his head on one side. The girl was cold and stiff. 'Hard to say until I do the temp with a body probe. But at a guess I'd say between eight and thirty-six hours. I don't think more than that. Once I start with the post-mortem, I'll also be able to give you a better idea about when she was moved.'

Mouton picked up the girl's hand and took a scrape from under her fingernails. He did a vaginal swab, too, bagging both of these and handing them to Riedwaan.

'Did you have to do that here, Doc?'

Mouton pulled the girl's short skirt down. 'Man, you are getting soft. It's hard to argue with evidence that's gathered before the body has been moved. Whoever did this to her took her dignity with her life. Don't you lose those, you fucker. You take that straight to the lab at Delft. And make them sign for it in their own blood.'

Riedwaan did not answer. He had seen enough rapists laugh into their victim's faces as they walked free. It just took one break in the chain of evidence – be it specimen or statement – and a clever defence lawyer would have a paedophile waiting for his little girl of choice by tea break. There was no way that this evidence would be out of his sight for one second.

Mouton leaned in close and looked at the slash across her throat. 'This is very high up,' he said. 'It's like he was trying to cut out her tongue. Like he wanted to do a Colombian Necktie, but didn't have the strength. Very sharp blade that he used, very sharp. Maybe a scalpel.'

'Look at her eyes, Doc. Surely she hasn't been dead long enough for that to happen,' said Riedwaan. The girl's eyes had sunken in. Mouton reached over and lifted an eyelid.

'*Ja*,' he said, 'he cut her.' He pointed to the incisions that formed a cross on the cornea. 'The eyeball is just a ball of gel. Make a hole in it like this guy did, and the eyeball will collapse.'

'When was she mutilated?'

'The hand while she was alive. You can see it from the crusted blood. Her throat – that was done after she died. Look here, there is no blood to speak of.'

'The eyes?' asked Riedwaan.

'Just before she died. Maybe as he killed her.'

Riedwaan shivered. 'I hate to imagine what she saw that needed to be removed so viciously.'

The mortuary van arrived. The mortuary technicians brought their stretcher around to pick her up. 'You ready, Doc?' asked the driver. Mouton nodded. The assistant was hardly older than the murdered girl. The boy struggled to stop his hands from shaking as he lifted her body. Mouton looked at the place where she had lain, but it had not been there long enough for any fluids to seep out.

'You coming to the post-mortem?' asked Mouton.

'You're doing it right now?' asked Riedwaan.

'*Ja*,' said Mouton. 'I've got a feeling this is going to get hot.' He looked back at the van. 'I don't think she's going to be your last either. I worked on the PMs when they were looking for that killer who was into bondage in KwaZulu-Natal. That girl didn't look like a once-off to me.'

'Don't jump to conclusions, Doc. They can lead you astray.'

The pathologist gave him a withering look. 'Are you coming or not?'

'*Ja*, I'll be there. I've just got to drop this stuff off at the lab. I'll be with you in an hour.' Riedwaan walked with Mouton to his car. 'Can I bring someone?'

'Who?' asked Mouton.

'Clare Hart. I'm thinking of getting her to do the profile for me. If you're right then we'll need one. She's worked with me before.'

Mouton put his hand on Riedwaan's shoulder. 'That's a strange way to pull women, Riedwaan, even for you. But if she's not in the police force, no way. You can tell her everything later. You can show her all the pictures if you can persuade her to go to dinner with you. But nobody who doesn't need to be there gets to watch my show.' Mouton opened his car and wedged his stomach behind the wheel. 'Jesus, man, I've got to lose some weight.'

'I'll see you back at the station,' Riedwaan called to Frikkie Bester, who pretended not to hear. Riedwaan shrugged. Not much he could do about trampled egos even if he had wanted to. He climbed into his own car, putting the swabs and samples down as if they were Ming porcelain. It was a pity Clare couldn't be at the PM but there was no way he would get Mouton to change his mind. He headed for the lab in Delft and handed over the samples. He was glad it was Anna Scheepers who took the case. She was meticulous about her evidence and brilliant in court. Riedwaan had seen her impale enough lawyers, lulled into complacency by the volume of her hair and the length of her legs, with her expertise in the arcane science of DNA testing.

On the way there he called Clare. She didn't answer, but he left a message asking if she would profile for him. She was the best there was. And he knew that he wanted an excuse to see her. Maybe this time he would fuck up less badly.

By the time Riedwaan headed for the northern suburbs hospital where Mouton presided like Orpheus in his basement laboratory, the last of the morning traffic had dribbled off the highways and his way was clear, delivering him to his destination sooner than he would have wished.

Riedwaan was not looking forward to the rest of the morning. Mouton supervised swarms of students, and they would be in full swing on the other trolleys while Mouton dissected 'his' girl. Mouton had phoned the ballistics experts and two of them were standing around discussing blades and angles, waiting for Mouton to get to the neck vertebrae to see what the marks on those delicate bones would tell them.

4

Riedwaan arrived back at the station late in the morning. He was about to sit down when Rita Mkhize put her head around the door.

'Superintendent Phiri wants to see you, Captain Faizal. He's in his office.'

'Thanks, Rita,' said Riedwaan. He felt her eyes on his back as he walked down the corridor towards Phiri's office. He was wondering why he was being summoned. He knocked on the door.

'Enter!' His commanding officer's affected military air never failed to irritate him. Phiri's desk was compulsively tidy. Riedwaan thought of his own warren of papers, files and dirty cups and was relieved that Phiri had not sought him out there.

'You wanted to see me, sir?' asked Riedwaan.

Phiri pointed to a chair. 'Sit down, Faizal.' Riedwaan sat and waited, the autopsy report clutched to his chest. 'How did it go with Frikkie Bester?' he asked.

'Thanks for phoning him, sir,' said Riedwaan. 'I don't think that he is too happy about me taking over. But he was okay. He didn't *klap* me, at least.'

Phiri put his arms on his desk and leaned towards Riedwaan. 'We go back a long way, don't we, Faizal?' Riedwaan nodded.

'I'm giving you a second chance here, so don't fuck it up. Is that clear?'

'Yes, sir,' said Riedwaan. Phiri eyed him. Riedwaan thought he was going to say something more, but he didn't. Instead he held his hand out for the preliminary autopsy report. Riedwaan handed it over, summarising Piet Mouton's preliminary findings. 'The scene was too carefully arranged for it to be a random killing. It doesn't look as if she was raped, or even that she'd had intercourse recently. No boyfriend, as far as we know. She was missing since Friday but Piet is pretty sure she died on Monday night – about twelve or so hours before she was found. We know she wasn't killed there. Someone took a big risk leaving her where he did.'

Phiri nodded, listening as he went through the report. 'I got a message that you wanted Clare Hart on your team?' Phiri closed the report and handed it back to Riedwaan. 'Why?'

'She's the best, sir,' Riedwaan replied.

'What makes you think you've got a serial killer here, Faizal? All you have is one body. Could be a once-off. She was in the wrong place at the wrong time.'

'With respect, sir, I don't think so.' Riedwaan chose his words. He knew what Phiri was afraid of. One whiff of another serial killer and the press would be circling like vultures.

'You think there'll be another one?' asked Phiri.

'Let's put it this way: I wouldn't be surprised if there is another one. Or if there have been other girls killed like this that we haven't heard about . . . yet.'

Phiri rubbed his eyes. It was two o'clock and he felt worn out. 'So why Clare?' he persisted.

'This is her area, sir. Femicide and sex crimes.' Riedwaan pointed to the bookshelf behind Phiri's desk. 'There's her doctorate.' *Crimes against Women in Post-Apartheid South Africa* was on the top shelf, its pages dog-eared and its margins filled

21

with question marks and comments in Phiri's precise hand.

'It's very good, meticulously researched,' conceded Phiri. 'But I'm not sure I agree that because we averted a civil war in South Africa that the "unspent violence was sublimated into a war against women. A war in which there are no rules and no limits", as she argues whenever she gets the chance.'

'It's not her fault, sir, that brutality against women and children is intensifying while conviction rates are falling.' Phiri was amused at how awkward the jargon sounded coming from Riedwaan Faizal, who went on to argue, 'She's profiled for the police since 1994, and she's been very successful.'

'She pisses off everybody she works with,' Phiri argued.

'Maybe because she's a woman and she's good.'

'Bullshit, Faizal. It's because she's a loner and she does what she wants.' Phiri looked at Riedwaan, then he laughed. 'That's why you like her, I suppose.'

Riedwaan smiled. 'Whatever her faults, you know she's the best, sir.'

'I'm going to get shit about that last case you two worked on.'

Riedwaan felt the old anger again. He and Clare had worked on a series of abductions. They had built an excellent case against a gangster who abducted homeless girls of between eight and thirteen for his brothels. But two witnesses had been murdered and the others withdrew their statements. DNA evidence was contaminated, and then a whole docket disappeared. The case collapsed, taking their tentative investigation with it.

'That wasn't her fault,' he said, the anger filtering through into his voice. 'That was because of someone inside. Dockets don't just walk.'

'Some people say a docket can get lost if the person

22

looking after it drinks too much. And when he doesn't sleep at home.'

Riedwaan suppressed his anger. 'What is the decision, sir?'

'Like I said, Riedwaan. Last chance.'

Riedwaan looked at Phiri. 'Last chance with Clare, too?'

Phiri nodded. 'Last chance, Faizal, all round.'

'Thank you, sir.' Riedwaan stood up to leave, the autopsy report in his hands.

He was about to open the door when Phiri spoke again. 'You catch him, Riedwaan. Not a word to the press yet. They will be on to this one like a ton of bricks.'

Riedwaan turned and looked at him. He didn't want journalists hounding him again either. 'Yes, sir.' Riedwaan pulled the door shut behind him.

Phiri stared after him. If Riedwaan needed Clare Hart's assistance, then good luck to him. And Phiri hoped that the killer, whoever he was, would still be fit for trial after Riedwaan had caught him.

5

Riedwaan threw the autopsy report onto his desk, ignoring Rita Mkhize's stare. He hadn't shaved that morning and he didn't look his best. The previous day, while Piet Mouton had taken blood, scraped fingernails and taken more swabs, he had waited and watched for any new bruises to bloom, but they hadn't. Mouton carefully cut open the body to remove and weigh the dead girl's organs, reading from them how she had lived while searching out the secrets of her death.

'Who is she?' asked Rita.

'Charnay Swanepoel. She was seventeen years old and in her last year of school. She also had a family. One younger brother. Parents alive, but separated. Father an auto-parts salesman who watched rugby on Saturdays. The mother a yoga teacher, New Age seeker, spiritual guide.' Riedwaan read from the file.

As mismatched as me and Shazia were, thought Riedwaan, sipping his coffee. Shazia was a nurse – and his wife. She had moved to Canada and taken their daughter, Yasmin, with her. Shazia was convinced that the distance, the safety, of Canada would erase the terror etched into their daughter during the endless hours she had been a hostage. Riedwaan had heard her voice. Her kidnappers had called the gang hotline Riedwaan had established for informers, recording Yasmin's terrified six-year-old pleas to her daddy to find her, for her mommy to come, for a drink of water, please, please. Riedwaan had not been able to prove it, but only Kelvin Landman had such a genius for cruelty. It had made him the Cape Flats' ultimate hard man.

Riedwaan returned to his desk and opened the folder. The smiling school portrait that Charnay's mother had given him in return for informing her of her daughter's murder smiled up at him.

'Here's a piece of cake for you,' said Rita.

'Just what I needed. Thanks, Rita,' he said, 'it's as sweet as you are.'

'That gender sensitivity course you were sent on is doing wonders,' laughed Rita.

She hovered next to his desk. 'What you got, Riedwaan?'

'I talked to her father yesterday. Chris Swanepoel. He sat the whole fucking Saturday watching rugby while his daughter was being murdered. You tell me how he did that?'

'I don't know, Riedwaan. But you know how people can panic. It freezes them. They just pretend nothing is happening and hope it will go away.'

'He told me he didn't want to make a mistake and report her missing to the police, and then she comes home with a *babalaas* or something.'

'*Eish*,' murmured Rita. 'When did they report her missing?'

'On Sunday. He says that when she wasn't home by lunchtime he started to look for her. Looked for her everywhere. That's when they reported her missing. Three days later.'

'Poor man,' said Rita. 'He must feel so terrible.'

'Your heart's too soft, Rita. You should have been a social worker, not in the police. I'm going to check out every move he made.' For Riedwaan, fathers – like boyfriends – were always suspects.

'What more could he have done, Riedwaan?'

'Found her. Alive. Reported it earlier.'

Rita looked at him and shook her head. 'You're a hard man, Riedwaan.' She went out, leaving him to his thoughts.

How could Swanepoel have failed to find his own daughter? Riedwaan had traced Yasmin to an abandoned warehouse by the faint signal emitted by the cellphone of the gangsters holding her, terrified that his discovery would be relayed through the metastasising web of gang informers and corrupt policemen. So he had gone in alone, and executed Yasmin's kidnappers as they dozed undisturbed by the little girl's desperate whimpering. Riedwaan had wiped his hysterical child clean of the blood spattered over her. But Yasmin still woke from her nightmares convinced that she was bathed in it. Riedwaan had found Yasmin, but as Shazia began telling him more and more frequently, that did not mean he had succeeded. There had been an investigation. The specialised and ruthless anti-gang squad he had established was dissolved. But community outrage at the rising number of child corpses in the latest bout of gang warfare had made it impossible to either charge or fire Faizal. His maverick justice had made him a community hero, so the best they could do was to shunt him sideways. He was posted to Sea Point, given a desk job and a pile of papers to shuffle. It was designed to make him fail – and he had. Shazia had begged him to leave the force but he refused. She then approached the Canadian embassy, filled in the form, and was gone. Just before the plane swallowed them, Yasmin had turned to wave at where she guessed he would be watching. A small, dark girl with a pink bag and memories Canadian children would not understand. He thought of calling Yasmin, but she would be asleep in Toronto. Her mother – still his wife, damn it – would fumble for her alarm clock, smoothing her long twist of black hair on top of her head. Unless she had since cut it, of course.

Riedwaan took a sip of his coffee. It was cold and bitter. He turned his attention back to the manila folder in front of him. He spread out the photographs that Riaan had taken at the crime scene. His stomach knotted. He couldn't save this girl, but he was going to make sure that whoever had done this to her paid in full. Then he thumbed a different number into his phone, imagining the rings slicing through the silence. Clare picked up her phone. She was startled, he could tell – she'd have been busy working, and had obviously forgotten to switch the phone off.

'Yes,' she said, annoyed with herself for answering.

'Clare, it's Riedwaan.' He paused, listening to her silence. His image of her was vivid – at her desk, papers, books, notes spread around her, laptop open, thick hair snaking between her sharp shoulder blades. Wing bones, she called them.

'Hello,' she said. What else was there to say?

'I have the preliminary report on that girl you called me about. I thought you might like to have a look.' Riedwaan waited.

'Okay,' Clare said. She wanted to ask why, but didn't. That would come later. 'New York Bagel, at six.' She hung up and took a deep breath. Thinking of him made her throat tighten. Talking to him made the skin around her nipples taut. If she ignored the feeling, she told herself, it would go away. She would meet him for coffee. He would slip her the autopsy report, some phone numbers, and that would be it. Yes, she told herself. That is what would happen. She would gather up the papers, do some interviews, send him the transcripts, give her opinion on who had committed the murder, Riedwaan would catch the killer, and that would be that. Clare reactivated her sleeping laptop. She needed a few more hours before her trafficking proposal would be ready to send. She would fit Riedwaan into the interstices of her busy working days as she did sleeping and running. This time, though, she would keep a proper perspective.

It was much later when her eyes drifted from her screen, her ears tuning out the hiss of her computer finding an Internet connection. Drifts of street rubbish eddied upwards, and dropped again. Her email sent, she shut down her computer. She decided to walk. It would give her time to compose herself before she saw him. She walked briskly to keep warm, the sky turning bleak as the sun set.

6

The restaurant Clare had chosen was a determined outpost in a creeping strip of hostess bars, peepshows and poolrooms. Muscled men leaned on barstools at the entrances of the strip clubs and adult entertainment centres with their blackened windows. Furtive, part-time street prostitutes, full-time junkies, loitered inside doorways, smoking, waiting. Riedwaan watched through the window. He saw a girl he did not recognise dart towards a potential customer. She looked fifteen under her amateur make-up. He knew there would be track marks creeping from the fold inside the elbow towards her wrist. The girl recoiled when the man spat at her. Riedwaan looked at his watch. Six o'clock. Clare was always on time. He looked down Main Road and watched her walk towards him, her stride easy, strong.

Clare walked faster, as most women did, when she went past the clubs. She ignored the speculative eyes of the bouncers who looked her over and then lost interest. She looked up, not towards Riedwaan but towards the crumbling art deco block across the road. The building was as notorious for its dealers as it was for the waves of desperate immigrants who crammed in there. They paid cash on the first day of each month to hard-eyed men who extorted ever larger amounts. Riedwaan had heard that the building had been sold. Nothing had changed, though. It didn't need to. It was a gold mine. You could get anything you wanted there, women, children – even infants – if you could pay. The police force was not going to do anything about it: anyone who tried ended up dead, or shafted. Like him.

Clare came in and unbuttoned her coat. She knew to look for him in the smoking section. She picked up a tray, two coffees, hot milk, a bagel for Riedwaan, and a croissant for herself. She exchanged the tray for the envelope that Riedwaan passed her with his greeting. She didn't kiss him. Sitting down, she scanned the report. Her stomach knotted at the pathologist's dry abbreviations of the horror of Charnay Swanepoel's death, the brevity of her life. There was a note to say that further pharmacology test results were pending.

'When did he cut her throat?' asked Clare.

'She was dead when he cut her throat,' said Riedwaan.

'Any maggots?'

'No,' said Riedwaan. He put down his bagel. 'But the weather's been cold. Mouton reckons that she was killed between Sunday night and midnight on Monday. She was dead at least eight hours before she was dumped.'

'Any indication where she was mutilated?'

'Could have been done there. Mouton thinks a very sharp knife or, more likely, a scalpel. The throat, that is. There was a small amount of leaked fluid on the collar of her shirt. Mouton thinks that he did her eyes before he cut her throat.'

'Same kind of weapon?'

'He's waiting for the ballistics report, but most probably yes.'

'The eyes?' asked Clare.

'Look on page four. Mouton says just before he smothered her.'

'So she was alive. How horrible. I wonder what she saw, what he showed her to make him do that.'

'We'd better find out before somebody else sees what she did,' said Riedwaan, hunting for his cigarettes.

Clare stared briefly at her untouched croissant. Then she returned to the secrets that Charnay's body might answer. Seventeen years old, wearing a skirt and top, high-heeled boots. No underwear. All her own teeth, six fillings. Appendix scar. Not a virgin. Not a needle user. Menstruating at the time of death. Bruising on the upper arms and thighs.

Riedwaan was smoking at the window. 'Sorry, Clare,' he said, waving his hands at the smoke.

'It's okay,' she said. 'Reading this makes me want one too.'

She looked down and continued reading. One tattoo on the left buttock – a symbol, not a picture of anything. Recent – maybe two weeks old – but healing.

'Any idea where she might have had the tattoo done?' she asked Riedwaan.

'Not sure yet. It's very distinctive, that mark.'

'What is it?' Clare asked. She studied the photograph. The tattoo was simple, elegant. Two decisive vertical lines bisected by an X.

'Dunno. Looks like a Chinese ideogram.'

'It's beautiful, in its sinister way. It's hard to tell with the scabbing, but it looks like a symbol. Can we ask Mouton to get an exact shape from the body?'

'I'll ask him,' said Riedwaan.

Clare went back to her reading. An incision across the left palm. Mouton had confirmed that it was done before death. Done with a very sharp knife across the hand that held a key. This hand had been intricately bound. Whoever had done it was skilled at bondage. The blood had crusted over the key, which had had to be prised loose. Blood group: A positive. Charnay's blood. Traces of ink under the blood where she had written a number or a name. These were very faint and

MARGIE ORFORD

it was not possible for the pathologist to decipher anything. Some genital trauma, hard to say how recent, no sign of semen in the body. Does not rule out the use of an object. Traces of semen on her clothes. Possible that her killer had masturbated to celebrate his achievement. It had been wiped clean but traces remained on the skirt. Also possible that it had been there before. Signs too of bruising on the right cheek. A cut next to the corner of the eye. Most likely an open-handed blow by a man wearing a ring. The soles of her feet were dirty inside the high-heeled boots. As if she had been walking without shoes. Toenails painted, fingernails not. Stomach empty. Traces of vomit in her mouth. Cause of death: suffocation.

Clare put the pages back into the envelope and slipped it into her bag.

'I couldn't bring the photos,' said Riedwaan. 'But I will let you know when we get the toxicology results. The ballistics tests are not conclusive about the scalpel or knife. Something very sharp, at any rate. She did struggle. Piet found some skin under her nails. But it looks like her efforts were feeble. Piet Mouton is sure that she was drugged when she was killed. Rohypnol or something like it.'

'That's typical, though,' said Clare. 'Rohypnol makes the victim confused and acquiescent. If they survive they won't remember. The survival instinct kicks in if your life is threatened with death.'

'Hence the bruising,' said Riedwaan. 'Piet says she was suffocated. The killer used his hands. There were tears on the lips. Her own teeth marked her lips too, so he used a fair amount of strength.'

Clare looked at the picture of the slender girl. 'Her throat was cut after she died? Why?'

Riedwaan nodded. 'That's your department, Clare. Why

32

would he want to silence someone who was already dead? Try and find out what she knew. It might not have any relevance, but it's something to start with.' Riedwaan handed her a slip of paper. An address and phone number were written on it. 'Her family,' he said. 'Call them. Talk to them. See what you can find out.'

'Have they been interviewed?' asked Clare.

'Of course,' said Riedwaan. 'You can read the transcripts.' He handed her another envelope.

'All right,' said Clare. 'What are you looking for?'

Riedwaan shrugged. 'I don't know. Just a feeling. The interviews didn't go that well.' He did not need to explain. Clare knew how short the station was on everything – staff, vehicles, computers. Unless there was another murder, the case would not get any additional resources.

'I'm doing an interview for my trafficking documentary tomorrow.' Clare stopped short. Then she stood up, putting on her coat, suddenly clumsy.

Riedwaan got up too. He put his hand on her arm, steadying her. 'Let me give you a lift home,' he said, his voice gentle despite himself.

Clare leaned towards him, his warmth. 'Yes, please.'

He could smell her hair, warm and alive against his lips. Then she pulled away.

'Actually, no, but thank you, it's not quite dark yet. I'll walk.' She turned and was gone.

Riedwaan watched, waiting for her to emerge on the street below. Her arms were hugged close around her body, as if she was carrying something heavy. He lit another cigarette, and when his eyes returned to the pavement below, she had disappeared.

He spent much longer than he had intended at the bar next to New York Bagel. He drove past Clare's flat on his way back to his cold, empty house. Her lights were on. He was glad she was safely at home.

Inside, Clare sat dead still. She held the familiar Tarot card, the envelope it had been sent in abandoned on the table with the autopsy report. She was looking at the card. The High Priestess. Or the Female Pope. The second card of the major arcana. The card that warned against the rational in favour of intuition. The card was both warning and summons to the dark world where her sister paced, hidden, full of fear and hate. Clare's heart was heavy with the knowledge that Constance had heard of the murder, had summoned her twin to see her.

Clare slipped the card back into the envelope, putting it into her bag. Then she settled down with the transcripts that Riedwaan had given her and tried to make sense of the girl's murder.

7

Clare cleared her thoughts of Charnay Swanepoel. This morning her obsessive attention was turned on Natalie Mwanga. Nosing her car into the traffic, Clare took the N1, slipping into the correct lane and peeling away on the road that skirted the edge of Atlantis. It was a desolate place. Drifts of young men gathered at street corners, hoping against forlorn hope for some work for the day. Clare glanced at her watch. Nine forty-five. Unlikely that those remaining would be picked up now. She drove past a boarded-up factory, looking for Disa Street. There it was. She turned, looking for the Vroue Helpmekaar Centre for Abused Women and Children. She drove straight past the nondescript house before registering the steel mesh on the windows. She parked under a tree that was bent double by years of relentless wind. Clare greeted the tall woman who came out to meet her.

'Welcome, I am Shazneem,' she said, enveloping Clare's smooth hand in her own. The lyrical name jarred with the shorn grey hair and the well-worn biker's jacket. 'We were waiting for you, Dr Hart.' Shazneem put an arm around Clare's shoulders, shepherding her towards the yellow front door, her large body positioned protectively between Clare's and the street.

'We'll talk in my office first.' Shazneem opened a door with

'Centre Director' and a colourful butterfly painted on it. 'And then I'll take you to meet Natalie. She is expecting you.'

Clare settled into the offered chair. Shazneem manoeuvred her bulk with surprising agility around the cramped desk and into her chair. Its tall back framed her, giving her the look of an Amazon queen. But when she reached over for her notebook and pencil, a wave of exhaustion played across her features and the illusion was gone. She was just a middle-aged woman doing a relentlessly demanding job.

'What can you tell me about trafficking, Shazneem? Do you think it happens?' Clare asked her first question, her pen clicked open, poised to write, her small tape-recorder whirring softly.

'I know it happens, we know it happens, and it is happening more and more. We see the women, the girls, who make it and find their way to the shelter. They are just the tip of the iceberg. But we can't prove it, can we?' Fury staccatoed her words. 'How do we prove it when so many of these girls are desperate to start with? Fleeing wars, fleeing poverty, believing that they are being offered a better life – and there is no law to protect them. For the gangsters who run the trade, it is risk free and the profits are enormous. Guns make money and, sure, drugs are profitable – but both are high-risk investments requiring complicated arrangements and a trail that is often not that difficult to trace back to the mastermind. With women, or children, there is almost no risk.' Shazneem calmed herself with a sip of water. 'The return on an investment that requires the smallest capital outlay – a plane ticket or a taxi ride and a bribe. It is limited only by the number of clients a body can service.'

'What proof do you have?' asked Clare.

'None that will stand up in court. The women are too terrified to testify.' Shazneem's eyes flashed with a rage that had etched deep lines onto her soft skin.

'I must warn you to be very careful, Clare. I don't know if this is connected, but yesterday we had a visit from three men. They came here, to the shelter, enquiring after Natalie. They said they were her brothers.'

Clare blanched. 'How did they know she was here?'

'Natalie has no brothers,' said Shazneem. 'But these men knew she was here. Or they know more about what you are doing than they should. I would be careful who you talk to about this investigation.'

The tendons in Clare's neck tightened. Silence stretched between the two women, deepened by the shouts and giggles of the shelter's children playing in the weak sunlight.

'Perhaps I should speak to Natalie now,' said Clare.

Shazneem stood up. 'Her room is at the back. It is safest there.' Clare followed her outside. They crossed a bleak courtyard, empty except for a shabby plastic jungle gym. The two little boys playing on it fell silent when they saw Clare. They did not respond to her greeting until instructed to by Shazneem. Then they turned back to their game, the visitor forgotten.

Shazneem knocked on the third door.

'*Entre.*' The voice was gentle. Shazneem opened the door and stood back to let Clare enter.

'Natalie, this is Dr Clare Hart,' she said, 'I'm the person who is doing the film on trafficking.' Before Clare could greet the woman seated on the bed, Shazneem turned and walked back the way they had come.

'*Bonjour*, Natalie,' said Clare.

'*Bonjour*, Madame. Please come in and sit down.' Natalie, silhouetted against the window, gestured graciously towards the chair. Clare sat down and waited. The room was very still. Sunlight filtering through the bars glanced off Natalie's angled face.

Natalie Mwanga looked at the woman sitting opposite her.

She guessed that she was about her own age. Clare's dark eyes were clear, but fear lurked around her soft mouth, hardening it. Clare Hart would have lines like vertical knifemarks on each side of her mouth before she was much older. Natalie had those lines coming too.

Clare waited for Natalie to decide whether to trust her with her story. It was a delicate moment that could be destroyed with one careless word or sudden movement. Natalie would look good on television, her beauty would sell her story.

The stillness took Natalie back to the chaos that had driven her from her home village. The first bout of noise and violence had come from her husband – who'd been chosen for her – and not from the war. Although once she left him, the war did catch up. Like a hyena, it snapped at her heels, driving her and her daughter from displacement camp to displacement camp, where Natalie traded her careful English for a bemused aid worker's spare tent, cooking pot, mosquito net. Like the other women who were young enough, she cajoled food from peacekeeping troops. She used charm when she could, or the temporary gift of her still-firm body when necessary. Her daughter she refused them, even when offered almost-fresh meat for her. She had made her way to Kalangani, where the fighting skirted the town and where she had some relatives. Here her daughter would be safe. But this, Natalie intuited, was not the story Clare wanted.

Natalie's voice bridged the distance between them. 'I will tell you, Madame, my story how I got here. For your film I will tell you. For my daughter.'

'Can I record this?' asked Clare, opening her camera bag.

Natalie shrugged her shoulders. 'Why not?'

Clare slipped the video camera out of her bag and flicked out the legs of the tripod to set up the camera. Natalie adjusted her hair, wiped the corners of her mouth, the instinctive gestures a camera elicits. She sat straight up in her chair and pulled her skirt over her knees.

'Shall I look at you or there?' she gestured towards the lens.

'Look at me,' said Clare. 'Forget about the camera. I'll ask you questions, so don't worry about saying things right or wrong. Just speak to me.'

Natalie nodded.

'Tell me who you are, where you are from,' said Clare.

'I am Natalie Mwanga,' she said. 'I am thirty-five years. I am from the Congo before I came to South Africa. The cousin of my father comes to me and he says you are suffering a lot. Why don't you go to South Africa, you will find a job, you will find everything. Go and find your new life. I didn't know what he thinks – what he means for me. When we came to South Africa he says, "You must do everything that I tell you." And in the afternoon I saw him coming with his friends, here in Cape Town. And he said, "If you make sex here with the people, you are going to find a lot of money." I was forced to do it.'

The woman's voice died away. 'Do you know what it feels like? What I feel like when it happens?' she asked. Clare shook her head.

'I just start to cry. I did feel bad, so bad. I just cry every day, every time. I am not used to do it.'

'Did they give money to your uncle?' asked Clare.

'Yes, they gave money to him. I don't know how much. When I asked him how much they gave him, he said, "It is not your problem. You eat here, you drink here, you sleep here. What do you want to know how much they give?" I was afraid of the HIV, about infection. But God loves me. I did the test and I am well. I am well.' Natalie's face transformed with the delight of this reprieve.

'How did you get away?' asked Clare.

'It was a Saturday, I think. He did lock the front door but

he forgot to lock the back door. I didn't go to the police. I also didn't know where they were. I didn't have any papers. When I asked my uncle for my papers he said, "Myself, I'm your paper." So I ran to my friend. She told me, "I can't help you. My house is small. Maybe my boyfriend won't accept you to stay here." She told me to go to the church. I went there and I got help. I spent four days at the church and then Shazneem came to fetch me from the shelter.'

'And your family?' asked Clare.

'I have one girl in my country. She is thirteen years. She is beautiful. I am so afraid for her.' Natalie had only needed one or two questions to free the river of her story, but now she fell silent.

'I was very afraid of that camera,' said Natalie. Her quiet voice agitated the motes of dust suspended in the light that lay between them.

'Why?' Clare asked. She reached over to switch off the camera.

'When I first come here to Cape Town some men make a film. These men, they pay my uncle.' Natalie stopped. Clare switched the camera back on.

'Go on,' she said. There was enough tape for another five minutes.

'They are men there and they take my clothes. They say they will teach me to make love. I say I am a married woman. That I know. They laugh and give me other clothes to put on. A lady helps me because I don't know how to wear these clothes.' She stopped and looked down at her hands. They are broad, strong, the nails bitten to the quick. 'I am very ashamed of that,' she whispered. 'They make picture and there is one man who say, do this, do that. He is like Hollywood and he has the camera too sometimes. Sometimes another man with a camera.'

'What did they want you to do?' asked Clare. Her tape ended, clicking into the silence.

Natalie raised her head. 'I don't want to say about it. I am very ashamed. More than the men because now I am here the men are over. I am safe. But in my film I am never over. Always I do the things, do the things in the film.' She wiped the tears that welled in her eyes. 'Maybe if you find that film you will bring it back to me so that I can stop.'

Clare switched off the camera again. 'If I see it I will try to get it. Thank you, Natalie.' She packed up her things and readied herself to leave.

'Dr Hart, I give you my story for your film. I would like to ask you for something,' said Natalie.

'What is that?' asked Clare. Her stomach knotted.

'With my daughter. Help me bring her here where she can be safe. Where she can eat and go to school.' Natalie handed her a sheet of paper. It was dog-eared, as if it had been smoothed open countless times. A young girl's face looked out at her from beneath the Red Cross letterhead. It was dated six months earlier.

'You know the right people. I saw your film on television,' said Natalie.

Clare took her phone out of her bag and dialled. The tension around Natalie's shoulders went as Clare gave the information about her daughter.

'They will do what they can. That was the director of the Southern African Refugee Centre,' said Clare. 'They will phone the shelter as soon as they have located her.'

'Good,' said Natalie, satisfied with their transaction. 'I will phone you and tell you what they do.'

The interview was over and Natalie looked exhausted. Clare felt exhausted too. She was glad that she had a flask of tea in her car. She was going to need it before the next part of her journey.

8

Clare sat in her car. She lifted her hands to her temples and pressed, trying to contain the horror that pulsed there. She turned the key and the car purred in response. The street was empty, desolate, as she paused, looking for running children before turning right. Someone had flanked a concrete garden path with petunias but the tender pink petals had been mutilated by the south-easter. Clare turned away from their defeat. She did not pay much attention to the white car ahead of her that indicated left towards the majestic solidity of Table Mountain.

She turned right, accelerating across the oncoming lanes when there was a lull in the traffic. She headed north, where the mountains petered out into hills and wheatfields. She was looking out for the sign to Serenity Farm, so she did not notice the white car pull over into a lay-by. Even if she had, she'd have been too far away to notice the fury that her sudden disappearance provoked in the driver.

As always, the faded lettering on weathered wood came too soon after the bend. Clare turned left sharply, a driver hooting in her wake. And then the sound of traffic was gone. Overhead, the ancient, ghostly gums reached their branches upwards and over. Their embrace created a dappled arch that extended like the nave of a cathedral towards the house in the distance. Clare drove down the rutted drive, avoiding the corrugations that had become worse over the years she had been taking this road. This suspended moment was the bridge between her world and the cloistered place that sheltered her twin.

Clare parked her car at the reception area and got out. She always remembered not to lock here. To do so would bring the fear of the world that surged back and forth on the freeway into this haven, but it took her some effort to override the instinct to both lock and double check.

Father Jones was waiting for her on the polished red steps. 'Hello, Isaiah,' she said, lifting her face to be kissed. He leaned towards her, breathing her in. His hand smoothed the familiar curve in the small of her back, and her body softened in response.

'Welcome, Clare,' he said. Twenty years had not diminished her feelings for him. When he hooked his arm at her elbow, as a brother would, they were aware of the loss – but it was one they had both accepted..

'I am glad you came.' There was no reproach. He understood her long absences. 'Constance has been so anxious since your call.'

Clare looked at him. 'More anxious than usual,' Isaiah amended. 'She's waiting for you.'

They walked down the narrow path, the plants they brushed against wafting sharp autumn scents up to them. Isaiah stopped at the edge of the clearing. On the other side of it stood the cottage, white, symmetrical, perfect, where her beautiful twin had purdahed herself. Isaiah pressed her arm.

'Thank you,' she murmured.

Clare stepped past the sundial to knock on the front door. Constance would not answer before she had allowed Isaiah to return up the narrow path. Clare listened for the susurration of her sister's skirts, her body alert as she waited for the door to open to reveal Constance. Her other self.

'Hello, Clare. I'm glad you came. Come in, you must be so tired.' A white hand reached from the dim interior and took hold of Clare's brown arm, drawing her inside. Constance closed the door. The sisters embraced, blonde hair mingling with black.

'Why did you send me this?' asked Clare, pulling away to show the enigmatic card to her twin.

Constance took it. 'The first card is the key to the present. This is the High Priestess.' She turned the card over in her hand. 'It's the Female Pope, the emblem of the law.'

Clare looked blank.

'This is you, Clare. Always thinking, never understanding.'

Clare followed Constance into the sitting room. She sat down, her arms tight around her legs, her body rocking now.

'Please keep it, Clare. You will need it.' Clare capitulated, putting the card back in her bag. Then she knelt beside Constance and held her. Her sister quietened in her arms.

'He's out there again. I feel him. He's moving.' She turned her face into the hollow below Clare's shoulder.

'No, he's not.' Clare did not believe her own lie.

'Who killed that girl, then? Who carved her up like that?' whispered Constance, her breath hot on Clare's face. 'Who?'

'The police will find him. I'm working with them. I'll find him.' Clare pushed her sister's hair away from her face. 'Try to rest now. You've not been sleeping, have you?'

Constance shook her head and leaned against Clare. There was nothing for it now but to hold her sister until she exhausted herself and fell asleep. Clare settled in to wait. It was dark before Constance fell asleep. Clare covered her and let herself out. The moonlight was cold as she crunched back up the path to her car.

As soon as she got home, Clare stripped and stepped under a scalding shower, trying to erase the ghost scars imprinted on her body when the real scars had in fact been carved onto Constance. She stepped out of the shower for her shampoo and stopped in front of her mirror. She had small, neat feet. Her legs were well proportioned with the muscular leanness to the hips and thighs that comes with running. Her waist curved inwards then flared towards small, curved breasts that had only recently started to soften. That could be disguised when necessary with a quick splash of cold water or a strategic run of a finger down her ribs. Her belly was taut, the unmarked skin stretched tight across her pelvis. She twisted her long hair on top of her head, revealing her elegant neck and the curve of her shoulders. It was a good body. One that had captured the attention of several men and one or two women.

But this body was not the body that Clare saw. The body she saw when she was naked was the body of her sister, Constance. They were the same height. But where Clare's body was muscular, Constance's was soft. Criss-crossed with scars, her thighs and breasts carried the knife emblems of the gang that had used her to initiate two new members. On her back, illegible now, were brutal signatures where they had carved their initials. Her left cheekbone was curved as sharply as a starling's wing, the other had been reconstructed out of the shattered mess left by a hammer blow that had glanced off her skull and spared her life. For some reason the men, how many or whom Constance could never say, had not struck a final blow. They were distracted perhaps, or bored with the messy pulp that she had become. And so she had lived, her hip-length hair hiding a shattered face and the cold snake of fear coiled inside her thin body.

This was the ghost-body Clare saw in her mirror. Clare let

45

her hair go, and its curtain fall ended the familiar hallucination. She returned to the shower and scrubbed. The water was so hot that she did not notice the tears coursing down her perfectly matched cheekbones.

9

The sliding doors were open: the dawn was surprisingly forgiving, despite the unsettled waves. Clare sat on the sofa, the sweat from her run already drying. She forgot her coffee as she watched the sun rise, the colours reflecting on the expanse of white flooring. The door to her bedroom was open, the room empty except for the bed and an exquisite view of the Atlantic and a wall covered with her books. These provided the only colour in Clare's sanctuary. The mountains, tinged pink by the sun, were an army frozen in its march up the bleak West Coast. She longed for that endless coast road snaking along the base of the mountains that led to the stone house whose low white buildings were screened by dusty eucalyptus trees. It was invisible from the road, secret. There Constance's voice still echoed happily with hers around that distant, long-abandoned farmhouse of their childhood.

Clare stood up, shaking memories from her as she stretched her stiffening muscles. She walked to the phone and, cradling the receiver in her hand, thumbed in the number without needing to think of the sequence. Three . . . four . . . five rings.

It was her defence against the work she did . . . seven . . . eight . . . rings. A ninth ring . . . Panic rose in Clare, as it always did if someone was not where they ought to be.

'Hello . . . Shit! The phone. Hello? Hello?' Her beloved sister, at forty, still unable to answer a phone without dropping it.

'Julie! I'm still here. It's me. Clare . . .' Her panic dispelled.

'Darling! How are you? Where have you been? Weren't you going to call me?' Julie had adopted their mother's way of speaking when they had still been very young children – an effusive torrent that swept along anyone in earshot. 'It's a bit mad here. But come for supper. Tonight, or maybe the weekend would be better. I've missed you. So have the girls.'

The thought of her nieces, both so alive, so protected, comforted Clare. 'Thanks, Julie. I'll see you tomorrow, then. Shall I bring something?' But Clare was talking to a dead receiver. Julie had turned her attention to Beatrice's breakfast and Imogen's frantic hunt for her homework and her hockey stick. Clare put the phone down, soothed by the domesticity of Julie's life.

She made fresh coffee and took it to her desk. The autopsy report and the interview transcripts were there. Riedwaan had faxed the ballistic reports. She fished them out of the tray and read them, letting her mind sift through the information.

There was one body. So far. Clare was convinced that there would be others. Or that there had been others that had not been picked up. She took the picture of Charnay out again and laid it in front of her. There were no injuries to suggest that she had been knocked out and then abducted. Charnay had gone willingly with her killer, so he must be personable. Charming too, to have access to a girl as beautiful as Charnay Swanepoel. It would have been later, when it was too late, that his abhorrence of women, of girls, emerged.

The phone rang. Riedwaan's name came up on the caller ID. She picked it up. 'Hi.'

'How are you doing?' he asked.

'I'm going to see the mother later today.'

48

'Good. And our man? What are we looking for?'

'You know it's impossible with one victim to have anything more than a feeling. Nothing, I suppose, from the records?'

'No. No murders. I did have a call from a friend in Jo'burg. They have an unsolved sexual assault there from about six months ago. The girl looked similar to this one: dark hair, about sixteen. Same sort of weird bondage, but on both hands. And a blindfold, she claimed, so she could give no description.'

'Any DNA?'

'There was some. Blood and semen. But different blood groups, so maybe there were two of them. The girl survived but she had been severely assaulted. He's sending the report down.'

'You don't know where she was before the assault?'

'I do,' said Riedwaan, shuffling through his notes. 'She was at the Da Vinci Hotel.' Clare had stayed there once. It was a replica of a Florentine villa in the heart of the sprawling chaos of Africa's wealthiest and most violent city.

'The friend who was meeting her was late and the victim had left by the time she arrived. It was busy – a Friday night – and no one saw her leave.'

'Our girl disappeared on a Friday too. From the Waterfront,' mused Clare.

'Toxicology reports show traces of cocaine in the girl's bloodstream. And Rohypnol.'

'Can we interview her?' asked Clare.

'I'm afraid not,' said Riedwaan. 'She's dead.'

'Dead? How?' asked Clare.

'Suicide, apparently. Two months after the rape. Her family didn't accept the verdict, but there was no evidence that indicated murder.'

Clare closed her eyes.

'There is one other thing, Clare. The victim was convinced

that her attacker filmed part of the assault. She said she heard the whirr of a camera.'

'Lots of home movies these days. The woman I interviewed who was trafficked, she also told me that she had been filmed.'

'We're going to stumble across a little nest of home-made porn,' said Riedwaan.

'It's probably all over the Net,' said Clare.

'You want to meet me for a drink later?' asked Rediwaan.

'Not tonight,' Clare answered. 'I've had quite a week.'

'Friday, then?'

'I'm going to my sister for dinner tomorrow night,' said Clare. 'Why don't you come?' Silence stretched between them.

'I don't think family is quite the thing for me, do you?' said Riedwaan.

'Maybe not,' said Clare. She was ashamed at how relieved she was that he'd refused. 'I'll email you the profile as soon as I've got something more coherent.' Clare cut the connection, wishing immediately that she had agreed to meet him that evening. She picked up her pen and started making careful notes, regret dissipating as she worked. She would be visiting the dead girl's home the next day.

10

Clare did not recognise the address – Welgemoed was not an area she ever had reason to visit. She was glad of Riedwaan's directions. A woman out of uniform might be easier for Charnay's family to talk to. It was a champagne-crisp morning, the light shimmered above the leaves of the trees lining the street she turned into. Here stolid face-brick houses, products of the affluent sixties, stood at the ends of long driveways. After the roar of the highway, the suburb seemed quiet. The only movement – the only sound – was a gardener pushing a lawnmower. It was as easy to find number 27 as it would have been to find any other house.

The house was silent. Every window was closed, with a net curtain blinding it. She thought she saw someone pass an upstairs window, but it could have been a shadow from the tree that blocked the sunlight from the house. Deep inside, a melancholy chime responded to her finger on the doorbell. The door flew open. A boy looked at Clare sourly.

'*Wie is daar*?' a voice called to him.

'It's that woman. About Charnay,' he replied, not taking his eyes off Clare. 'My mother is in there,' he said, standing aside. He pointed down the passage to an open door. From it, sunlight spilled into the gloom.

The dead girl's mother sat in the centre of the room,

hunched as if a knife was twisting low in her gut. Mrs Swanepoel looked up at Clare, her eyes emptied of all emotion except the knowledge that she was alive and her child was not.

'*Ek kan jou nie help nie,*' said Mrs Swanepoel. 'I cannot help you.' She remembered to repeat it in English. 'I told the police everything I know.'

Clare bent low and knelt next to the woman. She knew better than to touch her. The formulaic gesture of comfort would flay the woman.

'She was an angel,' said the mother, reverting to the familiarity of Afrikaans. 'That is why she was taken from me.'

Clare turned away from her, pinioned by loss on her suburban carpet. She did not need to talk to her, could not bear to ask her more questions to which she had no answers. She had read Riedwaan's interview transcripts anyway.

'Can I look through her room?' Clare asked.

Mrs Swanepoel did not move. 'J.P.,' she whispered. 'J.P., take Miss Hart to your sister's room.'

'*Ja, Ma.*' The boy who had let Clare in reappeared. Clare followed him up the stairs. Here all the doors were closed. He led her to the end of the passage. 'Friends Welcome, Family by Appointment' said the hand-drawn sign on her door – a remnant from a very recent childhood.

The boy opened the door and stood back to let Clare enter. The room was an orgy of pink: walls, curtains, carpets, bed – in every shade of the colour. Anything that could be flounced had ruffles and bows and flowers on it. It was oppressive. Clare wondered if the feeling of absence had been there before Charnay went missing. Clare repressed an urge to throw open the windows.

J.P. did not come in. 'I'll come back for you,' he said, closing the door before Clare could respond.

She was relieved when she did not hear the key turn. She stood in the centre of the room, at a loss, reaching for a sense of the absent presence of the girl. Every flat surface was covered in pictures cut from celebrity magazines. All of them were of Charlize Theron. Charnay seemed to have gathered every available image of the actress. On her desk was a scrapbook full of articles tracking the star's ascent from obscurity to the zenith of Hollywood fame. Clare sat down and read the notes that Charnay had made alongside the articles. They read like an instruction manual rather than a fan's obsession. The pictures might be of Charlize, but the focus was Charnay.

Clare settled herself, dislodging a small avalanche of cushions. She reached down to pick them up. There on the floor, revealed as she shifted the bedspread, lay a blue card. Clare picked it up and held it up to the light. A series of numbers had been pencilled there and then erased. There was a sound from the passage. Clare slipped the card into her pocket as J.P. opened the door.

'Look in her cupboard,' he instructed. Clare obeyed. It was stuffed with expensive, wispy clothes. A pile of high-heeled shoes tumbled out. She noticed the labels as she bent to put them back.

'Expensive, hey?' he sneered. 'I bet you could never afford them.' Clare did not correct him. 'How do you think she paid for them?' He stepped close to Clare. There was a sprinkle of pimples around his nose. His breath was rank. 'Think about how she paid,' he repeated. 'My mother thinks it was from modelling. But she believed anything that little *hoer* told her.'

His hatred was palpable. It was all Clare could do to stop herself from stepping back from it. It would give him pleasure, she was sure, if he sensed that he had unnerved her. 'Did she go to meet someone last Friday?' asked Clare.

'How must I know?' he spat. 'She never bothered to speak to me.'

'Where did she go when she went out?' asked Clare.

'To the Waterfront,' he said. 'That's where they always went.'

'They?' queried Clare. The boy shifted his weight, regretting his slip.

'Cornelle,' he said. 'They did everything together.'

'Did you tell Captain Faizal this?' asked Clare.

'Nobody asked me,' he replied. 'Anyway, she always told my ma that she was going to sleep at Cornelle's. And Cornelle said she was coming to sleep here. They were friends for so long that everyone stopped checking.'

'Except you,' said Clare. The boy looked awkward. He pointed to a framed photograph on the bookshelf. 'There's Charnay. And that's Cornelle.' The two girls were dressed in porn-star chic – like all girls their age. Cornelle was blonde and very slim, squeezed into clothes a size too small. She contrasted with the darker beauty of Charnay. Clare wondered how they had paid for these clothes. It cost a lot of money to look that cheap. Clare held the picture closer. It was difficult to work out where it had been taken. The blurred background did not look like someone's house.

'They worked well together,' said J.P. He was at the door, holding it open for her. Her time was up. She put the picture down.

'Where is Cornelle now?'

'At school,' he answered. 'She was in the same class as Charnay.'

Clare followed J.P. Swanepoel to the front door. 'J.P.,' she said, 'what were you doing on Friday night?' He was motionless except for the tic-tic-tic of a vein in his neck.

'Why?'

'I would like to know,' said Clare. 'Where were you?'

'On rugby tour.' His voice cracked a little. 'We went to the Boland on Friday morning. You can ask my coach.'

'I will,' said Clare, 'and you let me know if you think of anything else about Charnay.'

The dead girl's brother looked sullen. 'Like what?'

'Any new friends she might have made,' said Clare.

He laughed. 'She made a new friend every hour.' He closed the door behind her. He was still watching through the thick, ridged glass when she opened her car door. She waved at him, but he did not wave back. She drove around the block before calling Riedwaan.

'How did it go?' he asked.

'Interesting,' said Clare. 'I'll tell you when I see you. There was just one thing I wanted to check now.'

'*Ja*,' said Riedwaan. 'What?'

'J.P. Her brother,' said Clare. 'Did you talk to him?'

'Rita Mkhize did,' said Riedwaan. 'Why?'

'I just wanted to check on his alibi. Can I speak to Rita?'

'Sure,' said Riedwaan. He put his hand over the mouthpiece. 'Rita,' she heard him call. 'Clare wants to speak to you.' He took his hand away. 'I'll see you later?'

'I'll call you,' she said. Riedwaan handed the phone to Rita.

'Hi, Clare,' Rita said. 'What did you want to know?'

'About J.P. Swanepoel. What did you think?'

'Not my type,' laughed Rita. 'And I most certainly was not his type either. A little blast from the old South Africa past.'

'What did he tell you about his weekend?'

'He said he'd been on rugby tour,' said Rita.

'And?'

'I checked it out. His coach told me they left early Friday and were only back on Sunday evening. And that J.P. was there all the time.'

55

'Okay,' said Clare.

'There was one other thing,' Rita added. 'I'm not sure if it's important.'

'What?' asked Clare. Her pulse quickened.

'He was sent off twice. Once for punching an opponent, and once for kicking someone in the scrum.'

'Charming,' said Clare. 'Thanks.'

'Any time,' said Rita. 'Have a good weekend if I don't see you.'

Clare looked at her watch. It was close to the end of the school day. A chat to Cornelle would be worth the wait. Clare found Welgemoed High easily. There was only one exit – the rule now at government schools after a spate of assaults. She parked opposite a cluster of mothers chatting next to their Jeeps and BMWs.

11

Cornelle walked out of the school gates alone. She jerked at the book bag slung over her shoulder, reaching for the cigarettes in her blazer pocket as soon as she had rounded the corner. She swivelled, hip bones jutting above her grey skirt, towards Clare's greeting.

'Hi, Cornelle. I was hoping we could talk about Charnay.' Clare leaned over and opened the passenger door. 'Get in,' said Clare. 'I'll drive you home.' The girl narrowed her eyes, but the day was raw, and her cold hand was already reaching for the door. She folded herself into the passenger seat, shaking her blonde hair loose from its regulation ponytail.

'How do you know my name?' she asked. 'Who are you?'

'My name is Clare Hart. I'm part of the team investigating Charnay's murder.'

'Oh,' said Cornelle, interested now. 'How can I help you?'

'I was at Charnay's house earlier. J.P. showed me the photograph of you two. I just wanted to talk to you about her.'

Cornelle turned her head away, her hair curtaining her expression. She dragged again on the cigarette and then lit a fresh one from the glowing stump. Clare ignored the smoke.

'What was she like?'

'She was my friend,' said Cornelle. 'We used to do everything together. Before.'

'So what happened last week?' asked Clare. 'Where did you go? Where did she go?' Cornelle kept her face averted. She shrugged.

'I don't know. We didn't always spend our weekends together.'

'Charnay's mother thought you did. What about yours?'

'Mine doesn't give a fuck,' said Cornelle. She ground her half-smoked cigarette into the ashtray. 'She wouldn't even have noticed if I had disappeared.' Cornelle dashed the back of her hand against her cheek. Clare could not see if there were tears.

'Did you go out together last weekend?' Clare persisted.

'No.'

'I thought you did everything together?'

'*Ag*, we used to. But not so much lately,' said Cornelle. 'We didn't always *jol* together on the weekends. We had different friends sometimes.'

'Where do you live? I'll drive you there' said Clare. Cornelle directed her – left, right, second left, number 32. Then she was silent. The house she pointed out was shut up, blank. Cornelle scrabbled in her bag for her keys.

'Are you going out this evening?' asked Clare.

'I don't know. To the Waterfront, I suppose.'

'Shall I give you a lift? I'm going that way.'

Cornelle shrugged. '*Ag*, why not? Let me go change.' She didn't ask Clare if she wanted to wait inside. Clare looked at the depressing face-brick, blinds hanging askew in the upstairs windows, and was glad not to have been invited in. 'I'll be quick.'

Cornelle was gone in a flash of long legs. The look in her eyes, the tears, had not been grief, thought Clare. It had been fear. She watched the bathroom light go on and then snap off again. What was Cornelle afraid of? She put a call through to Riedwaan but his answering service kicked in before the first ring. She snapped her phone shut; Cornelle was hurtling out the door. Transformed in ten minutes by a tight black T-shirt and a skirt that could be mistaken for a belt.

'*Poes* pelmets is what my ma calls them,' giggled Cornelle, allowing Clare a glimpse of the child that she had so recently been. Cornelle turned back to the mirror to lacquer on her after-school face and the illusion was gone.

'What are you going to do?'

'Shop, I suppose.' There was a long pause. 'Maybe meet some friends later.'

Clare glanced over at Cornelle – imported designer skirt and sunglasses. An indiscreet double C on her handbag. 'Where do you get the money?' she asked, weaving in between the late afternoon traffic. 'Where did Charnay get her money?'

'Oh, we model,' said Cornelle with the nonchalance of a practised almost-truth. 'Sometimes we get gifts after a shoot. Got gifts,' she corrected.

Charnay's broken body flashed into Clare's mind. A driver hooted and she swerved back into her lane. 'Those are expensive clothes.'

Cornelle looked at her again. And again there was a shadow across her face.

'I work hard,' said Cornelle. 'So did Charnay.'

Clare dropped the subject. They drove in silence as darkness gathered, the elevated highway offering them a view of the glimmering harbour. Clare turned off the highway towards the Waterfront. Dockworkers and shop girls thronged home, shoulders hunched against the cold under thin jackets.

'Drop me here please,' Cornelle said. 'I'll walk the rest of the way.' Clare swung around the next third of the traffic circle and pulled over. She pulled the blue card she had found in Charnay's room from her pocket. 'Do you know this number?' she asked.

'I don't know,' said Cornelle, pulling her cellphone out of her bag. 'I'm so bad with numbers. Let me see if I've got it on my phone.' She peered at the number and dialled it. A name flashed onto the small screen. Cornelle ended the call, a flush rising on her pale neck. 'The Isis Club,' she muttered, not meeting Clare's eye.

'The strip club?' asked Clare.

'*Ja*,' said Cornelle. 'We auditioned there. Me and Charnay.'

'As strippers?' asked Clare.

'No,' answered Cornelle, her voice very low. 'They were making movies. We auditioned for a part.'

'Did you get one?' asked Clare.

'I didn't. It was too hard-core for me.' Cornelle looked down at her hands. The cuticles had been bitten until they bled.

'Did Charnay?' asked Clare.

'Not that I know of,' said Cornelle, reaching for the handle.

Clare put her hand on Cornelle's arm and handed her a card. 'Phone me if you want to talk,' she said.

'I will,' said Cornelle. 'I mean, I won't need to. I told you everything.'

The door slammed, muffling the thanks flung over her thin shoulder. Cornelle did not head towards the Clocktower with its evening jazz cafés. Instead she took the road wedged between the repair dock and an abandoned office block. Two men painting a Chinese ship watched her progress, turning back to their work when a directed wolf whistle failed to even register in her stride. And then she was swallowed by darkness.

12

Clare drove west, towards Sea Point. As she rounded the huge yacht basin at the Waterfront – eviscerated in preparation for new luxury apartments – she caught sight of Cornelle again and slowed, ignoring the impatient drivers behind her. The girl changed direction. She was walking away from the shops and cinemas – already starting to seethe with scantily dressed teenagers – towards the bunkered luxury of The Prince's Hotel. She dipped out of sight, obscured by the masts of the yachts anchored in the marina. Impulsively, Clare turned and drove back in the direction she had just come from. She parked deep in the shadow of an empty building. She grabbed her bag and, pushing her arms into her coat, walked down the access road that led through the luxury apartments to the marina. She looked for Cornelle, but she seemed to have gone into The Blue Room. The bar overlooked the most expensive yachts in the basin. Clare did not slow her pace. Instead, she walked around the hotel and entered the lobby. Her well-cut clothes earned her a welcoming nod from the concierge. She slipped past the receptionist busy on a call and took the narrow service passage that led to the bar. Then she slid behind a waiter and sat down at a table that was not visible from the mirrored bar.

The Blue Room was empty except for three men drinking

at a table near the entrance. Cornelle was sitting at the far end of the bar. She had exchanged her tackies for needle-heeled boots and adjusted the neckline of her T-shirt, displaying a generous cleavage as she leaned over to take a practised sip of her cocktail. As the barman turned to serve a new customer, the suited man who had bought her the drink tucked a bloated finger between her breasts, pushing her top down further. Cornelle pressed her arms against her body and smiled, spilling more of herself towards the man. Clare stared at the exposed tattoo on her breast. The same elegant verticals bisected with an X. The same design as Charnay's. The man edged closer to the girl, slack mouth wet with anticipation. Cornelle avoided looking at him by checking her hair in the mirror behind the bar. She caught sight of Clare and shame blazed briefly in her eyes, which then glazed over. She turned her smiling mouth to the man whose left hand was moving up her naked thigh towards her crotch. His wedding band flashed in the light and then disappeared under Cornelle's skirt. Clare saw him squeeze hard at some imagined resistance. Cornelle's thighs parted at once. She smiled when he twisted her nipple into pertness as the barman came to take Clare's order.

'A whiskey and water, please. No ice.' The young man went back to his station, busying himself with bottles and glasses. The man put a hundred-rand note on the counter and handed Cornelle her bag. She followed him obediently into the night. Clare sipped her drink, hoping that the alcohol would stop the churn in her stomach.

Clare went to pay for her drink. She passed a picture of Charnay over to the barman with the money.

'Do you know her, Tyrone?' she asked. He looked startled, then touched the silver name tag on his shirt. 'I'm Dr Clare Hart.' He shook her outstretched hand.

He picked up her picture. 'Shame, it's that girl they found in Sea Point, isn't it? This is a better photo than the one they put in the paper.'

Clare nodded. 'Charnay. Charnay Swanepoel. Did she ever come in here?'

Tyrone glanced towards the three men drinking steadily at their table, then he nodded.

'She did come in here once or twice.' He looked back at the picture. 'She was pretty. My type. She looks like a fairy princess with all that hair.'

'When was she here last?'

'Last Friday,' he said reluctantly.

'Who was she here with?'

The barman did not look Clare in the eye. 'Nobody. She left early. By herself.'

'Why did you not tell anybody?'

'I didn't know that I had to,' he replied.

Clare's hands curled into fists. She put them into her pockets. 'A girl is dead. Surely that worried you?' He shifted from one foot to the other, but he didn't reply. Clare turned away from him and walked down to the yachts rocking in the wind-chopped water. The engine of a gleaming blue and mahogany yacht purred to life. Clare had managed to control her rage – and then the barman appeared at her side.

'She went in this direction,' he said. 'The same way you walked when you left – this way down to the marina.' Clare looked down – there was a broad deck that stretched out into the water, providing access to the vessels moored there.

'Do you know what she was doing?' Clare asked.

'Same as you, I suppose. Looking at the lights. It's beautiful.' It was. The lights gleamed like pearls in the inky black water. The mournful bellow of a seal was all that punctuated the quiet. The blue yacht manoeuvred – graceful as a dancer –

around the quay and towards the channel that led through the harbour to the sea.

'What a beauty,' said the barman.

Clare admired the sleek lines of the yacht as it sliced its way down the channel. The pedestrian bridge across it reared skywards, and the tall vessel sailed out towards the open sea.

'Who else was here last Friday when Charnay was here?'

'No one. Only those guys you saw this evening – they are always here. It seems like we are their new hangout. They pay, though,' he added. 'And they tip well. Which is more than some of these yachting *ous*.'

'No one else?'

'No, nobody that I remember. But I was a little bit late coming in that evening. The trains were all over the place. As usual.' He grimaced. 'What do you need to do to get a boat like that?' he asked, staring at the gracious yacht sailing away.

Clare smiled. 'Get lucky, I suppose.' She handed him a card. 'You call me if you think of anything else. Anything about Charnay. Doesn't matter if it seems trivial.'

He put the card into his pocket. 'Thanks. Take care now.'

Clare headed towards the Waterfront. Two glasses of wine and a nigiri platter took the edge off the day. It was later than she thought when she headed back to her car, and the evening crowds had thinned. The bar at The Prince's Hotel was busy, but the evening was chilly and the outside tables had been stacked away. She held her bag closer and quickened her stride, her key braced in her hand. She scanned the darkened street. Nothing. She let go of the tension in her shoulders and unlocked the door.

'Hello, Dr Hart.' The voice in her ear was chilling, the fingers gripping her elbow ice tentacles. Clare forced herself to turn and look at the man trapping her between his hard body and the car.

'I hear you've been looking for me. Here I am. I thought you'd recognise me.' He sounded disappointed.

Clare forced her mind to function. He was so close she could feel the heat of his body, but the man made no further move towards her or her car. She looked at the face, lit by a distant street lamp. It was familiar. Then he moved and the white scars etched down his cheek were visible. 'Kelvin Landman,' she whispered.

'The same.' He smiled, mouth turning up, wrinkling his scar, his eyes untouched. 'I hear you are looking for a star.'

Clare's mind had been so far from her film that it took her a few seconds to remember that she had put the word about that she wanted to talk to Kelvin Landman, to interview him for her film. She swallowed. 'I wanted to interview you, yes,' she said. 'Get your side of the story. See how the business works.'

Kelvin Landman shrugged. 'I am a simple man. Bit of import, bit of export. Bit of pleasure. It's a service that I provide. There's a demand – so why not?' He smiled, the muscles in his neck taut.

'Did you know Charnay Swanepoel, the girl whose body was found in Sea Point?' Clare was irritated that her voice quavered.

'Why? Should I?'

'It's meant to be your territory now,' said Clare. She tried to free her arm from his grip. Landman held her for a single menacing second, his physical power needing no other demonstration. Then he held the door open for her.

'Let's do lunch. It sounds like we might have some interests in common.'

Before she could respond, he took her hand. The silver pen flashed like a knife in the moonlight. He wrote a phone number on her exposed palm. 'Call me,' he said, folding her hand closed, closing the door. He waited until she'd started her car and driven back towards the exit. When she glanced into her rear-view mirror he was nothing but a shadow between the trees. She kept her eyes on him as she waited for a gap in the late-night traffic. As she slipped into her lane the shadow moved in the direction of the marina.

Clare started to shake, but she managed to keep the steering-wheel steady. Rear-view mirror. Brake. Breathe. Indicate. Turn. Park. She rested her forehead on the steering-wheel. The panic was gone. She was home.

13

Dinner with Julie and Marcus was at eight. Clare reversed her car out of the garage and set off across town for her older sister's house, a bottle of cold wine on the seat next to her. She stopped to buy sunflowers before turning up the steep road that led to the house. The grey mountain, its flanks lit for the tourists, loomed like a ghostly elephant above her.

The security gate slid open before Clare could ring the bell. Beatrice, who could now just reach the button if she stood on tiptoe, had been looking out for her. She bulleted down the stairs, and into Clare's arms. Imogen was just behind her to rescue the wine and flowers and to be kissed on the cheek. Beatrice patted Clare's body expertly until she came to the pocket with the chocolate bar in it. This she wolfed down before her mother was out of the front door to greet Clare.

'Hello, Julie.' Clare kissed her sister and accepted the affectionate hug from her brother-in-law. 'Hi, Marcus.'

She carried Beatrice inside and plonked her on her bed. Beatrice ferreted around in the drift of soft toys. A plump and triumphant arm brandished the book she'd been looking for.

'Read me a story, Clare. Please read me a story.' Beatrice was already flicking through the old fairy-tale book.

Clare settled down next to her. There was no point in

resisting Beatrice. One story would settle her, and then the adults could eat in peace. Clare drew her small niece inside the crook of her arm, delighting in her grubby warmth. 'Okay, Bea, what shall we read? Cinderella? The Lemon Princess?'

'Bluebeard,' said Beatrice, bouncing with anticipation. 'Bluebeard. He's so bad!'

Clare prickled with horror at the lurid picture of Bluebeard's wives hanging in their secret chamber. The youngest wife stood stricken, key in hand, watching the indelible bloodstain spread.

'It's her favourite.' Imogen spoke from the door. She must have been watching for a while. Only a few years before, it had been Imogen demanding a bedtime story from Clare. 'It's gross, but she loves that story. Especially the bit when the brothers come to kill Bluebeard at the end.'

Curled against her aunt's body, Beatrice stuck her tongue out at her big sister. She stabbed a plump finger at the old book. 'Read, Clare, read.' Clare read.

> '*Blue Beard: the Moral*
> Ladies, you should never pry,
> You'll repent it by and by!
> Tis the silliest of sins;
> Trouble in a trice begins. There are,
> surely – more's the woe
> Lots of things you need not know.
> Come, forswear it now and here –
> Joy so brief that costs so dear!'

'No morals,' interrupted Beatrice. 'Just the story.' Clare could feel the small body softening towards sleep. She held Bea closer, shielding herself from thoughts of the dead girl on the promenade. Clare did not want to bring her here into her sister's house. The story ended and Bluebeard's resourceful wife was rescued by her brothers. Clare kissed Beatrice and tucked her in, leaving the little girl to dream of sword-fighting and vengeance.

Julie had a glass of chilled wine ready for Clare when she came through to join the rest of the family by the fire. Clare sipped it, drifting on the conversational flow of a family catching up with itself at the end of a busy day. The evening might not have been as comfortable if Riedwaan had been there. Julie carried in a gleaming copper pot and they ate at the fire – big bowls of soup and chunks of bread.

'What happened to your hand?' Julie touched the plaster.

'A dog. Can you believe it?' Clare replied.

'Nothing to do with your investigation into human trafficking?' Julie looked suspicious.

'No, no,' said Clare. 'There's a new security guard on that empty building site near me, and his dog was off the leash. He appeared from nowhere, they both did.' Clare rubbed her hand – it must be healing because it was starting to itch. 'I'll be fine, Julie. Didn't need stitches and I had a tetanus shot.'

Julie looked sceptical but Clare couldn't see any point in telling her how odd the incident had been. 'Sorry, Dr Hart,' the guard had leered, leashing his dog. 'Perhaps this is not such a safe place for you here.' That he knew her name had given her more of a chill than the dog's unprovoked attack.

'The Osiris Group bought that land,' said Marcus.

'Did they? When? I thought it belonged to the city council,'. said Julie.

'It did, but Osiris has acquired a whole lot of land. Their plans are flying through council. I heard that the mayor was trying to get the planning division sorted out, but this is something else.'

'I had a letter the other day asking if I wanted to sell,' said Clare. 'They have been quite persistent. Who are they?'

'They're quite new,' said Marcus. 'Well, in Cape Town anyway. I got one of those free property magazines, and it was fawning over Osiris and Otis Tohar, who owns the company. He's like a rash all over the social pages, by the way. His father was a doctor who made his money somewhere in the Middle East. But his son seems dead set on making his own money. Apparently his mother was from Cape Town, hence his feeling of belonging here. He has been behind some of the new developments in Bantry Bay and Clifton.'

Clare hated how the gentle curves of the Atlantic seaboard were being eaten away by serried ranks of steel and glass high-rises that stared at the setting sun. 'I am not selling. And if I have to, I'll take him to court. There are strict limits to what can be built there,' Clare said.

'Be careful,' said Marcus. 'Otis Tohar is very well connected.'

'That's no problem.' Clare had dealt with corrupt politicians often enough not to fear them. 'I've been invited to the launch with the rest of the press. It should be worth it.'

'It'll be interesting to see who's there,' said Marcus. 'I've also heard that he is in the pocket of some very powerful people who are not concerned about what the press says about them.'

Clare remembered the guard's cuff of blue prison-gang tattoos, revealed when he had leashed his dog. 'Who?' she asked.

Marcus held his hands up. 'This is third-hand, but I have heard that Kelvin Landman has helped him with a couple of cash-flow tight spots. That advertising producer, King I think is his name, has apparently also invested. Must have money to burn. Or launder. The construction business is a brilliant way of getting dirty money clean. So much cash, so many costs, so many places to hide the money and then pop it out later as legitimate profit.'

'Not a pleasant combination,' said Clare. 'Kelvin Landman

turns up all over the place. He's the guy I have been angling to interview for my new documentary.'

'Who wants pudding?' asked Julie, adding a log to the fire to dispel the sudden chill in the room.

'I'll get it,' said Imogen, getting up.

'Come, I'll help you,' said Clare, gathering their plates. They walked though to the kitchen together. Clare stacked the dishwasher while Imogen set bowls, spoons and Julie's lemon ice cream on a tray.

'My friend knew her,' said Imogen.

'Who, darling?' asked Clare, rinsing glasses in the sink. Imogen didn't reply. 'Who knew who?'

'That girl they found near you.' Clare looked up. Imogen was watching her. 'My friend Frances knew her. The police came to speak to Frances. That guy we met once. He came.'

'Riedwaan?' said Clare.

'*Ja*, him. And a woman. Rita someone. Frances had to make a whole statement.'

'How did your friend know Charnay?' Clare asked.

'She didn't know her well, but she'd seen her at the Chili Club and once or twice at Dolce's at the Waterfront.' In fact, Clare had picked Imogen up from both places before. 'Frances says she saw her last week,' said Imogen. 'She was sitting at a table next to hers at Dolce's. I had flu so I couldn't go out. Frances says she was boasting that she would soon be a star. And that we should all get her autograph now because she was going to be the next Charlize.'

'Why did she say that?' asked Clare.

'I don't know. Maybe she had finally got a part. She was always going to auditions. Frances says she ignored her.' Her face was pale, the set of her mouth adult beyond her sixteen years.

'Did anything else happen?' asked Clare.

'Nothing,' said Imogen. 'She went to see a movie.'

'What time was that?' asked Clare.

'It must have been a quarter to eight,' said Imogen. 'For the eight o'clock show. So, yes, a quarter to eight.' She picked up the dessert tray. She paused at the kitchen door. 'That was the night she disappeared, wasn't it?'

Clare nodded.

'So where was she all that time before she died?'

Clare looked at Imogen. She was no longer a child. Imogen might even have some idea of what the dead girl had endured in the days before she died. Clare shook her head. 'I have no idea yet.'

'She was a pain, that girl,' said Imogen, pushing through the swing door. 'But she didn't deserve what she got.'

'Who does?' said Clare to the door, which had swung closed behind Imogen.

Clare followed her back to the fire but she found it difficult to settle down. She couldn't finish her dessert. She felt tired and she suddenly needed to be alone.

'I think I'll be on my way,' said Clare, standing up. She carried a tray of glasses through to the kitchen.

'Don't worry,' said Marcus. 'You look exhausted. I'll finish cleaning up.'

Clare kissed his cheek. 'Thanks,' she said. 'I am tired. Thanks for supper.'

'Bye, Clare, we'll see you soon.'

Julie walked to the car with her. 'How was Constance?'

'She's the same, Jules. Always the same.' Clare started her car. 'Thanks for supper.' Julie stood and waved, returning to her family when Clare turned at the bottom of the hill.

14

Clare drove home through quiet streets, avoiding the weekend frenzy building up near the strip of clubs that snaked up Long Street. It was later than she had intended, but immersing herself in Julie's domesticity had restored her. She let herself in, relieved to be home. Fritz wrapped herself around Clare's ankles, reminding her that she had not been fed. Clare ignored the cat's disdain at the dried food clattering so late into her bowl. She made herself a cup of tea, added a shot of whiskey to it, and checked for email. She held her breath as it downloaded.

'Yes,' she exhaled. 'Yes!' There was the go-ahead for her documentary on trafficking. Her refusal to alter or dilute her story had paid off. There was nothing but the caveat that she should not glorify the bad guys, or airbrush the victims into unrealistic innocence. There was a note from the executive producer to follow up on the money-laundering angle. Dates, accounts, companies, front companies – her weekend was mapped out for her. How did they manage it, making money *that* dirty 'clean' again? Clare sat wondering after she'd sent her elated reply.

It was already past one by the time she got into bed. The phone rang just as she had settled in, Fritz curled in the small of her back. She ignored it, but it started to ring again. Clare sighed, pushed aside her duvet, and went to pick up the cellphone she had left in her study.

'Jakes,' she said, reading the name that came up on her screen. It was his home number. 'What are you doing? It's one in the morning.' Clare could hear music, glasses clinking in the background.

'It can't be that late.' He had been drinking. She could feel the irritation welling up in her, despite the lure of his flirtatious voice.

'It is. What do you want?'

'Don't be so bad-tempered, Clare. I'm sure you're not busy right now.'

'Jakes, I've known you long enough to know that you weren't sitting at home worrying about how lonely I might be. What do you want?'

'Clare,' he said affectionately. 'Always straight for the jugular.' He paused, waiting for her to defend herself. When she didn't, he decided that he may as well get to the point before she put the phone down. 'Clare, baby, are you by any chance invited to that Osiris Group party?'

'Osiris, Osiris, Osiris. Everybody is talking about them and they are ruining my neighbourhood.'

'Well, are you?' insisted Jakes.

'I am invited.'

'Don't you need a date?'

Clare said nothing.

'Come on, don't be such an ice-queen,' he wheedled.

Clare sighed. This was how he got women into bed: there didn't seem to be anything to do except give in. 'Okay, Jakes. Just this once.'

'Can I pick you up?' he asked.

'Okay,' said Clare. 'Pick me up at seven. And remember – you owe me.'

'Of course,' said Jakes. 'I'll see you then.' She heard a girl's sultry laugh behind his voice. Clare switched the phone off. She knew what that girl would look like – slim, supple, hair brushing honey-brown shoulders. No more than twenty, seventeen if Jakes had his wish. Clare got back into bed smiling. She reckoned Jakes had, at forty-five, about two more girlfriends to go before he'd have to pay by the hour for his dream girls. She turned out the light. Jakes Kani was a good photographer. Even though he sold his pictures to anybody who'd pay, he knew how to make a woman enjoy her body. He had loved her, in his way, and he could make her laugh.

The Osiris party would be more fun with him there. She turned over to sleep, wishing for a moment that the warm weight against her back was not a cat, but a man.

15

Apart from a long run on Saturday afternoon and a hastily eaten bowl of pasta at Giovanni's, Clare worked on the documentary all Saturday. She was up and working again on Sunday morning, tiredness banished by coffee. She emailed Riedwaan, asking him to check the logs of the private yachts at the Waterfront marina. She wanted to know who owned them and who had skippered them during the time Charnay had been missing. Clare had arranged to see the old man who had found Charnay. He lived five blocks from her flat so she walked, the sun warm on her back. She scanned the name tags that accompanied the buzzers outside the San Souci apartment block. There he was, Harry Rabinowitz: 8 A. She pressed. A voice crackled. 'Dr Hart?'

'Yes, it's me.'

The door buzzed and she pushed it open. The foyer had that deserted feeling holiday flats have out of season. Post was piled in lopsided heaps on top of full letterboxes. The yellowed indoor plant was forlorn in its dry pot, choked by a ruff of discarded cigarette ends. The lift was clean, though, and had recently been serviced – Clare checked this before pressing the button for the eighth floor. She tamped down the small flicker of panic that came with the uprush of the steel box.

The doors opened, Harry Rabinowitz was waiting for her.

He was older than she had imagined. His wiry, athletic body belied the whiteness of his hair. He had been wearing a cap when she had seen him cover the dead girl.

'Welcome, Dr Hart.' His handshake was firm, his warm skin paper dry. He shepherded her towards his flat at the end of the dark corridor. He opened the door and sunlight splashed over them. The view was breathtaking, the expanse of ocean cradled by the crescent of land that curved north. The sturdy weight of Robben Island gave the view focus. It contrasted with the red and blue cargo ships heading towards the harbour. A tray was laid with delicate china, silver sugar tongs. The aroma of fresh coffee was strong.

'Do sit down, Dr Hart.' He pointed to a red leather chair and waited until she sat down. 'Can I offer you some coffee? Some cake?'

Clare wanted neither, but accepted both. 'It's very kind of you to see me.'

'Not at all. The pleasure is mine.' Clare looked around the flat. It had been tidied in preparation for her visit. Loneliness had trans formed a stranger coming to ask questions into a rare social occasion. There were amateurish swipes in the dust on the dark tables that cluttered the space between the chairs. She set her cup down and got up to look at the framed photographs on the crowded bookshelf.

'Your children?' she asked, turning to him, holding the first picture that came to hand. It was of a man with his arm around a too-thin woman whose smile failed to mask her irritation. Seated in front of them were three children in the unattractive dress of a formal photograph. The boys were suety, sullen. The girl, about sixteen, was arresting: a sculpted face surrounded by a shock of curls. Winged brows framed her black eyes.

'What a beautiful girl,' said Clare.

77

'My Rachel. My son's daughter. They live in New York.' He stared at the photograph, perhaps musing on the girl who was now moving into a complex American adolescence that he could not comprehend. A beloved stranger to him.

'The other girl.' He hesitated, unsure how to go on. 'The one I found – would she be the same age?' Clare nodded. She did not point out how similar the two looked. Perhaps that was something that Mr Rabinowitz would prefer not to see.

'Would you take a walk with me?' she asked. 'Back along the promenade? Perhaps you could tell me what you saw.' He looked anxious. 'I know it will be painful, but maybe you will remember something else. Something more than you told the police.'

He weighed that up. 'All right, my dear, all right.' He walked back to the hallway and picked up his coat. A woman's coat hung next to it, some ten years out of date. It had not been moved for a long time. The creases formed on the hook had faded. The fabric would eventually disintegrate. Clare still had her coat on, so she picked up her bag and stepped ahead of him through the front door. She held the lift while he locked and relocked the security doors that kept him safe. They were silent in the lift – both watching the winking light that indicated the progress of their journey back to street level.

They crossed Beach Road, taking a short cut through the park where a couple of children played, watched by their bored nannies. The vagrants had stirred to life and were drifting into the cold day. Mr Rabinowitz greeted some of the older ones. The younger men – less battered, more bitter – he did not seem to know.

A woman was selling flowers. 'The flowers,' Mr Rabinowitz said more to himself than to Clare. 'At least there was something lovely with her.' The old man stopped. 'Which would be best for a young girl, Mavis?' he asked.

'Those irises. Just thirty rand a bunch. I'll give you two for fifty,' she said. Harry handed her the money and the flower seller wrapped the flowers.

'She's *mos* a pretty girl. Lucky,' the flower seller said, winking at Clare.

'I usually walk every day, my dear, but this is the first time I have been out since I found her.' He fell into step with Clare on the curve of the promenade. The sea wall obscured the ocean, but every now and then the hidden waves tossed up arcs of spray that pirouetted then splashed at their feet. They were approaching Three Anchor Bay, where Charnay Swanepoel's broken young body had been found.

'I was out earlier than usual that morning. I had a meeting with my accountant and I didn't want to be late.' Clare already knew this, as she had read Riedwaan's interview transcripts. Xavier Ndoro, the security guard, had not seen him leave. According to his interview, he had been making coffee, and usually no one left before six in the morning. So Mr Rabinowitz must have let himself out.

'Tell me what happened,' said Clare. 'Everything. Each detail. As if you were replaying a movie. Tell me details that might seem unimportant, out of focus.' Harry pointed to a bench and they sat down. The wind had shifted around and was coming hard off the sea. There was ice on its breath.

'I came out of my building as usual. It was dark. No one about. The homeless were all huddled together around those ablution blocks there.' Clare looked at them, five hundred metres from where they sat, from where the girl had been found. She was glad she was too far away to smell the foetid air they exuded. 'It was misty. I remember hearing the foghorn as I stepped onto the promenade.'

'When did you notice her?' asked Clare.

'It was as I rounded this corner where we're sitting now.

See those tamarisks?' He pointed to the wind-crippled trees. 'They're small, but they obscure your view of this little bay here. As I came round here, I saw her near those steps.' He dabbed at his watery eyes. 'I thought it was a dead dog. Or a heap of rubbish. I was nearly on top of her before I realised it was a girl.' Harry Rabinowitz leaned forward and rubbed his foot. 'She was very beautiful.'

'Have you hurt yourself?' asked Clare, looking down as he rubbed.

'I stubbed my foot against something that morning. Maybe one of those manhole covers. The council is so hopeless with maintenance these days that people are always hurting themselves.'

They got up to walk to the place where Charnay had lain. The flowers people had left for her had been whipped away by the wind or scavenged by vagrants and sold for a few rand. Enough to buy cheap wine or a bottle of methylated spirits.

The old man took off his hat and closed his eyes. Clare looked up from where the body had lain, towards the sea. There was a flight of stairs fifty metres away, which led down to the jagged rocks that were exposed only at low tide. High tide had been at five forty-five the morning the body was found. It had been full moon, so the water would have been deep. At spring tide the rocks were submerged, so a small craft could have reached the bottom of the steps.

She turned her back to the sea. The car park was close enough for her to make out what takeaways people were eating. Whoever had dumped Charnay could as easily have parked there. It would have taken ten seconds to carry the girl – she had only weighed fifty kilograms – and place her here for Harry to find, posed as carefully as a model for a shoot.

Clare pulled her coat closed and walked back. The large

manhole cover was set into its frame. Either this was not the one that had injured Harry's foot or the council had fixed it. Harry, she noticed, had replaced his hat. She sat down next to him.

'It was so quiet that morning,' he said. 'You know how the fog sometimes absorbs sound back into itself?' Clare nodded. 'There was no traffic either, but I thought that just after I found her I heard a car engine. I looked up because I was hoping for help. But there were no lights, no movement. Just the sound, but as if it was coming from below. The fog distorts things, disorientates you. And then someone came. That group of lady walkers. Some time afterwards, the police. They were quick. The station is right there behind the garage.' Harry did not know that Clare had also been there, that she had seen him looking at the dead girl, his face suffused with yearning and anger.

'Anything else you remember, Mr Rabinowitz?' Clare asked into the long silence

'You know, Dr Hart, I did hear that car again after I found her. It sounded as if it idled for a bit. Maybe waiting for the lights to change.' Clare checked the road. There were no traffic lights. 'Do you know what kind of car it was?' she asked.

'Oh, I don't know. I did look up, but the driver must have just accelerated because all I registered was a flash of something low, dark.'

'Was it black?' Clare asked.

Harry sifted through the fragmented memories of that morning. 'I don't know,' he said. 'I think it was blue. A dark blue. Powerful engine, too.'

He turned from her and took the irises out from the shelter of his coat. He separated the most perfect one from the bunch and put it where the girl's body had lain on the gum-pocked pavement. The rest he took to the water's edge. He flung the

81

violet blooms into the air and the wind lifted them, carrying them for a few seconds before discarding them to the churning waves below. Harry put his hands back in his pockets and headed back home. Clare watched the flowers, glad that the old man did not see them being dashed against the rocks till they blended with the snared rubbish.

She caught up with him and they walked in silence till they reached her car. 'Thank you so much,' she said. 'I'll head for home from here.'

'Well, good luck, my dear.' He was disappointed she wasn't coming up for a second coffee. Harry watched her until her car turned the corner, then he went upstairs to his flat. Once inside, he heated a cup of coffee in the microwave and went to sit at his computer. No one would phone him today so it didn't matter how long he spent on the Internet. He wrote a long email to his son in America. He knew he wouldn't get more than a two-line reply. Mr Rabinowitz wondered if his boy even read them. Later he would email Rachel, glad she was far away from here. She, at least, would answer.

16

Clare picked up the Sunday papers and a takeaway on her way home, remembering to get cat food too. Fritz had been incensed that morning when she hadn't been fed. The phone rang as she was fumbling with the key of her security gate. She got in just in time to answer it.

'Clare?' It was Rita Mkhize.

'Hi, Rita. What's happening?' asked Clare, anxiety tightening her throat.

'It's bad news, *sisi*. Bad news. Another girl is gone.'

'When? Who?'

'Today. Right now. I took the call but I can't get hold of Captain Faizal. He's not picking up his phone. I thought maybe he was with you.'

'He's not,' said Clare curtly.

'Sorry, Clare . . . I didn't mean anything, but we need him.'

'I'll go past Riedwaan's house and see if he's there.'

'Thanks, Clare. There is chaos down here.'

Clare quickly poured some food into Fritz's bowl and went to find Riedwaan. Parking on Signal Street, she crossed the cobbled road. There was no sign of life, but she could hear music. She knocked. Nothing.

'Riedwaan?' she called, knocking louder.

'Who's there?'

'It's Clare. Let me in.' The door opened.

'What are you doing here?' he asked. 'It's Sunday.'

'Your phone was off. Rita called me.'

Riedwaan stiffened. 'Now what?'

'Another girl is missing. Here, speak to her.' Clare dialled Rita Mkhize's number and handed the phone to Riedwaan. She followed him inside. It looked as if Riedwaan had been doing housework. There was a pile of laundry on the kitchen floor. The sink was filled with a week's worth of dishes.

'Mkhize? Riedwaan Faizal here.' He picked up a pen and jotted down notes. He handed Clare's phone back to her, his face grim.

'Who?' asked Clare. 'Where?'

'Amore Hendricks: the only daughter of elderly parents, a dancer, current Miss Panorama High. Slim, seventeen, long black hair. Last seen on Saturday when a family friend dropped her off at Canal Walk shopping mall to meet a friend. Reported missing by her father. I'd better get down to the station. Rita's waiting for me – and so is Phiri. He's on the warpath, as you can imagine, worrying whether the press has already got wind of it. We'll get the interviews started.'

Riedwaan had his keys in his hand. Clare handed him his jacket. 'I'll call you when I've got some news.' He touched Clare's cheek.

'No news won't be good news,' said Clare, closing Riedwaan's door behind them.

'I hope you're wrong.'

Clare grimaced, then drove home into the cold fog settling along the promenade.

17

Rita Mkhize and Riedwaan interviewed everyone who had recently seen Amore Hendricks, but three days' work produced nothing. Chief-Superintendent Phiri decided to keep it from the press, which Riedwaan opposed bitterly, trying to convince Phiri that someone might have seen the girl, that they might come forward. Phiri had not wanted any more accusations of police incompetence and had refused to budge. Riedwaan passed everything on to Clare, but there was little to go on. Because there was nothing else for her to do, Clare immersed herself in her film research.

It was late in the afternoon when she eventually switched off her computer, so she had to rush to get ready for the party. The dress code for the Osiris Group Launch was formal; no allowance made for the 'traditional' that covered a multitude of sartorial sins. Clare dressed carefully in pared-down black, and pinned her hair up. She poured herself a whiskey, glad that Jakes was a few minutes late. It gave her time to collect her thoughts. She took a closer look at the promotional material that had come with the invitation. A piece of parchment fell into her lap. Intrigued, Clare smoothed it out. It was the story of the Egyptian god Osiris, betrayed by his brother then dismembered and thrown into the sea. His sister Isis eventually rescued him, restoring both body and crown to him.

On the next fold was a short CV of Otis Tohar and the Osiris Group – the two entities indistinguishable. Clare skimmed it, drawn by the grainy family photographs. Otis Tohar was the only son of a South African mother and a Lebanese father – an ambiguous identity. His father had been a doctor. The family had moved from Cape Town to Johannesburg, then to Kimberley, to Lebanon and to Sierra Leone. Tohar's father had died, leaving his fortune to his only son. Otis Tohar had consolidated his fortune by building – so the blurb on the invitation claimed – on 'the great humanitarian legacy of his father'. Clare was sceptical. Sierra Leone was notorious for blood diamonds and child soldiers, not humanitarian effort.

No mention was made of the shadowy girl; a sister, Clare guessed, judging by the matched black brows and luxurious hair in the photograph. She was a few years older than the awkward little boy her arm encircled. Tohar's mother had named her son after Otis Redding. His song 'Sitting on the Dock of the Bay' had reminded her of her youth in Sea Point and her walks along the promenade. It was this, gushed the brochure, that had prompted Otis Tohar to return to the place his mother had been forced to leave in her youth.

Tohar had been very busy since selling up in Lebanon and abandoning whatever was left of his business in Sierra Leone, mused Clare. He seemed to have limitless cash. Block after beautiful art deco block had been sold to him. These were being razed, though, and in their place steel and glass titans were rearing up from the subdued land. Clare turned the parchment over in her hands as she stared ahead of her. Tohar's latest acquisition blinked its blind neon eyes across Three Anchor Bay. It would need a very quick return on such a huge investment for him to make a profit. But the Cape Town city council, notorious for its geriatric slowness, was passing plans and quashing objections at an indecent rate.

The doorbell interrupted her thoughts. Fritz's eyes slitted in disgust as Clare pushed her off her lap to gather her bag and cloak.

Jakes Kani had pulled up right by her door, but still her stockings and shoes got wet. 'Cats and dogs,' said Jakes, leaning over to kiss her cheek. He handed her a towel and she rubbed herself dry. 'You look gorgeous, Clare,' he said.

'You don't look too bad yourself,' Clare shot back, 'considering your age.'

He laughed, hands going to the balding spot on his crown. 'Hey, Clare, you know I don't fight dirty.' He started the old Mercedes and bumped off the pavement.

'What do you know about Otis Tohar?' Clare asked.

'Not much,' said Jakes. 'Nothing concrete, except that he has clambered up Cape Town's social ladders. But who wouldn't if they had enough money?'

'Don't be nasty, Jakes, tabloid photographers like you will always hit the snakes,' said Clare. 'Tell me whose ladders, and how. I'm curious to know why I was invited.'

'He loves the media, being a celebrity. That explains you, I suppose,' Jakes looked at her sideways. She was still damn good looking, that might explain it too, although he didn't say anything to Clare. But she really was rather past it, for some of Tohar's sidelines. 'I know that the mayor had his birthday party on Tohar's yacht, the *Isis*.'

'Does he berth it at the Waterfront marina?'

'He does,' said Jakes. 'I've also heard that Tohar and Kelvin Landman are pretty close.'

'A delightful couple.'

'Landman moved faster up the ranks of a Cape Flats gang than anyone I've ever heard of,' said Jakes.

'How did he do it?'

'He's sharp, has a nose for business. He consolidated business and turf. If you didn't agree, you were dead. If you did, you were rich. Everybody figured it out after a while.'

'He's moved beyond local stuff, though,' said Clare. 'The information I've got about human trafficking is that it is very organised. Nothing ad hoc about this at all.'

'I know he was in Jo'burg for a while. Not sure what he did there, but he must have made an impression. He got into trouble with the police at some stage – and next thing you know, he was asking for asylum in Holland just before '94. He was there for years, and that's where he really got into the big league.'

'I suppose everyone who's anyone in international organised crime moves through Amsterdam at some stage.'

'*Ja*,' said Jakes. 'He developed some very cosy bilateral ties with the South Americans. I put out the word that you wanted to interview him about the import/export side of his business,' said Jakes. 'Has he contacted you?'

Clare remembered Landman's fingers hard on her elbow. 'He did. Thanks. Do you know what his focus is these days?'

'He's moved into town now,' continued Jakes. 'He bought a mansion in Clifton and he's going legit. He's moving into property too. That's where he and Tohar have connected. The bastard will be submitting a tax return soon. Apparently he's opening branches of The Isis Club from Bellville to Benoni and making a fortune. Two Isis Safari Lodges have also just opened, one outside Pretoria and one here in Cape Town. Have a look, I've got a brochure in the cubbyhole. Very upmarket, very secluded, specialising in catering to their overnight clients' "wildest jungle fevers". That is what their ad says, anyway. You'll love their slogan: "Your wish: Her command".'

'You know a lot about him,' said Clare.

'We met last month. The Isis has started making films and I was asked to do some stills for a film shoot. For a video cover, actually. I did it, but their speciality is not really my thing. There is an almost limitless profit – if you make the right kind of movies and have good distribution,' said Jakes as he turned into the parking area for the party guests.

'What kind of films?' asked Clare.

'Oh, they do a bit of fuzzy erotica, but mainly it is the very end of the legal hard-core spectrum. I prefer women with a bit of spirit. I can't see the fun in tying them up and gagging them before you hang them from the ceiling,' said Jakes.

Jakes handed his keys to the valet who was dressed in Egyptian blue and gold. Clare and Jakes made their way across the thick red carpet that led to the old Sea Point Tower Hotel. The party was in the revolving pinnacle of the building. Otis Tohar had acquired the whole place eighteen months before and had kept the three floors below the original revolving restaurant as his penthouse. The rest of the hotel had been sold off as luxury apartments. Clare glanced at the guest list as the bouncer searched for her name. There were several names that she recognised – politicians whose names had been associated with shady land deals and golf estates, two ex-beauty queens, and a few entrepreneurs whose businesses would have been difficult to explain to the taxman.

'Hart. Doctor.' The bouncer smiled at Clare, his large finger dwarfing her name. 'And Partner. Go up.'

They stepped into the plush private lift. Before they had a chance to draw breath, the doors opened on the top floor. Clare gasped at the view. The city lights were stitched together by the threads of the evening traffic – white headlights, red taillights. The rain had stopped and the clouds parted to reveal the moon on the horizon. The restless waves were contained behind the sea wall. Then the gap closed again.

A girl silently materialised, her hair in an elaborate Egyptian wig. She gave them champagne and took their coats without meeting their eyes. As she turned from them to greet the next offering to emerge from the elevator, her short shift parted to reveal a tattoo. Clare stared, startled by its familiarity. The girl, sensing that she was being looked at, turned around. Her hostess's smile evaporated, leaving her face blank, her eyes expressionless. Then she turned back again to smile and wiggle for the man who had stepped out of the lift. He tested the firmness of her bottom as one would test a peach before eating it. Clare turned and followed Jakes into a room that had been converted into an opulent Pharaoh's court for the night.

'Money certainly doesn't buy you taste,' said Jakes under his breath while waving at someone across the room. Clare circulated with Jakes, admiring his social dexterity. He already had several fading models around him, competing for lens space.

'Chick magnet,' Clare muttered. She went in search of a drink.

An obese politician, whose incompetence seemed directly proportional to the number of companies desperate to have him on their boards, cornered her at the bar. Clare extricated herself as the man piled his plate high with canapés offered to him by a succulent waitress.

Going over to the window, she noticed with surprise that she could see her flat from up there. She had bought it with the first royalty cheque she had received for the book she had written about the gang rape of her beloved twin. Blood money was what Julie called it. Clare had divided the income. Half for her, half for Constance.

She scanned the promenade where Charnay Swanepoel's body had been dumped. If the girl's family had made a shrine, the rain had washed it clear. The investigation team was no closer to solving Charnay's murder, even though the police lab had analysed the DNA traces on the body and it looked like they might be searching for two men. The blood group of the skin under the dead girl's nails was one group, the semen traces indicated another. Riedwaan thought there could be two or more people involved. Clare thought not. The posthumous mutilations spoke to her of one man. Nothing had turned up. No cellphone records, no witness. Nothing on the CCTV. The police had checked – only to find that the camera along that stretch of the promenade was fake. Clare felt a surge of guilt that the days since Charnay's murder had stretched first into one week and then another. That silence was ominous. And now another girl had vanished. Clare suddenly wished she was home.

She turned back to the vast room, which was swathed in blue velvet. It was filling up rapidly. She greeted a senior policeman who had an expensive-looking woman on his arm. Clare had once interviewed him about proposed anti-trafficking legislation. He shifted uncomfortably when he recognised Clare, apparently unable to remember her name.

Otis Tohar had not yet arrived, but Kelvin Landman was there. He was sprawled on the largest of the couches, surrounded by his entourage. Clare walked closer, but stopped as a waitress brought them a bottle of single malt. One of the men pulled the waitress towards him, grinding her into his lap, one hand mauling her small breasts. Landman watched, amused.

Just then, a soft flurry of sound blew from the entrance through the scattered conversations. Otis Tohar, tall and striking, paused just long enough to be sure that all eyes were on him. Trailing in his wake was a woman who wore her exotic beauty like a mask. Clare jumped at the sudden hand on her arm. One of Kelvin Landman's companions was at her elbow.

'Excuse me, Dr Hart. Mr Landman says you must join us.' Clare looked across at Landman. He inclined his head towards her in greeting. The waitress, Clare noted with relief, had escaped.

'Hello again, Dr Hart,' said Kelvin Landman, standing as Clare reached the table. 'Please join us.' A glance dislodged two of the men seated close to him. Clare sat down. 'Can I offer you a whiskey?' He handed her a glass, not waiting for her to reply. Clare took it but did not drink.

'A fine couple, Otis Tohar and Tatiana,' said Landman, looking speculatively at the woman.

Clare looked over at Tohar. 'Tatiana? That sounds Russian.'

'Could be. Cape Town is an international city these days.'

Clare added some water to her drink.

'I'm glad to see you, Dr Hart. I hope your research is going well?' He paused, the question hanging between them.

Clare smiled at him, holding his gaze. 'I have spoken to some of the women. I look forward to hearing what you have to say.'

'I create work,' said Landman, leaning forward. 'With forty per cent unemployment in the country, that can only be a good thing. Where I come from, people are proud of me. They eat. Their kids go to school.'

Clare swirled the whiskey, the crystal refracting the golden liquid, and waited for him to continue.

'I provide a service. Where there is a demand, I find a supply. Look at these girls.' He gestured towards the half-naked waitresses, several of whom looked far too young to be up this late. 'If it wasn't for me these girls wouldn't be working, their families wouldn't be eating.' Landman smiled, top lip curling back, revealing his teeth.

'Why don't you come to one of my clubs, Dr Hart? Come to the Isis. You'll be my guest. You can meet some of my girls.' He handed her a card. On it was a familiar city address. 'Eleven o'clock, Saturday?'

'Thank you,' said Clare. 'Shall we record the interview there?'

'Why not?' he replied. He leaned towards her, placing one manicured hand on her exposed knee. Clare shivered involuntarily. 'But no cameraman. No sound man. Only you.' Clare swallowed. His physical presence was unnerving. She looked down at the card.

'Fine,' she agreed. She slipped the card into her bag and got up to leave. 'I'll see you there at eleven.' Her knee felt hot when he removed his hand.

Otis Tohar's guests were drinking steadily. He circulated, slapping fawning politicians on the back, complimenting the overweight wives of eager businessmen. Clare watched Tatiana as she drifted unnoticed out of his orbit. She had bruises blooming like bracts of irises up her arms. She turned to see where Tohar was, then drew aside a heavy blue curtain and stepped behind it.

Clare followed her into the concealed passage. Ahead was a staircase spiralling down to the floor below and into Tohar's private quarters. Clare heard whimpering. There was a sliver of light from a door at the end of the passage. Clare pushed it open to reveal an editing suite and, behind it, a home cinema. The woman was folded into the director's chair, her back to a phalanx of video cases packed into glass-fronted shelves. Her slender arms were clenched with knuckle-whitening force around her knees. Her head was bent, the black hair a parted curtain. On her exposed neck was the tattoo: two verticals scored through with an X. Clare repressed the urge to reach out and touch it.

'Excuse me, Tatiana,' said Clare. 'Is something wrong?'

Tatiana's head snapped up, a video cassette in her hand.

93

Her eyes were blank for a moment and then they blazed with fury. She stood up and pushed past Clare.

Clare looked at the cover left behind on the desk. It was blank. There were banks of tapes, but the shelf above the edit suite was locked. Each of the videos had the Isis logo stuck to it. The lock was flimsy. Clare tried to twist it open, but before she could do so, she heard voices. She slipped back into the passage, her heart pounding. She was halfway up the stairs when whoever it was turned into the passage and closed the door that Clare had left wide open.

Clare pushed the curtain aside and walked straight into Otis Tohar. She was so close she could smell the sharpness of him beneath his expensive cologne.

'Dr Clare Hart. Were you lost? In search of entertainment?' he said, pulling her away from the curtain as he shook her proffered hand. The arm that slipped around her waist brooked no resistance. She allowed herself to be propelled across the floor towards the bar.

'I was looking for you. My friend, Kelvin Landman, tells me that you are going to be interviewing him for your latest film. Tell me, I have a special interest in film.'

'I'm researching a documentary on the business of trafficking women and children,' said Clare.

'How worthy,' said Tohar. 'You know, I suppose, that we have refurbished all the Isis clubs?'

'We?' said Clare.

'Oh, yes, I acquired several of the buildings where the Isis Clubs were established. And the land for the new Isis Safari Lodges – secluded, exclusive. Everything a busy man could want. You might be interested in doing a story. Not at all what you'd expect to find. Willing girls. Happy customers.' His eyes trailed over her body. Tohar put his arm around Landman who had materialised next to him.

'It's a growth industry, isn't it, Kelvin?'

Landman nodded. 'Unlimited. Just have to hold onto our wilder dreams while we keep an eye on the cash flow.' His voice was laced with honeyed menace. Tohar turned back to Clare. 'We are both very interested in movies. I am sure that it is going to be most interesting working with you, Dr Hart.'

'I'm sure,' said Clare. 'But I don't do promotional work.'

'Very principled,' said Tohar. 'Now, if you will excuse me, I must see to my guests.'

He and Landman walked towards the busy gaming tables set out in a corner of the room. Clare attributed the icy feeling in the pit of her stomach to hunger, not fear. She went in search of Jakes and something to eat.

18

The boy walked ahead, his buttocks moulded by the tight trousers, T-shirt clinging to his slight chest. The path across the beach to the tidal pool was slick with rain and seaweed abandoned by the receding tide. He turned into the lee of the wind, sheltered by the curved wall that led to the open sea. Waves thrashed over the black rocks, waiting for the return of the lulled storm. The first real storm of the winter, thought the boy, absenting himself from what was coming. Fifteen minutes of being there but not being there, and he would have the money he craved.

The man – fiftyish, paunchy, yet still muscled – braced himself against the rough concrete. Unzipped himself.

'Strip.'

The boy hesitated.

The man yanked him forward. 'Strip. And kneel.' The boy capitulated. What did it matter being cold for a while, having mussel shells cut into his knees? It would be over so soon. The boy took off his clothes, his dark skin goose-pimpling in the cold. The man pushed him down, hands clamped at the base of the boy's slender throat. He moved him slowly at first and then faster. The boy obeyed the terse orders, drifting loose now above the pool. Mind closed. Eyes, on instruction, open. It was when the man pulled him back for a final, choking plunge that he saw her lying between the rocks. The man finished, pushed him aside, enjoyed watching the boy scrabble for the negotiated notes he threw at him. And was gone. Back for dinner with his wife and daughter.

The boy pulled on his clothes, his eyes held by the pale undulation of the girl's body. He picked his way over to her, chilled by her stillness. He put his hand out to draw the wisp of her expensive top over the displayed breasts. He draped a ribbon of seaweed across her face, shutting out the blinded eyes. She was ice-cold to the touch. He felt sick as he ran back towards the road, away from her. He looked back once when he stopped to tuck the money into his pocket, then he caught a taxi home.

He heard his mother's soothing mutter calm his stepfather as he took the staircase up to his bedroom. His curtains were open. On the other side of his window Lower Main Road, deserted now and wet, trailed away towards Salt River. He shut his eyes, but all he saw was the girl, alone and dead on the rocks. Her long hair would be floating on the tide soon. The boy opened his eyes again but still she lingered, her right hand arced in a ballerina's beckoning, a mute plea.

He had to help her, but there was no way he was going to call the cops. He picked up his phone, checked for airtime. There was enough for an SMS. He riffled through the heap of papers on his desk. Right at the bottom was the folder he had kept from the documentary course he had done in the holidays. Dr Clare Hart. That was her name. She had given him a card when he had talked to her after a screening of one of her films. He had seen in the paper that she was involved in the investigation of the other murdered girl. His thumbs whirred across the tiny keys, forming the condensed message. He pressed 'send' and the icon swirled back and forth across the screen. Then it was gone. The boy sighed with relief:

the dead girl was gone too. She was someone else's problem now.

He drew the curtains, then felt behind his abandoned tennis racket on top of the cupboard. The small wooden box had not been moved. In it was everything he needed to bridge him into the next day. He took the syringe out, admiring its slender elegance as he fitted the needle. The burner was lit, then the powder dissolved on the spoon and was drawn into the syringe – the vein on his thigh eager for the needle. He avoided the soft inside of his arm. It was the first place an inquisitive teacher would look, and it made his clients wary. They liked to sully his innocence themselves. He pulled the blankets over himself and subsided into a chasm of sleep.

19

Clare was extricating Jakes from a cluster of women when the text message came through. Her anxiety, always circling below the surface, surged at the jarring beep. She opened her phone – 'Girl's body. Graaff's Pool.' She froze. She checked the message details. 'Private number' came up on her screen.

'What is it?' asked Jakes, sensing her distress. She held her hand up and walked to the window facing the sea, dialling Riedwaan's number.

The clouds lay low over the sea, but the rain had worn itself out. She could just make out Graaff's Pool. There was no one there, no one walking, no one loitering. A cold drizzle had driven even the hardiest vagrants off the benches and under the construction sites along Main Road. She shivered as she imagined a body out there, beyond the night-blackened sea wall.

Riedwaan answered. 'Did I wake you?' Clare asked.

'*Ja*,' he yawned. 'What is it?'

'Someone's found another body, Riedwaan. A girl.'

'Where is it?' Riedwaan was wide awake now. He was already out of bed and dressing, phone in hand. 'Where are you?'

'I'm at a party. Someone sent me a text message. I'll explain later. Meet me at Graaff's Pool. That's where the SMS said the girl's body was.'

'I'll be there now,' he said.

Clare wanted to say more but the words stuck, sharp in her throat. She snapped her phone shut.

Otis Tohar was standing next to her. 'A beautiful view, no?' He pointed in the direction she had been looking. 'One never knows what a night like this might bring, does one? Who were you calling?'

'A friend,' said Clare, surprised into answering his intimate question.

'Someone to meet for a nightcap? How lovely for you.'

Clare did not correct him. Instead, she thanked him for the party and fetched Jakes. The lift sank to the basement with a sigh. Clare pictured Otis Tohar watching the blue flash of police lights, the red of the ambulance from his eyrie, and the fear she had repressed came rushing back.

'What was the big rush?' Jakes asked as they turned onto the wet street.

'I need to go down to Graaff's Pool,' she told Jakes. 'Drop me at home so I can fetch my car.'

'Graaff's Pool? That's not a good place in the middle of the night. I'll come with you, be your knight in shining armour.'

'It's fine, Jakes. Just take me home.' But Jakes was weaving his car through the late-night taxis towards the beachfront. Clare was too tired to argue with him, and she did not really feel like waiting there alone. Jakes parked with the exaggerated accuracy of someone who has had too much to drink.

Riedwaan's car was not there yet. It would take him twenty minutes to get there from the Bo-Kaap, where he rattled around alone in his too-large house. Clare was out of the car before Jakes had switched off the engine. She walked down the path, past the walls blocking the pool from public view, and the discarded condoms. Clare waited for her eyes to adjust to the flickering light as the clouds scudded along, hiding then revealing the moon. The tide was coming in. If there was a body here they would need to move it soon – before the water reclaimed it. The rocks were jagged black teeth against the night sky, the sand a grimy white. Clare surveyed the rocks. She could see nothing soft, nothing human. She ventured closer to the encroaching water's edge, empty mussel shells crunching under her heels.

The slim body was wedged into a shallow crevice, the dark hair haloed around her face. Clare felt faint. She stepped back from the body and phoned Riedwaan. 'Call Piet Mouton and your scene of crime officers,' she said. 'We have a serial killer on our hands.'

A wave rushed forward then pulled back with a sigh. The girl's long boots with their spiked heels were flecked with foam. Clare switched her phone to camera and circled the body at a careful distance, taking photographs. The rising tide would soon obliterate any evidence. One breast was exposed, the other covered by the flimsy fabric of her top. There was a tear near the shoulder, as if someone had tried to cover her. Clare's blood ran cold when she zoomed in on her hand – a bound, bloody pulp in which a dull metallic gleam was discernible. It would be a key, Clare was sure. The waves pulled back and Clare balanced herself over the rocks to photograph the girl's feet. The girl's head pointed south, towards Signal Hill, the rounded hillside that framed the tower block that Clare had just come from. The girl's eyes were sunken, and the blood had dried into a mocking harlequin's tear on her soft cheek.

Jakes gasped when he saw the body.

His camera would give them far better photographs than her cellphone. 'Where's your camera?' Clare asked, 'It could take a while before the police photographer gets to the scene.'

'It's in the boot,' he replied. 'I'll get it.' She walked back up with him, steadying herself on his arm. She felt him shake and held onto him more tightly.

'How the hell did anyone get a body here without someone seeing him?' asked Jakes.

'Rent boys and their clients are not likely to rush to the nearest police station,' said Clare.

'I don't know. It's peculiar,' said Jakes. 'It's quite a way from the road to the pool.' Jakes opened his boot and was taking out his camera bag when Riedwaan pulled up. He got out of his car and looked from Jakes to Clare, noting the absence of Clare's car. Riedwaan's hostility was palpable when Clare introduced the men.

'I took some pictures with my phone,' said Clare as she led the way back down the path. 'The tide is coming in so fast that I was worried any evidence might be obliterated. I've asked Jakes to take some more pictures with his camera. In case your guys take a while.'

'How helpful,' Riedwaan said. Jakes had gone ahead, camera at the ready. Riedwaan put both hands onto her shoulders. 'How did you know about this, Clare?' He could see the hesitation in her eyes. 'You have to tell me. Otherwise we are both in shit.'

'I told you, someone sent me an SMS.'

'Who?' asked Riedwaan.

'It's a private number,' said Clare. 'Do you think Rita could track it down?'

'*Ja*,' said Riedwaan. 'I'll get her on it ASAP.'

Riedwaan bent down to look at the dead girl. 'Amore Hendricks,' he said, his voice heavy with pain. He was going to have to tell her parents. His face would forever be the one that lurked in their nightmares of their daughter's death.

Riedwaan turned to greet the scene of crime officers. Within minutes the area was taped off and lights had been set up.

102

The police photographer was taking pictures of the body and the beach sand around it. A uniformed officer bent down and was checking every footprint in the vicinity. Another officer was collecting anything that could be collateral evidence; anything that might show how long the killer had spent with the body, what he had done here. Clare would add this to what she already knew to draw up a profile of the killer. The work of shifting from a single murder case to a special investigation would keep Riedwaan very busy. Clare envied him his preoccupation.

'I'll see you tomorrow, Riedwaan,' she said

'Okay. You can come and make your statement. I'll give you the preliminary autopsy report then.'

Jakes was waiting at the car, smoking a bummed cigarette. He gave her the roll of film he had shot, opened the door for her and drove towards her flat without a word. Riedwaan watched the car until it merged with the late-night clubbing traffic. He turned back to the task at hand, attributing the tightness in his chest to the horror before him.

Riedwaan waited for Piet Mouton to arrive, which he did, ten minutes later. Mouton looked around. 'The bloody tide is coming in fast, man. Not much to see here any more.' He straightened up, wheezing at the effort. 'You're lucky you found her at all. If the tide had got her, you would have had fuck-all to compare with the last one.' Mouton shook out a cigarette, and offered one to Riedwaan. The match hissed as it hit the water. 'Who found her?'

'Clare did. Somebody SMS'd her. Rita's tracing the number.'

'Jesus, Riedwaan, stay away from that woman. She's a corpse magnet.' Mouton put his pudgy hand on Riedwaan's shoulder and gave it a squeeze. 'She's a bit too clever for me and too skinny, also. Not my type.' Piet didn't have a type. He had Mrs Mouton. Soft, plump, could cook like an angel, allowed no mortuary jokes in her house. She would be waiting for Piet with a slice of cake and a pot of tea when he finished the autopsy.

'Are we going to autopsy her tonight?' asked Riedwaan.

'You trying to show up the rest of the police force, man?' Piet asked him. Riedwaan shrugged.

'Okay,' said Piet, looking at his watch. It was well after midnight. 'The night is young and it doesn't look as if the two of us have much else to do.' A wave splashed his shoes. 'There's nothing I can do here with the tide rising so fast.' Mouton made a series of quick sketches of the girl's body and tested her limbs for rigor mortis.

'How long has she been dead, Doc?'

'Hard to say. It's been bloody cold tonight, but I'd say pretty much the same as the other girl. Thirty-six hours max. I'd say he likes to keep them with him a while once they are nice and quiet.'

'You going to do swabs here, Doc?' asked the older of the two mortuary technicians. He was blowing on his hands to keep them warm. A freezing drizzle was drifting off the sea.

'No,' said Mouton. 'You boys can pack her up. We'll get her inside. I'll do everything in the lab. That rain looks like it's here for the night.'

The two men lifted the girl gently and settled her onto the stretcher. Mouton zipped up the body bag, covering her blinded face just as the rain began to come down in earnest.

20

Riedwaan followed Piet Mouton to the mortuary, stopping to buy coffee on the way. He would phone Clare in the morning. He did not want Jakes answering the phone. What he felt like doing was punching the bastard in the mouth. That would wipe the smug smile off his face. Riedwaan's fist was clenched around the polystyrene cup. It spilt, burning him. He balanced the coffee in the open ashtray to avoid doing any more damage to himself, then parked next to Piet's car. Theirs were the only two in the parking lot. He keyed in the entrance code to the lab and took the lift up. Piet was already setting out his instruments and containers. Riedwaan pushed open the door and gave the pathologist his coffee.

'No cake?' asked Mouton.

'You're fucking too fat already, Doc. Let's go.' Riedwaan sipped his coffee, keeping his eyes off the girl's mutilated face. He picked up a clipboard and made some notes. Her hand was tied up – just like the last girl. He looked at her long dark hair. A piece had been cut off, close to her scalp.

'A souvenir for the killer?' he asked Mouton.

'Can't tell, but probably. Sick bastards.' Mouton was scribbling his own notes.

'Time of death, Doc?' Mouton had inserted the probe into the girl's body. He always did a sub-hepatic probe, moving the metal behind the liver. He didn't approve of the rectal scope. In a sexual assault case you didn't want to mess with evidence. 'I'd say at least eight hours, maybe more. She's cold.' He put the instruments down.

'When was she moved?' asked Riedwaan.

Mouton turned the body over. 'I'll have to do some more tests, but take a look at this hypostasis. The red blood cells fix after a while. I'd take a bet she lay on her side for some time before she was moved. Maybe even since last night.'

'So when was she moved?' asked Riedwaan. 'It couldn't have been last night because the tide was up in the morning.'

'I'd say this evening. Her hair is only slightly damp from the rain.' He pulled a finger through the girl's thick hair. 'I would guess not long before she was found.'

'Such a public place. How? Why there?'

'You ask your lady to figure that out for you.' Mouton was bending in close to the body again, tweezers in his hand.

'What you got there, Doc? More semen?' The pathologist grunted. 'Not this time. Looks like bird shit to me.' He dropped the tiny fibres he had picked off the girl's back into the bags he used for samples. 'I'll send it away for testing.' He moved around the body, picking up one of the girl's hands, then the other. Then he moved to her feet, eased off the high, tight-fitting boots, and scribbled again on his notepad.

'What happened to her feet, Doc?'

'Same injuries to the extremities as the other girl had. I'm not sure what they are. Gnaw marks. Rats, maybe. Most of the bodies we see that have been left outside for some time have bites from scavengers on them. In the northern hemisphere most dead bodies are found indoors. Makes it much easier to place time of death because you get a constant ambient temperature. And, of course, a body that's inside is not going to be interfered with by packs of dogs.'

106

'Thanks for the free lecture, Doc.'

Mouton straightened up. 'You could do with an education, Riedwaan. But these boots were put on after death, after she'd been alone somewhere long enough for the rats to chew her.'

Mouton crouched down beside the girl. 'Come and look here.' Riedwaan crouched next to him. He could smell a trace of perfume on her skin, she was that close.

'The throat is cut in the same way. Another Colombian necktie,' Mouton turned to Riedwaan. 'The South Americans moving in?'

'Not that I've heard,' said Riedwaan. 'I don't think this is drug related, do you?'

'Thinking is not my job, Riedwaan. I'll leave that up to you. But if you asked my opinion, I'd say no. Whoever did this has some unresolved business with women.'

Piet Mouton reached over for the instruments he used to expose the most intimate recesses of the human body. 'Okay, let's get to the real work now.' Riedwaan's stomach heaved, but Mouton's patient dissection would reveal where Amore had been in the last few days of her life and the first day of her death. Finding out where and teasing out how she died were the keys they needed to unlock the secret of who had killed her. The mortuary was quiet. Riedwaan prepared himself for a long night.

21

Clare dreamt of the dead girl, but, to her surprise, she awoke refreshed – and, to her shame, elated to be alive. She lay in bed listening to the pre-dawn silence, drifting between consciousness and her hovering dreams. There was something on the periphery of her mind, but whenever she shifted her mind's eye to look at it, it disappeared. She gave up when the first call of a dove pulled her into the morning. She stretched and got up, pulling on her running clothes. She felt chilly, despite the warmth of her heated flat, so she put on an extra top and set off. Outside it was dark, except for a cold gleam in the slitted yellow eye of the horizon. In spite of her unease, she ran in the direction of Graaff's Pool.

The flurried activity of the previous night was gone. Chevroned police tape was looped around the whole area. Clare could see a guard drawing on his cigarette as if it might warm him. The rising sun provided no warmth and Clare was getting cold. She turned to continue her run. She followed the promenade's paved ribbon to the end before heading home again. By the time she was back at Graaff's Pool the forensics officers had returned, searching a wider arc now for anything that Amore Hendricks's killer may have left behind. So far, there was nothing. The tide had risen high the previous night, and if anything had remained it would have been obliterated. Clare doubted they'd find anything.

The way the two bodies they had found so far had been arranged, and the symbolism of the wounds – almost like stigmata – pointed to a killer who made careful preparations. He was not someone who would easily make a mistake. Also, by now the tide would have washed any little slips away. Clare watched for Riedwaan. He had called her last night, keeping the call businesslike and brushing aside her attempt to explain Jakes. He told her that Rita Mkhize called to say that the SMS had come from a phone belonging to Clinton Donnelly. Clare remembered the name – he'd been an enthusiastic student at a lecture she'd once given. Clinton lived in Observatory, a cramped suburb where attempts at gentrification had never really succeeded; it was a place that Clare generally avoided. He had sent the message from a house in Campbell Road.

The mournful wail of the foghorn demanded her attention. She looked towards the rhythmic flash of the lighthouse that accompanied it. It was due east. Then she looked back towards Graaff's Pool, where the girl's body had been laid out along a precise north/south axis. Her head had pointed south, as had the blood-soaked bound hand. Clare stood still, the threads of morning mist twisting wraithlike, receding ahead of the breakers before they disappeared. The precision of the arrangement of the corpses – the head of the first one pointing east, this one south – tugged at her mind. She shivered, praying that there would be no west, no north.

The wind was cold, so Clare sheltered in the lee of a small building. The tide was retreating. Clare watched the pattern the waves made as they rushed forward onto the rocks. Their energy spent, they fell back into each other. Foam formed where the crests thrashed against the rocks, and one another, then retreated for respite towards the open sea. This white spine of foam ran along the deep, navigable channel between the rocks. Clare stood up on the bench she had been sitting on. The body had been placed at the end of that channel. Had the killer brought her in there by boat? Last night's weather would have made this difficult – but then nobody would have have been around to notice, either.

A flash of blue in a rock pool caught Clare's eye. Something stranded by the receding tide, or rubbish from one of the vessels anchored off the coast, thought Clare, as she leapt down to the beach. She picked her way across the rocks. A bedraggled bunch of flowers tied together with gold ribbon, washing out, and then returning with the tide, dislodged a shard of memory. An old man with a bunch of plastic-wrapped blooms. Clare pulled the flowers out of the sea, even though she was outside the police cordon. She walked over to the tape and called to one of the forensic detectives searching across the beach sand.

'Joe,' she called. He came over to her, rubber gloves stretched tight across his plump hands.

'Hi, Clare.' Clare had known Joe Zulu all the years she had worked with the police. 'I hear it was you who found this one.'

'*Ja*, it was horrible. Someone I know told me the body was here.' Clare handed him the flowers and pointed to the beach below. 'By the way, I found these over there – they seem so out of place here. Also, Harry Rabinowitz mentioned that there were flowers with the first girl. I didn't see anything in the report, though. I'll check Riaan's photos again. Harry Rabinowitz told me there were flowers with the first girl too.'

Joe placed the flowers in an evidence bag. 'They're almost the same colour as the ribbon her hand was tied with,' observed Joe. 'Who knows what will help solve this?' and he turned in the direction where Amore's body had lain. The tide had made sure that any visible trace of her had been erased. But you never knew until later about invisible traces of evidence left behind.

'Let me know what you find, Joe,' said Clare. 'I'll speak to you later.' Joe waved and went back to work.

Clare checked her cellphone for messages as she climbed the rough steps that led from the beach back to street level.

'Hello, Dr Hart. I see you are a morning person too.' Otis Tohar's voice raised every single one of the tiny hairs on the back of her neck. 'Are you a runner?' he asked.

'As you can see,' said Clare, irritated that he had so unnerved her. Tohar was dressed in an expensive tracksuit, but he did not look as if he had been running. He had several newspapers under his arm. Clare made out a headline that clearly relished the sales spike the murder of a beautiful girl would result in. Her heart sank. Chief-Superintendent Phiri was going to throw a fit: it wouldn't be too long before the history of the case officer came out. Ever since Riedwaan Faizal had punched a journalist who'd questioned his relationship with some of the local gangsters, he'd not been that popular with the more liberal papers.

'You did not strike me as a vulture, Dr Hart.' Tohar leaned in close to her. The acrid smell was there again. Clare's nostrils flared in distaste. This seemed to amuse him. He moved closer, trapping her between his body and the sea wall. 'Curiosity seems to be a habit with you.'

Clare contained her claustrophobia and stepped away. 'It is my profession.'

'It has brought you luck so far?'

'Not luck,' Clare replied. 'Knowledge. Why are you here so early?'

'I have so much invested here.' He gestured behind him.

The cranes loomed above the road. 'I need to be sure of what is going on around here. But also to see if I can help.'

He was not the only one. A crowd was gathering around the police cordon.

'I'm going to fetch Tatiana from gym. I think you met her last night?'

Clare wondered if Tohar knew about their brief meeting in his video library.

'No,' she risked. 'We weren't introduced.' He turned to go.

'Mr Tohar, I hear that Kelvin Landman has put quite a bit of finance into some of your more recent projects.'

'Who told you that?'

'You know what Cape Town is like with rumours, especially about other people's money.'

Tohar hesitated. 'We work very well together. Mutual interests. We should really do lunch some time. Call me, Clare.' He wiped a sudden sheen of sweat off his forehead and made his way back to his car. The clouds parted temporarily and the sky gleamed a deep blue. The engine of his car started at once with a rumble, a bass note to the whine of the accumulating morning traffic.

Clare went back to checking her messages. There was one from Riedwaan to say that he had dropped a copy of the preliminary autopsy report off for her. She went home, picking up the envelope he had put in her letterbox. Clare phoned Riaan, asking him to let her have a set of his pictures from the murder scene, and then she had a shower. She was forcing herself to eat a slice of toast with her coffee when the doorbell rang.

'Who is it?' asked Clare, pressing the intercom.

'Delivery. Small package, madam.' She buzzed the man in and signed for it.

She ripped it open, knowing already who had sent it. She

shook open the slim envelope. The face of the Devil, fifteenth card of the Tarot leered up at her, the carnal card, the grinning symbol of desire and entrapment in bodily lust. Clare picked it up. The second card of any Tarot reading revealed past influences. But whether these were her own, or the killer's, Clare was uncertain. She tucked the repugnant card into her handbag, leaving her breakfast unfinished. She sat at her desk, determined to face her day with composure.

22

Riaan dropped off the copies of his photographs of Amore Hendricks. Clare ignored his request for coffee and opened the envelope as soon as she had got rid of him. She set the photographs alongside those of Charnay Swanepoel, checking them carefully, looking for similarities, for differences. The killer had twinned the bodies with uncanny exactitude.

She looked closely at all the pictures of Charnay Swanepoel. There it was – a small heap in the gutter that could be flowers. She called Riedwaan to tell him.

'Won't you ask Rita to check which florists use gold ribbon? Joe will have the sample of it,' said Clare.

'I'll do that – could work. But most florists will be closed now, so it'll have to be tomorrow. What do you think they mean, the flowers?'

'Maybe some kind of apology. Or maybe it's part of some wedding fantasy, an ultimate union. White irises are sometimes used for wedding bouquets.'

'The ones you found were purple.'

'I know. I'm just thinking aloud.'

'Give me a call after you've talked to the boy,' said Riedwaan.

Clare then drove to Observatory. She found the café the boy had suggested as a meeting place. She looked at her watch again. Five-thirty. She hoped that the boy hadn't changed his mind about coming. But he arrived just as the waitress sloshed Clare's cappuccino onto the table.

'Dr Hart?' He was very nervous, but his handshake was firm. His blazer hung elegantly on his athletic frame. Yet his beautiful face was strained, and there were dark circles under his wide-set brown eyes.

'Hello, Clinton,' said Clare. She was relieved to see him. 'Would you like something?' The boy looked through the menu, ordered a Coke and a toasted cheese.

'I'm glad you came,' said Clare. 'I was beginning to think you wouldn't.'

'I'm sorry about being late. I had band practice at school and it went on a bit. I'm a trumpeter.' The waitress placed his Coke and cutlery on the table. 'Thanks,' he said, and the young woman beamed at him.

Clare leaned towards him. She placed her small tape recorder in front of them. 'It'll be useful to everyone if I tape this,' she explained. 'Tell me about last night.'

Clinton shifted, as if his seat had hardened.

'Tell me how you found her. Why were you there?' Clare's voice was gentle but Clinton recognised the steel in it. He picked at the small tear of skin on his left thumb.

'I was at Graaff's Pool. I saw her lying between the rocks. I read in the paper that you were involved in the investigation, so I thought you'd be the best person to tell.' He stopped, sucking at the bead of blood welling on the edge of his nail. 'She looked so peaceful there in the moonlight. So perfect.'

'What time was that, Clinton?' He hesitated. 'Try to remember. It is very important.'

'It must have been about eight-thirty. The rain had stopped then. I went there. I saw her. Then I sent you the SMS.'

'I got the message after eleven. Why did it take you so long to tell someone?'

'I was busy. There were things I had to do,' he muttered.

'Who was with you?' Clare's eyes were unwavering on the boy's face. He looked away.

'I was alone. Just me.'

'At Graaff's Pool?'

'I went there to look at the view. To think.'

'No boy is alone there for long. So what were you thinking there, Clinton?'

He turned to look her straight in the eye for the first time. 'I was thinking how lucky that girl is.' Clinton reached for his Coke, but his hands shook so much that he put it down without taking a sip.

'You knew her?' asked Clare in surprise.

'I didn't recognise her that night. But when we saw it in the paper my mother remembered her.' He stopped, as if regretting that he had told her this.

'How did your mother know her?' prompted Clare.

'We were at the same junior school,' he explained. 'My mom knew her mom. Then they moved to Panorama and built a house there. Then my dad died and when my mom got remarried we moved to Observatory. Later I got the music scholarship to the larnie school I'm at now.' He stopped speaking, his breathing hurried.

'But when you saw her last night you did not know who she was?'

Clinton shook his head and picked up his Coke again. His hands were steadier now. He looked pleased, as if he had negotiated a rough stretch of water. Clare softened her voice and put her hand on his. 'Tell me who you were with, Clinton. It will come out, you know.'

'With Rick.' His hands flew up, as if to catch the name, take it back. 'That is what he said his name was.'

'Who is Rick?' asked Clare, her voice gentle but relentless.

'Rick the Prick.' His childish giggle was laced with revulsion. Then the bravado evaporated and the boy's shoulders slumped forward. He had capitulated. Clare re-angled her tape recorder.

'Who is he?' asked Clare.

'I met him that night at Lulu's.' Clare knew the bar he was talking about. It was at the heart of Sea Point's red light district, catering to men who liked young boys. The seventeen-year-old in front of her could pass for fourteen in the right light.

'Come on, Clinton, why are you trying to protect him?'

'All right.' Anger flashed across his face. It vanished as quickly, leaving tears in its wake. 'He was a regular. He called himself Rick, but I saw his ID when I went to a party at his house. It said Luis Da Cunha.'

'Whose idea was it to go to Graaff's Pool?' asked Clare.

'Usually I just do him in his car quickly. But this time he insisted that we go there.' Clinton's voice was almost inaudible. 'I don't like it there, it's so creepy. I hadn't been since those guys were attacked there last year.'

'Why did you go this time?'

'He offered me double. I needed the money. I needed to get home.' Clare touched the smooth skin on the back of his wrist. He turned his hand over and gripped hers. His shoulders quivered as he repressed a sob. Clinton leaned forward and pulled up a khaki trouser leg. 'Look here.'

Clare saw the puncture marks like ritual tattoos following the vein that traced the contour of his calf muscle and disappeared into the back of his knee. 'This is why I need the money. This is why I take the risks. Rick said that is where we must go. It seemed to turn him on like anything.' Clinton stopped.

'Go on,' said Clare.

'He wanted a blow job,' said Clinton. He shuddered. 'I just look somewhere else and pretend it's not me doing it. That's when I saw her lying there. She looked like a mermaid on the edge of the water. That was when I wished I was there where she was. With everything just over.' He paused and managed a shaky sip of his cooldrink. 'Rick was finished. He threw money at me, more than we'd agreed, and then he was gone.'

'Did he see the girl?' asked Clare.

'He had his back to her, so I don't think so. He didn't say anything. He just threw the money at me and went home to his wife.'

'I thought you didn't know anything about him.'

'I don't, but I can recognise a wedding ring when I see one. Most of my regulars are straight men. Married. They seem to like me. Maybe it's because I look like a girl so they can carry on pretending about themselves even while you suck them off.'

'Did you go over to her?'

'I got dressed again first. I was freezing. And then I went over to her. Amore. Her name didn't help her, did it?'

'How long were you with her?'

'I don't know. A few minutes,' he said. 'Should I have stayed longer?'

Clare shook her head. 'Did you touch her at all? Pick anything up?'

Clinton looked trapped. 'I tried to cover her. She looked so cold lying like that.'

'Like what?' asked Clare.

'With her top pulled down like that. I tried to cover her up but her shirt was stuck underneath her. I heard it tear. When I pulled, her head moved and I could see where her throat had been cut. That gave me such a fright. Then I left her. I had to be home. Otherwise . . .'

'Otherwise what?' Again the deadness in his eyes.

'My stepfather *donners* me if I'm late. And then he *donners* my mom. For giving birth to a worthless thing like me.' He put his face in his hands, fingers opening, closing on his short dreadlocks.

'What will happen to me?' he asked Clare.

'The police will need to interview you. And they will need to find Rick and talk to him too.'

'Ha!' said Clinton. 'He'll deny that he has ever even laid eyes on me. And who will believe me? Rent boy versus businessman – great odds.'

'You have to take that chance. The people at Lulu's will recognise him too,' said Clare with more confidence than she felt. 'But right now you need to do something about your other problem. The one that got you into this situation.' She passed him a name and number she had written onto one of her cards. 'Call him. He knows where you've been: he's been in the same place himself.' Clinton looked at it with a sneer. But he put it into his pocket before he stood up to go.

'There is one other thing,' he said, as he gathered his bags. 'There was a drag mark on the sand near where she was lying. I don't know if it means anything, but I thought it was funny because it had rained so hard earlier. So it must have happened after the rain stopped. That gave me the *grils* – it really got me that someone had put her there just before we got there. That he might have been around there somewhere. Watching.' He looked nauseated.

'What time did you meet Rick?'

'Oh, it was just before. He came into Lulu's at about eight-fifteen, and he came straight over to me. As if he had checked it out before. Planned it, planned me. He bought two drinks and brought them over, but we didn't finish them. He wanted to get going straight away. He was very excited.'

'Did you drive?'

'No. It's close. We walked down Joubert Road to the pool.'

119

'And when he left? Where did he go?'

'He crossed the road to his car. I had the feeling that it was in the direction of Three Anchor Bay. And then I caught a taxi. Can I ask you something, Dr Hart?' Clare nodded. 'Will my mother find out?'

'She will. You'll have to give a detailed statement to Inspector Faizal at the Sea Point station. You should tell her yourself. Maybe she will go with you. Also, when the police catch this man, you'll be a witness.'

'Will people know what I was doing?'

'Yes,' said Clare.

'He will kill me. He'll kill me and that will kill her.' He walked out into a blast of winter air. Clare watched him until he disappeared around the corner. She put down her cappuccino. It was ice cold.

She was waiting for the bill when her phone beeped. There was a text message on it from Clinton. 'Rick,' it said. 'Apt 2, 473 Victoria Road, Clifton.'

It would be an interesting interview. She didn't think that Riedwaan would want to miss it. She called him. 'Turns out Clinton was paid for his time. I've got the client's address,' said Clare. 'What do you say we drop in for some late supper?'

'I was just thinking how hungry I am,' said Riedwaan. 'Why don't you pick me up? I persuaded Phiri that I needed a special ops room and he gave me that old caravan at the back of the building. Generous bastard. Thank God it's not summer, otherwise we'd all die of heat out here. Much more pleasant to freeze.'

'I'll see you in half an hour,' said Clare. She couldn't help feeling a surge of hope that they might have something at last. Mr Da Cunha was certainly well off and mobile. He wouldn't be the first killer to pay a visit to a corpse. If it was him, of course, Clare cautioned herself – if it was him.

23

Clare found Riedwaan swearing into his cellphone. He banged it onto the desk when she walked in. 'I can't get a land line and I can't get a computer. Can you believe this: Admin says it will be stolen. I told the woman that we are the police and she said that our station has no security guards, so our computers "just walk". I have to get permission from the provincial government if I want a computer in my caravan. How the fuck am I meant to catch a serial killer without any support?'

'Maybe Joe will have more luck,' said Clare. 'He knows how to chat up those ladies with the forms. Will you give it a try, Joe?'

Joe nodded, smiling. 'Riedwaan, you go with Clare and interview that rent boy's client. Leave me to get the equipment. What else would you like?'

'Try a coffee machine,' said Riedwaan. 'Maybe pigs will fly.'

'Well, you'd better fly away.' Joe held up an espresso machine. 'I've got one already.'

Riedwaan laughed. 'What truck did that fall off, then?'

He turned to Clare. 'Shall we go?' She nodded. He held the sagging caravan door open for her. 'We'll see you, Joe. You can ward off crank confessions while you freeze your balls off in here.'

'I've got a heater, Faizal. But thanks for caring,' said Joe.

'I don't know how you do it.' Riedwaan slammed the door shut.

'Have you had some cranks already?' asked Clare as she unlocked her car. Riedwaan got into the passenger seat.

'Two already. But I think it's the same guy,' said Riedwaan.

'What did he say?'

'He said he fucked them and then he shot them.'

'Delightful,' said Clare. 'Have you traced him yet?'

'We did,' said Riedwaan. 'It's someone in Pollsmoor Prison. Either a warder or a prisoner on cleaning duty who has been using the phone.'

They were in Clifton now. Luxurious blocks of flats loomed on either side of the narrow winding road. 'It's number 473,' said Clare.

'There it is. Park here, this will be fine.' Riedwaan got out and crossed the road. 'What number is the flat?'

'Apartment 2B,' said Clare.

'The lights are on, so somebody's at home,' said Riedwaan, pressing the doorbell. 'Shall we go and see who it is?'

'Yes?' came a disembodied female voice.

'This is Inspector Faizal. I was hoping to come up with my colleague and talk to Mr Da Cunha. Is he in?'

There was a muffled conversation before the door clicked open. Riedwaan and Clare entered the lobby where an enormous vase of lilies and orange blossom was perched on a table with delicate legs. They took the steps and headed up for the second floor. There were only two apartments on that level, and the door of number 2B was ajar. Riedwaan pushed open the door and went inside. The opulence was overwhelming.

'Good evening.' A woman with a faint moustache bore down on them. 'Do come and sit down. My husband will be home any minute. Can I get you anything?'

'No, thank you,' said Riedwaan. 'We're fine. We'll just wait until he gets in. I hope we aren't disturbing you?'

'Not at all,' said Mrs Da Cunha. 'We always eat late. It's a Mediterranean habit that is hard to break. This is my daughter, Ana-Rosa.' She introduced the pretty, plump teenager who came in with two cups of coffee on a tray, the girl blushing scarlet at the mention of her name. Clare was glad of the hot drink.

'My husband is usually home by nine,' said Mrs Da Cunha. She looked at her watch. 'He should be here any minute now. Tell me, why do you want to see him?'

'We just want to ask him a few questions. Does he usually work this late?' asked Riedwaan.

'He does work late. He has fishing boats, so they come in at different times. He also goes to the Portuguese Club on some evenings, doesn't he, Ana-Rosa?' The girl nodded, then blushed again and twisted her skirt in her hands. There was a sound at the door. 'That must be him. I'll bring him in here. Come, Ana.' She swept from the room, the girl in her wake.

Mr Da Cunha came in, closing the door behind him. 'Can I help you?' he asked, proffering a hand to Riedwaan and nodding to Clare.

'Good evening, Mr Da Cunha. Or can I call you Rick?' Riedwaan asked.

Da Cunha sat down abruptly. 'Why do you call me that?'

'We know a friend of yours,' replied Riedwaan. 'A very pretty boy called Clinton. He tells us you were with him on Wednesday night.'

'I don't know what you're talking about,' said Da Cunha. 'I was at home on Wednesday evening.'

'I'm sure you were,' said Clare. 'But your wife tells us that you usually eat late. So where were you before dinner?'

'I was at work. Then I went to the club and had some drinks. Then I came home.'

123

'Funny, that. The barman at Lulu's told me that you were ordering double whiskeys from him at seven forty-five. You ordered two. One for you and one for your little friend.'

'Okay, I was there. So what? What harm does it do? He's not underage, is he?'

'I'm not sure,' said Riedwaan, contempt in his voice. He leaned close to Da Cunha. 'But perhaps you would care to tell me exactly what you did on Wednesday. And what you were doing last weekend. And don't leave anything out. We will be checking everything.'

'Are you from the tax office?'

'No,' said Riedwaan. 'I am a serious and violent crimes officer and we are investigating a murder.'

Da Cunha's eyes widened. 'Who died?' he asked.

'A young girl. About your daughter's age,' said Clare. 'Clinton found her body just after he had finished servicing yours.'

'We found it curious that you were so insistent that you went to Graaff's Pool. Perhaps you could fill us in,' Riedwaan prompted.

'I like it outside,' Da Cunha said. 'It's wrong, I know, but I like it with that boy. And outside it feels free. I grew up on the sea. That is all there is to it.' He raised his eyes and looked at them. 'You can check. I was at work all day. I left at five-thirty and went from work to play cards at the Portuguese Club in Green Point. I went to Lulu's on the way home and I had dinner here at nine.'

'And last weekend?'

'I went with my family to our house in Betty's Bay. We had some of my wife's friends there. You can check with them.'

'We will,' said Riedwaan. He towered over the seated man. 'We most certainly will.' He handed Da Cunha a notepad. 'Put their names and phone numbers down there, if you don't mind.'

Da Cunha took the pad and wrote down several numbers.

This took him some time – he was shaking, which made it difficult for him to get the numbers from his cellphone. Riedwaan glanced at the piece of paper.

'Thanks.'

'Did you notice anything unusual when you went down to Graaff's Pool?' asked Clare, her voice deceptively gentle.

'No, nothing really,' said Da Cunha, averting his eyes from Riedwaan with relief. 'I did notice that they seem to have finished the work on the tunnel, though.'

'Which tunnel is that?' asked Riedwaan, interested.

'That old tunnel. The Graaff family used it to get from their house to the beach. It was them who had the wall put up because they liked to swim naked. The tunnel wasn't used after they donated the pool to the city. But I heard that it had been repaired.'

'Thanks,' said Clare. 'I'm sure we'll be meeting again.'

Da Cunha saw them out. Clare and Riedwaan heard his wife, her voice shrill and loud, launch into a tirade as Da Cunha closed the door. They heard the daughter's pleas, too, as they made their way down the stairs.

'What do you think?' asked Riedwaan.

'Check him out,' said Clare. 'I don't like what he does, but I don't think it was him.'

The car doors slammed. 'Interesting about that tunnel,' said Riedwaan. 'I didn't know it was open.'

'There's a boulder that screens the opening. You wouldn't see it if you didn't know it was there. It leads under Main Road. Nowhere else, as far as I know,' said Clare. 'Will you check if there was any CCTV footage there? I think it would be worth searching that, too.'

Riedwaan flipped open his phone. 'I'm going to ask Joe to get it sealed off. Then we can search it tomorrow when it's light.' Riedwaan rattled out a series of instructions to Joe.

'Let's get something to eat before we go back to the station,' suggested Clare.

'Okay.' They stopped and ordered Thai curries to take away. Clare headed back to the station to drop Riedwaan.

'You coming in?'

'Yes,' said Clare. 'I want to get working on this now. I'm never going to sleep tonight.'

They passed Joe Zulu as they entered the caravan. 'I'll see you later,' Joe said. I'm going to get that tunnel cordoned off. How did you know about it?' he asked them.

'A fluke,' said Clare. 'We were questioning the man who was with Clinton at Graaff's Pool, and he mentioned it had been repaired.'

Clare opened the polystyrene containers. The food was delicious. She hadn't realised how hungry she was.

24

Clare stretched her arms up in the air. It was very late, and the roar of Beach Road had dropped to a hum, indistinguishable from the distant crash of the sea along the promenade. She and Riedwaan had spent the evening in the special ops caravan, shuffling the information they had, trying to make sense of the girls, of their killer. Riedwaan had gone home earlier, leaving Clare to transcribe her interview with Clinton Donnelly.

She should really go home, she thought, and log her interview with Natalie Mwanga. Her documentary deadline was bearing down on her. She had been following up on what Natalie had told her. But she needed corroboration from a border official. One of the long-haul taxi drivers would be ideal. Clare thought about getting a cup of coffee, but she'd already settled into her bones. She did not move.

Giscard walked towards the police station, obscured by the late-night shadows that hung from the buildings. He had long ago learnt to be invisible. It was this that had enabled him to survive in Cape Town. Tonight, though, his stride was hesitant – something that a refugee soon learnt to hide if he wanted to avoid being noticed by the police. He hesitated at the door, looking in through the meshed glass. There was just the woman there, the one he'd been told was trying to find out about the sale of women. She looked so slight. He watched as she slipped her headphones onto her shoulders.

Giscard opened the door but she did not hear him.

'Good evening, Madame.' The accented voice startled her.

'Can I help you?' She guessed he was an illegal.

'Madame, I saw something. You must go there now, please, Madame.'

'What is your name?' Clare asked.

'You can call me Giscard. That is enough.'

'Tell me what you saw,' said Clare. She reached over for her notebook, clicked the pen against the palm of her hand.

Giscard reached into his pocket, producing a scrap of thumbed newspaper. The phone number had been written with the careful deliberateness of one who has taught himself to read and write. Clare took the paper, jotted down the number, and gave it back to Giscard.

'What, Giscard, what did you see? Start at the beginning.'

'I called that number.' He spoke in a rush in case his fear silenced him. 'It is a man who answered. I tell him my name. That someone give me the number and tell me that he needs a security. The man say to me: are you strong? I say yes.'

Clare noticed the taut muscles across his shoulders, the broad hands, the gentle eyes. A kind father's eyes, she thought. His words flowed now.

'Madame, I say yes and he say I must come to see him. And I go.' Clare knew how much it must have cost him to come in here: no papers, desperate to avoid all contact with an officialdom that would send him back to the violent mayhem he had fled.

'Madame, I go there. It is an apartment with many locks. Bars on the window. It is there in Main Road. A man lets me in. He says I must wait – that the man I talked to is coming. I do that. I wait while he goes to call someone. He comes back with another man. They ask me: can I be good security? Can I keep quiet? Do I have papers? I say yes. I say yes. I say not yet. They say I must work at night until nine a.m. I ask them what is the job and they laugh. They say that my job is to forget what I see every night. To forget who I see. They say they know men from my country. How we make our money from our women. I say nothing. We talk about the money. But there is a noise outside. The men go out. I hear them talking, shouting. I think that they are talking on their phones. They go out the front door – I hear the lock sliding – I think that someone is coming. I wait. It is very quiet. I am waiting there then I hear a very small noise. I listen. It sounds like a child that is crying, a girl crying. The men are gone, so I get up. I cannot leave the crying. I think of my own children in Congo. I go through the curtain where the second man came from. There I see more doors. One is open a little bit and it is there that I hear the crying. I go in. Madame.' Giscard's voice is soft, urgent. 'Madame, there is a child. I am afraid for her. She is too much in pain. You must go there now. It is a very young girl that is crying there. She looks very, very bad. I see her hand is bleeding. Her face, it is hit many times.'

'Where is she?' asked Clare, reaching for notebook. 'Can you take me?'

'No, Madame. I cannot! But you go there, please. Take the other men with you.' He pushed a scrap of paper towards her. On it was an address she recognised. A block of flats on a notorious stretch of Sea Point's Main Road. 'Please, Madame, I cannot tell you more. Can you go there now? Can you fetch the child tonight?' A car pulled up outside. Clare went to the window to see who it was. She turned round, a question on her lips. But the caravan door was open, and Giscard was gone.

Joe Zulu came in. 'Who was that guy leaving?' asked Joe, placing a cup of coffee in front of her. Clare did not answer.

She was punching a number into her cellphone.

Pick up, she willed. He did. 'Riedwaan, it's Clare. I have a report of an abduction. Can you come?' she closed her eyes, willing him to come. Then she thought of him in bed, imagined her hand moving down his hairless, brown chest.

'Clare.' His voice was irritated. 'I asked you: where?'

'In that block on Main Road. I think that we need to visit tonight.' Riedwaan's hesitation was palpable on the other end of the phone. Clare thought she could hear someone else's voice asking who and what and why so late?

'Okay,' he said. 'I'll pick you and Joe up at the station.' The phone went dead.

'What's happening, Clare?'

'Riedwaan's picking us up to investigate an assault. Looks like an abduction. Someone came to report it while you were next door.'

Joe folded his arms. 'You don't think it's a set-up?' he asked.

'For what?' asked Clare. 'Why would an illegal take the risk of coming to the police station?'

'Who knows? To cause trouble for someone else. Because he was paid to,' said Joe. 'I wonder how he got past the gate security.'

'Jesus, Joe, you could drive a tank past those guards and they wouldn't wake up after ten o'clock.'

Clare brought her car round from the parking lot at the back and was waiting for her heater to warm up when Riedwaan arrived. He came over to her window and held out his hand. She handed him the slip of paper with the address scrawled on it.

'I hope you know what you're doing, Clare,' he said. 'Who gave this to you?'

'He called himself Giscard. Congolese, I'd say.'

Joe came out of the station. 'Hey, Riedwaan. Shall we go?'

The two men got into Riedwaan's car and Clare slipped into their wake. At 12.30 only the most desperate women were displayed along the road in their high heels, skinny thighs blue with cold.

Riedwaan and Joe parked near the block they were headed for and waited for Clare. The three of them then picked their way over the bodies of sleeping street children and made their way to the entrance. A young Somali woman, bright scarf pulled tight around her face, stood aside, eyes glazed with relief when they walked past her.

Riedwaan took the stairs two at a time, with Clare close behind him. Joe, still smoking twenty a day, wheezed after them. On the third floor Riedwaan checked the number that Clare had given him and looked for number four. There was nothing on any of the doors so he counted along. The door he knocked on opened immediately, as if they had been expected. The man who answered was tattooed and wore a tight T-shirt.

'Can I help you, gentlemen?' He leered at Clare. 'Lady?'

'You going to let us in, Kenny?' said Riedwaan, matching his bulk against that of the doorman. Kenny moved aside just enough for them to pass through. Clare brushed against his bare arm, and recoiled.

'We had a report that a child was being held here, Kenny. A very unhappy child. You know that means we can inspect the premises, don't you, Kenny?'

Kenny looked confused. 'For sure, man. I know that. But I scheme you'll find yourself on a wild goose chase.' Kenny sauntered down the passage, pushing doors open. There were women in all the rooms. 'My sister,' said Kenny, 'so keep your eyes front. And my cousins from Malmesbury.'

'What about that door?' asked Riedwaan.

'It's empty. Check it out yourself.'

Riedwaan opened it. Kenny was right. Except for a bed,

the room was empty. Kenny went over and closed the window, shutting out the cold wind billowing the tattered curtain.

'That's all, folks,' said Kenny, shepherding Riedwaan and Joe down the passage. 'You came, you checked it out, there was nothing to see. You did your job. Now fuck off.'

Clare slipped back into the empty room. Her nostrils flared: she could smell the trace of someone who'd recently been there. She pulled back the cheap floral quilt. Beneath it was a naked mattress streaked with drying blood. She put her hand down to feel between the wall and the mattress. Wedged there, was a single earring. She slipped it into her pocket as she stepped over to the window. There was a three-metre drop to the roof below. It was possible someone had made that leap. Someone very desperate. A fragment of cloth caught on the razor wire whipped wildly in the rising wind, alerting Clare to a narrow alley snaking up behind the buildings. About halfway up the hill the filthy passageway led to a flight of steps, but Clare couldn't make out any movement.

'Clare,' called Riedwaan.

She turned away reluctantly and closed the door behind her. Riedwaan propelled her towards the front door. 'Your little bird has flown and we can't do anything more without a fucking warrant,' he whispered. 'Do you want me to get into more shit with your crusades?'

'You know as well as I do that there was someone there,' Clare retorted, furious at the rigmarole of laws and warrants and having to be fair to scum like Kenny. 'There's blood all over that mattress.'

'And there is nothing I can do about that or the so-called cousins from Malmesbury without a search warrant. And there is no way we will get a warrant without your mystery Giscard. Now let's go, before Kenny decides we are infringing on his undeserved civil rights.'

132

'Where has she gone?' Clare wondered aloud as they went down the stairs.

'She could be anywhere,' said Joe. 'If she is still alive she'll be terrified beyond speech. She's not going to come to us.'

Riedwaan slammed the car door in impotent fury.

'I'm sorry, Riedwaan,' said Clare.

'It's nobody's fault. Those guys would have cleared things up in seconds after they realised that your friend had taken off. But without him there will be no case. No witness, no warrant, no evidence.'

'No girl,' said Clare.

'That too,' Riedwaan said. 'No bloody girl. Not yet. I'm going to put out an alert so that everyone is on the lookout for her. She'll need help if she's been with these guys for a while.'

'I wonder if she looked like the other two,' said Clare. There was no need to elaborate.

'She'll turn up. Alive, I mean,' said Joe. 'I don't think these gangsters killed the other two. They didn't look like initiation victims to me: there usually isn't much left of them when we find them. And pimps don't like destroying their assets. Beatings, yes, torture for fun, but killing a girl usually means things got a little out of hand. Nothing was out of control when Charnay and Amore were murdered.'

'I hope you're right, Joe,' said Riedwaan. He started the car. 'Are you coming back to the station, Clare?

She looked at her watch. It was past one. 'No. Not now. It's so late. I think I'll just go home.'

'Okay, see you,' said Joe.

Riedwaan didn't try to dissuade her. Clare got into her car, automatically pushing down the central locking. Maybe whoever had been with Riedwaan earlier was waiting for him. Maybe he had just been watching the late-night movie. She watched as the two men drove off.

25

Clare sat in her car, thinking of that scrap of material whipping back and forth on the razor wire. The girl must have escaped along the passageway and up the hill. Moving away from people, as a wounded animal would. Then Clare's heart lurched as she saw a hand pressing on the passenger window.

'Madame, is me, Giscard.' Clare looked again.

'You gave me such a fright.' She rolled down her window. 'We didn't find her. I don't know where she is.'

'She got away,' said Giscard, quietly. 'I saw her.'

'Where is she?'

'I come back here after I see you. I watch to see if you come with the police. That is when I see her climb out the window.'

'Where did she go?' asked Clare.

'I followed her but she ran when she saw me.'

'Yes, but where did she go?' Clare's voice was a low, urgent mutter.

'I followed her to Glengariff Road. There is a building site halfway down. Maybe you look there?'

'Thank you, Giscard.' Clare did an abrupt U-turn, driving up steep streets through sleeping mansions snug behind walls and electric fences. Alarm systems winked their red Cyclops eyes as she passed. A security guard shifted in his chair, raising his arm in a tired salute. She turned left into the late-night emptiness of High Level Road. The houses here were smaller, the security more makeshift. She stopped at the red light on Glengariff Road. The street was shrouded with trees, their branches hanging low over the pavements. The lights changed and Clare turned down the hill. The building site was on the left. Clare parked, feeling inside the cubbyhole for a torch. To her relief, it was there. She got out of her car and picked her way through the debris. The old house was gutted, the ribs of the roof eerie against the sky. Clare checked the exposed basement. It was empty. She was about to return to her car when she noticed the partially covered skip. She picked her way over to it and called softly.

'Hello? Are you there?' she called softly. There was silence. Clare shone her torch past broken floorboards and lumps of cement. The beam caught a pair of eyes gleaming in the dark like a terrified cat.

'I won't hurt you,' said Clare. The girl shrank back into the shadows. Clare climbed into the skip and crouched next to the girl.

'Come with me,' said Clare. The girl shook her head, but did not resist when Clare put an arm around her and helped her to the car. She collapsed onto the seat, her long hair matted over her shoulders. Clare reached over and buckled her in. The girl winced.

'I'm taking you to a hospital,' she told her as she got back into her seat. She spread a coat over her. The girl's legs were streaked with blood, her left eye swollen shut, her hand a bloodied pulp. And the familiar tattoo on her back.

'What is your name?' asked Clare, more to keep the girl conscious than anything else. Her shaking hands were slippery on the wheel.

'Whitney,' was the whispered reply.

'Who did this to you?'

'Nobody. Nothing happened.' She scrabbled for the door handle with her good hand; the left one she kept cradled against her bruised body. 'It was an accident.'

'I won't hurt you,' Clare reassured her. 'I'm taking you to see a doctor.' Whitney fell back into her seat.

Clare drove to the emergency entrance of the private City Hospital. She half carried Whitney from the car into the admissions room. Whitney answered none of the questions put to her so Clare gave her own details and signed endless forms before Whitney could be seen by a doctor. Then Whitney was wheeled away, leaving Clare bereft in the chilly room. A night nurse brought her a cup of tea and told her that the doctor would be out soon to tell her about her daughter. Clare did not correct her about the relationship. She sipped the lukewarm tea with gratitude, exhaustion starting to bite.

Clare was almost asleep when the doctor came to find her.

'We've patched her up and sedated her. I'm Erika September.' She shook Clare's hand. She seemed too young to be doing this work. 'She has been very severely assaulted. The extent of her injuries points to a sexual assault perpetrated by several different people. A gang rape. There are signs of healing, though, so my guess is that this took place over a number of days.' The doctor paused, waiting for Clare to explain. When no explanation was forthcoming she continued. 'Whitney will need emergency trauma counselling. I have set something up for tomorrow morning. This also needs to be reported to the police.'

'I'll leave that to Whitney to decide,' said Clare. Erika September turned to go back to Whitney. 'You can see her now,' she said over her shoulder. 'I hope she presses charges. I see too many like her.'

'What about anti-HIV treatment?' asked Clare as she followed the young woman down the dimly lit passage.

'She has just had the first dose. You'll need to monitor the treatment carefully. She must come for her follow-up.' The doctor paused with her hand on the heavy door. She looked directly at Clare. 'She has been assaulted over an extended period. If it was more than seventy-two hours then the medication won't work if she is infected.' She opened the door and stood back, letting Clare into the treatment room. Whitney lay on the high bed, curled into a tight foetal ball under the covers. She had been sponged down and dressed in a white hospital gown.

'Whitney,' said Clare, bending close to her. 'It's Clare. I brought you here.' There was no response from the girl. Clare touched her arm but Whitney flinched as if Clare's cool fingers were a branding iron. Clare did not remove her hand from Whitney's arm. She felt the flesh recoil instinctively at her touch, and then slowly relax again when no hurt followed.

'Whitney,' she whispered into her ear, 'how do you feel?' The girl curled up even tighter. 'Who did this to you?'

'Nobody.' Her voice was cracked, broken with her body. 'It was just an accident. Nobody.' Clare traced the girl's delicate shoulder blades under the gown. A yellow ooze had seeped through, staining the starched cotton.

'What's this?' she asked Dr September, who was standing on the other side of the bed.

'It's burn ointment.' Erika September had grown up on a farm. She felt certain that Whitney had been burnt with a branding iron – just as her father had marked each year's new batch of heifers. 'There are cigarette burns on her hands and thighs too.'

Clare's stomach contracted. 'Whitney,' she tried once more. 'Can we call the police in the morning?' Whitney shook her head. 'Where is your family? Can I phone your mother?' Again just a shake of her head.

Dr September took Clare by the arm and moved her towards the door. 'It won't work. I see more and more of these "accidents". She won't report anything. I am sure she is terrified that whoever did this to her will do it to her mother, her little sister. Or to her all over again. That is what they will have told her.' Dr September's voice dropped. 'We have collected all the samples for analysis. So, if by some miracle she does press charges, we'll have evidence.'

'I'll come and see how she is in the morning,' said Clare. 'Thank you, Doctor.'

'Her body will heal, she's young. It's the rest of her that I'm not so sure of,' said Dr September, looking back at Whitney.

Clare picked up the pathetic heap of clothes, the cheap skirt, the torn black T-shirt with its jaunty white swoosh. She hung up the long coat Whitney had been wearing when Clare had found her. A small, shiny crucifix earring clattered to the floor. She picked it up and reached into the pocket of her jeans. The earrings made a perfect pair. She closed her hand around them and left the hospital, flicking open her phone the minute she was in her car. Riedwaan answered. He hadn't been sleeping, and there was a sharp edge to his voice.

'I found her,' she said.

'Where?' Riedwaan asked.

'Hiding in a skip on a building site in Glengariff Road. I took her to the City Park.'

'How did you know she was there?' asked Riedwaan.

'Giscard saw her escape and followed her up the hill. He told me.'

'And you didn't think of calling me?' Silence stretched tautly between them.

'I thought that it might be better for her if a woman fetched her,' said Clare eventually.

'Did she tell you what happened?'

'Not a word,' said Clare, 'but I found her earring. It matches the one I found in the room.'

'No chance of her reporting this?'

'I doubt it. The doctor is good, though. She collected what evidence she could.'

'Why do bastards like Kenny ever get let out of jail?' Clare could hear the rage crackle in Riedwaan's voice.

'What is his background?' Clare asked.

'Kenny McKenzie?' said Riedwaan. 'Kenny worked for Kelvin Landman years ago when he still lived on the Flats. He was released from Pollsmoor recently, where he was very upwardly mobile in the 28s prison gang. His parole officer said that he had gone through an extensive skills-training process, and that he was now only going to be an asset to our community.'

'Working with Landman, do you think?' asked Clare.

'Hard to tell. Kelvin Landman seems to have gone so squeaky clean you'd swear he was going to run in the next election.' Riedwaan paused. 'You on your way home now?'

'I was. Shall I come over?' Clare's voice was tentative.

Riedwaan knew what it cost her to ask him this, but still he answered, 'I think I need to sleep now, Clare.' He heard the sharp inhalation of breath, and felt perversely happy that he had hurt her. 'Bastard,' he muttered to himself. He picked up his whiskey glass. He would feel like shit tomorrow. But what was new?

Clare blinked quickly a couple of times, even though there were no tears, and drove home. Too exhausted to change her clothes, she just kicked off her shoes and collapsed into bed. The duvet was comforting but sleep took a long time to come. When she did finally fall asleep, her dreams were haunted by the battered girl.

26

The phone buzzed malignantly. Clare picked it up. 'Hello.'
She peered at her alarm clock – not yet six.

'Dr Hart,' said a clipped voice. 'This is the City Park Hospital.'

'Yes,' said Clare, sitting up wide awake. 'What is it?'

'The young lady you brought here is discharging herself. We cannot take responsibility for that as it is against the doctor's wishes. She is being disruptive.' There was a disapproving pause. 'And there is the matter of the bill.'

'I'll be there in ten minutes. Make her wait.' There was a muffled exchange. Then the woman was back on the line, her voice compressed with thin-lipped disapproval.

'She'll wait. This is not the right procedure at all.' Clare put down the phone, cutting her off. She showered and dressed, putting clean clothes for Whitney into a basket. The city was still half-asleep as she hurried across town, terrified that Whitney would vanish again.

The girl sat hunched on a hard plastic seat that was the furthest from the admissions desk. She looked up when Clare opened the door, and handed her a parcel of clothes.

'It's freezing outside, Whitney,' said Clare. 'Go and put these on and I'll take you home.' Whitney stood up with difficulty and limped to the bathroom. Clare went over to the woman on duty. She glared at Clare – the light harsh on the skin swagged beneath her eyes – and shoved an account at her.

'Settle this now, please.'

Clare looked at the figure and wrote a cheque. The woman snatched it with a red-tipped claw, her eyes assessing it with practised scepticism. She clipped the invoice and the cheque together and pulled over her receipt book.

'Sluts,' she muttered as Whitney came out of the bathroom wearing the borrowed tracksuit. 'What do they expect?' She tore out the receipt and gave it to Clare. Clare took Whitney's arm as the colour drained from the girl's face.

'Come,' she said, 'I'll take you home.' The girl followed, exhausted by this final display of will, collapsing into Clare's car.

'Where do you live?' asked Clare. There was no answer. Clare glanced at Whitney, her face pale in the morning light. 'I'll take you home with me. When you've rested we can decide what to do.'

Clare drove through streets rapidly filling with scurrying office workers and school children. Newspaper vendors had materialised at the traffic lights, selling yesterday's deaths to commuters. Whitney stared at her lap. Clare parked and helped Whitney out. She took the plastic bag holding her clothes and helped the girl inside. Clare was relieved that there was no one around to see them.

Whitney stopped just inside the front door, swaying on her feet. Clare took her hand as soon as she had slipped the dead bolt back into place.

'You need a bed.' Clare guided Whitney into the spare room and folded back the covers. Whitney sat down gingerly and then collapsed back onto the pillow. Clare covered her, tucking the duvet in against the back of her neck as she had always done for Constance. Whitney closed her eyes. 'Thanks,' she whispered as she eventually slipped into sleep.

Clare drew the curtains across the orange morning and stepped out, pulling the door silently closed behind her. She leaned her forehead against the passage wall. It was cool and reassuringly solid. She breathed in deeply, stilling her panic at having another person so close, so dependent. Clare then willed herself away from the wall. She walked to her desk, reached for her Rolodex and found the number for Rape Crisis, then made the necessary arrangements. There were others who were trained to cope with these things. When Whitney woke up, she'd tell her where her mother lived and Clare could take her back home. Perhaps her family would get her to press charges.

Clare switched on her laptop, trying to focus her scattered thoughts on her film. The picture of the web of organised crime, freelancers and corrupt officials that eased the flow of people from one place to another was coming into focus. The pieces of her puzzle were falling into place, but there were several things she needed to know: how local distribution worked and what happened to the money. There were rumours of laundering in the usual places – beauty parlours, restaurants, construction, property – but it was difficult to prove. Clare skimmed through her notes, frustrated at what she was still missing.

First prize would be an interview with Whitney, who could well be the key Clare needed. Whitney's family might talk, even if she refused.

Clare checked on Whitney at ten. The juice next to her bed had been drunk, but Dr September's potent sleeping pills had suspended Whitney once again in a dreamless sleep.

Clare went back to her careful mapping of routes and detours on the trafficked women's journeys to Cape Town. She pulled out a jaunty tourist map of the city, trying to guess Whitney's route to San Marina Mansions. The name was familiar. Clare reached for the file that held her interviews, excitement mounting. She ran her finger down the index she had started. There it was: San Marina Mansions. The place where Natalie Mwanga had been put to work was in the same building they'd found Whitney – who was clearly from one of the poorer suburbs of Cape Town. Clare reached for her phone. 'Hi, Marcus,' she greeted her brother-in-law. 'You're not by any chance going to the deeds registry today, are you?'

'I am. What are you ferreting out now?'

'Can you check who owns a block in Sea Point? San Marina Mansions. The address is 148 Main Road. Thanks.' She blew him a kiss over the phone. 'Bye.'

A tiny click made her turn. Whitney was standing in the doorway.

Clare smiled at her. 'Do you want something to eat?' The girl nodded. Clare led her to the kitchen where she toasted white bread, sliced some cheese, and made a mug of sweet tea. Whitney ate, making herself chew then swallow, chew then swallow, determined to stay alive. Clare sat opposite her, hands cradling her own hot mug. Fritz leapt up onto Whitney's lap, purring. The girl stroked the cat gently, her small hand childlike against the grey fur.

'Where do you live, Whitney?' Fritz's purr stopped. Clare's voice was loud in the kitchen quiet. 'I have to take you back. Your mother will be frantic.' Whitney shifted her eyes over onto Clare's face, but she was silent. Clare reached for the notepad and pencil next to the phone. 'Write it down for me.' Whitney hesitated and then picked up the pen and wrote, pushing the paper back to Clare.

'Twenty-three Regent Street, Retreat? Shall I take you

home?' Clare asked. Whitney nodded, struggling to swallow the last piece of toast. She got up and fetched her coat, moving carefully. She had the small bag of clothes – torn top, short skirt – in her hand. This she shoved into Clare's dustbin and headed for the door. She hesitated on the threshold for a few seconds and then stepped outside. Clare followed, locking the house, opening the car. Whitney stared blindly at the traffic as Clare rounded the circle and headed towards the highway that would take them to the urban sprawl that stretched between the slopes of the mountain and False Bay.

Half an hour later Clare turned off, driving into the warren of dilapidated cottages huddled on either side of the streets. Homeward-bound workers and housewives shopping were gradually replaced by knots of young men on the street corners, and the women here were older, scurrying home, hands clamped tight around the fists of small children. Windows were curtained, doors were shut tight – and graffiti proclaimed which gang owned this or that street. Hard, speculating eyes followed Clare's car as she nosed her way into Regent Street and looked for number twenty-three.

The front door opened as Clare parked, and a woman flew down the path. She grabbed hold of Whitney, pulling her out of the car. The girl eventually relaxed the iron grip she had on her body, melting back into the enveloping flesh of her mother's arms.

'My baby,' she breathed into her daughter's hair. 'Come inside.' She turned her child away from the gathering curiosity in the street. 'Come inside, please,' she said to Clare, who followed mother and daughter inside.

The house was immaculate. The woman must have polished and scrubbed her way through the days of her daughter's disappearance. In the lounge, Clare sat on the covered armchair with its crotcheted cloths.

144

'I am Florrie Ruiters.' She held her hand out to Clare. The woman's tears pooled, then overflowed. Clare watched as she took her child into the bedroom and covered her, switching on the electric blanket in an effort to warm her shaking body.

'I'm Dr Clare Hart,' she introduced herself when the woman returned. 'I found Whitney last night and took her to the hospital. She refused to stay but it was only today that she told me where she lived. I brought her to you as soon as she told me.' She did not know what else to say.

'Thank you for bringing her back.' Mrs Ruiters twisted her pink housecoat. 'I thought I would never see her again.'

'Where did you report her missing?' Clare asked. She had not seen anything in the papers.

'My husband looked for her. And her brothers.' Mrs Ruiters looked at Clare then dropped her eyes, as if in shame. 'They looked in all the places we usually find the girls when they are finished.' She set the pills from the hospital out neatly on a small tray on the coffee table. 'But we could not find her.'

'And the police?' persisted Clare.

'No police, Dr Hart. No police.' She stopped twisting her dress, her face resolute. 'We will take care of her.'

'Who abducted her?'

Mrs Ruiters's face closed down again. 'I can't tell you, Dr Hart. But thank you for bringing Whitney back to me.' Then she stood up.

Clare took a photograph out of her bag and handed it to Florrie Ruiters. The colour drained from her face. 'Why are you showing me this?'

'That is the tattoo that Kelvin Landman marks his girls with. It was on a girl who was murdered,' Clare explained as the photograph slipped from the woman's trembling hands. 'Her body was dumped in Sea Point. Your daughter has the same tattoo now. On her back.'

Mrs Ruiters shook her head, determined. 'You must go now, Dr Hart. There is nothing I can do. There is nothing that Whitney can do. Her life is not worth it. We don't know this Kelvin Landman.' Her voice dropped to a whisper. She gripped Clare, her bony fingers hard on Clare's arm. Her sleeve slipped back, revealing the same distinctive tattoo on the tender skin inside her elbow. Clare traced it with her free hand. Florrie pulled back, as if Clare's touch had seared her skin.

'Can you find your way out, Dr Hart?'

'Take this, please,' Clare wrote down the number of a rape counsellor. 'Phone her. It might help you both. My number is there too if you change your mind about the police.' Clare hesitated. 'Or if you need anything.'

Mrs Ruiters pushed the scrap of paper into her pocket. She looked up at Clare, her face a faded shadow of her daughter's beauty, layered with years of hardship and fear.

'How can talking make her right?' she spat.

'It is a miracle she survived,' said Clare. 'Maybe it can help her heal.'

'The body survives.' Mrs Ruiters picked up the photograph of Charnay's dead, tattooed body. 'But the spirit?' The question hung in the air between them as she handed the photograph to Clare. Mrs Ruiters only moved when summoned by her daughter's plea: 'Mammie, come.'

In the hallway there was a picture of Whitney radiant at a school dance – she was with a boy wearing a suit. Clare let herself out. She got into her car, ignoring the three men pimp-rolling slowly down the pavement away from number twenty-three, and made her way back home. Dropping her things on the hall table, she went to tidy the spare room. Clare turned back the duvet. The shell-curl of Whitney's body was still there in the slight impression on the sheet. On the white pillow was the indentation her head had left, and also one long

146

black hair. Clare straightened the bed and pushed back the curtains. She glanced around the room, the used glass in her hand.

The only thing out of place was the top row of the bookshelf. Her books were so tightly packed that she could see at once that a book was missing. It was the one she had written about Constance. She sat down on the bed; her head slumped onto her knees. She hoped that her sister's story would help Whitney, although she doubted it. Constance was still trying to read, to get others to read, what had been scripted with such violence onto her naked body twenty years before. Clare thought of Mrs Ruiters's question about her daughter's spirit. Hot tears, shocking because so rare, slid down Clare's arms, running between her fingers. She had been too late, she had failed to help. The guilt she usually assuaged with her crusading journalism dragged a moan from her hidden self. She did not know how long she had sat there, rocking herself, but she was stiff when she got up to answer the shrill phone. She did not recognise the number that flashed on her caller ID, so she waited to see if there would be a message.

'Hello, Dr Hart, I was waiting for you to get home.' The sibilant voice was familiar. 'Just to remind you that we have a date. See you at eleven. Give your name to the doorman. He's expecting you, and he'll bring you up to me.' Clare felt sick. Kelvin Landman and his Isis Club. 'I hope you enjoyed your little drive.'

Clare had forgotten about him, could not bear the thought of being anywhere near him. She was about to call back and cancel, when she noticed the flash on the machine telling her there was another message waiting for her. She pressed 'play'. It was from her producer in London.

'Hello, Clare. I need rough footage to prove that you've reeled in your pet gangster. We're not going to swing it without

147

that. I'll have it some time on Monday, won't I, darling? Lovely weekend – weather's lovely here. Bye.'

'That's it, then,' said Clare to herself. She showered, feeling soiled by the phone message. Landman's timing was uncanny.

For once, she found it difficult to decide what to wear. In the end she settled for plain black. No jewellery. She called Riedwaan at home.

'I'm going to interview Landman,' she said.

'What for?'

'For my documentary,' said Clare. 'I am meant to have another life, remember?'

'It's no coincidence that he's talking to you just after you take that girl home. Be very careful,' said Riedwaan.

'I will. I'll be in public with him.'

'Watch your back.'

'I'm always careful,' said Clare. 'Will you be at home later?'

'Maybe. Why?'

'Just wondering,' she replied.

27

Its gold door handle distinguished the Isis Club from the half-hearted businesses that operated on the shabby eastern fringe of the city. Blackened windows prevented people from looking in. The doorman appeared when cars arrived. Some he directed to an empty parking lot. For others, a snap of his fingers summoned a valet. Clare decided that she would take the risk and park in the street. She was surprised at how self-conscious she felt going to a strip club alone, and was glad for the weight of her camera bag. It grounded her, announced her occupation to anyone who might stare at her. The doorman opened the door before she reached the handle, leaving her hand raised uselessly. She let it drop back to her side, disconcerted.

'Clare Hart?' he asked. The muscles around his neck bulged against the stiff-collared dress shirt.

'That's me,' she answered, relieved that she did not need to explain. 'I've come to see Kelvin Landman.'

The bouncer nodded, picked up his cellphone. 'She's here. Will someone come down?' An eager press of men was gathering behind Clare. Her back prickled uncomfortably.

'Miss Hart, do you mind stepping into the bar and having a drink? Mr Landman will be with you shortly.' The bar counter was a majestic sweep of gleaming russet wood. Clare took the leather stool she was offered and ordered a whiskey from a girl tagged: 'Melissa. I know I can help you'. The weight of the name tag made her transparent top sag strategically, to expose a rouged nipple.

Clare looked around the room as she waited for her drink. Opulence was blended with restraint. On the dark walls hung a range of erotic prints, coy French maids beckoning, black and white Japanese illustrations with strategically placed slashes of crimson, leering English squires bending rosy-cheeked milkmaids over rustic fences – it was a connoisseur's collection. Deep leather armchairs in gentleman's-club green and red huddled around low tables, were occupied by groups of paunchy, slack-mouthed men. A few had awkward wives with them. More animated than these were the guests with unabashed young women draped over them.

'Hostess service,' said Melissa, bringing Clare an excellent single malt. 'Three hundred an hour for one. Five hundred for two. Meant to be no touching.'

'That must be difficult,' said Clare. She was watching a short-skirted blonde work her breasts up a man's bare arm as she moved her pouting lips against his ear. Whatever she was saying made his tongue – wet and pink – protrude.

'Ja, those guys wreck your clothes. There's meant to be no touching now – just getting them ready for the show or the private rooms. Afterwards is open to negotiation, of course.'

'Who's that girl?' asked Clare.

Melissa followed Clare's gaze. 'Cornelle, I think. She's new. Do you know her?'

'We've met before,' said Clare.

'Do you want to speak to her?' asked Melissa. Cornelle turned, sensing that she was being watched. She blanched when she saw Clare.

'I don't think she wants to talk to you,' said Melissa.

'I think you're right.' Clare took a sip of her drink.

Melissa looked Clare up and down. 'We don't often get ladies,' she said. 'Hardly ever on their own.'

'Who do they come with?'

'The older ones come with their husbands usually, hoping it will stop him getting bored with their saggy tits and everything. The younger ones come with their bosses. They quite often buy the underwear. Would you like some? I can give you a catalogue.'

'Thanks,' said Clare. 'I would like one.'

The girl reached under the counter and handed Clare a brochure; embossed in gold on its cover was the outline of a woman's sumptuous body. 'Cool, hey,' said the girl. 'They're new. The whole place is going upmarket. The new owner bought all those expensive pictures to hang. And our movie catalogue is going to be great too.'

'I didn't know Isis made films,' said Clare.

'Oh, yes,' said Melissa. 'We used to just order from America or Holland and then sell them on. Now we're making them here. Cape Town has such a great film industry. Really skilled technical people, you know. And that will make things much more professional for us.' She wiped the counter and set out dishes of stuffed olives.

'What sort of movies are you making?'

'It's all under Isis Productions. I've been in two already. I got to choose my own costumes too. But those were only soft-core. There's also hard-core, girls-only *flieks* – all the usual stuff. Some of our customers like to star in their own blue movies. So we've been doing some of that too. Some only like to have the lapdances filmed. Others like more. It's cool for them. Quite expensive, but cool. There are also some girls who do live webcam stuff – so anyone who can afford it can do pay-per-view from home.'

151

'Did you ever meet a girl called Charnay?' asked Clare.

'Charnay . . . that's a good name. Was it her real name?'

'It was. Charnay Swanepoel.'

'What did she look like?'

'She was slim, tall, very long black hair. About seventeen. Apparently she was interested in making films too.'

'I can't remember. Maybe I saw her. Check our website. There are pictures of all the girls who have been in anything to do with Isis.'

'I will,' said Clare. 'How old are you, Melissa? Where are you from?'

'Me? I'm from Beaufort West. You can't imagine how boring the *platteland* is. I came here when I was seventeen, but I'm nineteen now. But I look young still, hey?' she pulled her mane of blonde hair into two pigtails and batted her eyelashes. 'I do quite a lot of the barely-legal stuff – you know how many guys just freak for the schoolgirl look.' She was thin, fragile even. In a uniform, without make-up, she would pass for fourteen. Or less.

'Who is the new boss?' Clare asked. Melissa's effervescence was gone. The colour drained from her face, leaving her blusher starkly scarlet on her white cheeks. She fumbled with the glass she was wiping. Clare looked into the mirror behind her. Kelvin Landman stood in front of the thick velvet curtains.

'Hello, Clare. You look lonely.' He smoothed her hair. 'I'm glad that Melissa has been keeping you entertained.' His diamond cuff links glinted as he leaned against the bar and snapped his fingers – boldly displaying his power. A drink materialised and Melissa was gone, taking a tray to check on already scrupulously tidy tables. Landman picked up his glass.

'Come through,' he said. 'The show is about to start.'

Clare followed him, bringing her drink with her. Landman held the heavy curtains aside and she went through. The room was an updated Moulin Rouge: the ubiquitous kitsch of commercial sex. The low stage was draped with plush red and gold. A low ramp thrust its way into the centre of the room. Men clustered at the tables, moving the chairs to be closer to the promise of the dancer's ramp. The mandatory poles were present, painted shiny black and red. Kelvin Landman's table was on a small raised dais, his entourage smaller than when Clare had met him at Otis Tohar's party. 'Where would you like to set up your camera?'

'Here,' said Clare, positioning the tripod so that the strippers would appear behind him when they came onstage. 'This is perfect,' she said, clipping the camera into place, checking batteries, tape, light. She pinned the mike under his shirt, startled at how smooth, how cold, his skin was. Then she sat back, watching him preen. The lure of celebrity that a lens promised was irresistible. Clare gave her standard caveats, that she was recording this interview, that he should answer in full sentences so that she could be edited out later, that he should look into the camera's eye and not hers. She asked him to tell her who he was, where he came from.

'Kelvin Landman. Born in 1968 in Cape Town. I grew up on the Flats. I had my troubles with the law. I was involved in street gangs where I lived in Manenberg. But who wasn't, there?' he grinned broadly at Clare. Then he remembered her instruction and looked back at the camera. 'I had some trouble with politics too, so in the eighties I went overseas. Into exile.'

'Where did you go? How?' prompted Clare.

'To Amsterdam. My uncle was in the merchant navy at that time. And as you can imagine, there are many places to hide on a boat, especially if you are a pretty boy. Which I was, in those days, believe it or not. I worked my way over and jumped ship in Amsterdam. I met some people working there, started at the bottom and worked my way up. Then I got asylum papers, so I was legal.'

'What exactly were you doing there?'

'A bit of import, bit of export – luxury goods. They've got it sorted there, I tell you. Hash bars and the women selling themselves with no problems from the police. I learnt how to run a business.'

Clare's face was wiped clean of expression. 'Explain the import-export thing to me.'

'You figure out what is in demand and then you supply. You can get what you want as long as you are willing to pay the right price. That is the business principle I have applied since I came back to Cape Town. We import vodka and hot Thai chilli. And we have lots of sweet things to export – wine, peaches.'

One of the men sitting listening sniggered. 'Shut the fuck up, Benny,' snarled Landman. 'Whose fucking interview is this?' Benny held his hands up in submission and cowered into his seat. Turning to Clare, Landman took a deep breath. 'Where were we?'

'You were telling me about supply and demand. What about here? In this club?'

Landman looked around, genuinely proud. 'I supply my clients with what they need.' He pointed to the men waiting along the ramp. The music throbbed. 'And I provide employment.' He grabbed a passing hostess, her buttocks exposed in tight black hotpants. He twisted her flesh, his eyes holding hers, daring her to do anything less than smile delightedly through the pain. 'What else would these girls find to do?' he asked, dismissing her. Clare watched her retreat, a welt emerging on the smooth skin. 'I suppose you could call me a philanthropist. I give men what they need and women what they deserve.'

The lights suddenly dimmed, releasing Clare from the

interview. A pulsating drumbeat filled the air, the rhythm unmistakable. Clare turned her attention to the stage. A spotlight cut through the darkness, illuminating a girl, naked apart from the intricate metal bondage gear biting hungrily where her flesh was softest. She was tightly blindfolded. Her tongue glistened red behind her parted lips. Two corseted women, strapped into high, shiny boots, stepped out of the darkness to spreadeagle her and handcuff her to a pole. Both held whips that they flicked first across their hands and then across the girl's breasts. The sound cracked sharply in the silence, and the girl's nipples stood erect. Slowly, the music began to pulse faster, and the lights went up a little. The strobe turned slowly, tattooing the girl with flickering pornographic inanities. Each new word brought fresh blows from the stiletto-heeled dominatrixes. The girl writhed, either in faked agony or orgasm. Clare watched, mesmerised.

Landman touched the inside of her knee. 'That is Justine. I see you like it. This is "Fetish Night" – very popular, as you can see.' Some of the men were taking turns now, at a hundred rand a time, to bring a velvet horsewhip down on the bound body that now hung limp against the pole.

Clare shook herself, switching her mind from the degradation on the stage back to Landman. 'Where do these girls come from, how do you recruit them?'

He turned his attention back to the camera. 'Some are local. Quite a few are foreigners – they're often better dancers,' he explained, 'more committed to the profession. Fewer piercings, fewer drugs, no families to worry about. But you can check, there are no illegals here. All of them have their papers. With the unique skills these girls have, it's not so hard to get Home Affairs to comply.'

'Your mother must be proud of you,' said Clare. 'You have done so well.'

Landman spat. 'My mother was a *dronklap* who forgot to feed me when I was baby and who loaned my sister out to any "uncle" who'd buy her a *dop*. Right now she can't remember her own name, let alone that she ever had a son.' He paused and swivelled around to watch the show. It had shifted to a complicated harem scene that involved yashmaks and lapdogs. 'But we are doing well.'

'We?' asked Clare.

'My business partner has bought this building. And another one recently, in Sea Point, for the next Isis Club. We're building a chain that will challenge the other operators. Much less tame, much more extreme. Our next move will be Isis Safaris – "Where all your wildest fantasies come to life".'

'That's an expensive investment.'

'Sex is a very lucrative business, Clare. The demand is always there and the supply is limitless.'

'What has your strategy been?' asked Clare.

'We're consolidating, branding our products, developing our niche market – for the connoisseur who thought he had it all. There's so much growth potential: products, spin-off goods, movies. That's where you make your money.' Clare thought of the elaborate edit suite she had glimpsed at Tohar's apartment. The memory called to mind Tatiana's sobs as she huddled there, alone. Landman continued, on a roll with his newly acquired business-speak. 'Movies are where you really make your money. You can, for one, sell the same girl over and over again. She doesn't get tired, doesn't get her fucking period, doesn't get thirsty. It's perfect. And because it's the movies, you can make all sorts of things look as if they really happened – when in fact they didn't. Some men pay a lot to see their darkest fantasies come alive.' He laughed. 'Or dead.'

A waitress brought a fresh round of drinks to the table and

cleared away the ashtray and dirty glasses. Landman's phone rang. He picked it up and checked the number. He didn't answer. It rang gratingly four more times. 'We just have to keep our main man steady.' He put the phone back into his pocket. 'Keep him convinced that teamwork is the best.' The interview was over. Clare repressed the urge to down her whiskey. Instead she packed up her camera, hoping that Landman would not notice that her hands were shaking.

'Thank you,' said Clare. 'You have been most informative.'

'Sure,' said Landman. 'Any time. You let me know.' He slapped her bottom. 'You're going to make me a star, aren't you, baby? Move over, Patrice Motsepe, Mr Oppenheimer. Watch this space: here comes Kelvin Landman.'

Clare zipped her bag closed and said through clenched teeth, 'I don't know about being a star. But probably famous for a day or two.'

She desperately needed to get out. The cool night air was cleansing, and she gulped it in as soon as she was outside. She felt complicit in Landman's misogyny and ambition. And defiled by her own fascination with what she had watched, by the pulse she had banished from between her legs only after it had left its wetness behind. She opened her window wide, hoping the sea air would blow her clean. She would have another shower, scrub herself, as soon as she got home.

But the road home took her past the turnoff to Riedwaan's house. Clare took it without thinking. She slowed as she descended the steep one-way road where he lived. The lights were on, and before she had even thought about what she was doing, she'd parked her car and knocked on the door. Riedwaan opened it and drew her inside without a word. His hands were on her body before he had latched the door behind her. He pushed her against the wall and kissed her, obliterating from her mind what she had watched all evening. The tension that had held Clare so taut melted away. Then Riedwaan led her to his unmade bed.

Later, Riedwaan got up and poured them both whiskeys. He lit a cigarette and pushed Clare's hair aside, stroking her naked back from shoulder to flank.

'Isn't it your birthday tomorrow?' he asked.

Clare turned her head to look at him. 'How did you know?' she asked.

'I remember these things.' He leant over and kissed the curve of her waist. 'What shall we do? Croissants? A walk on the mountain?' He flipped her over, moving his hand down her belly towards her thighs. She didn't resist when he put his glass down and pulled her on top of him again. She couldn't give him an answer because he was kissing her again. Like a drowning man. He fell asleep as soon as he had come, but Clare lay wide-eyed long into the night. She was not looking forward to the hours she'd have to spend over the next few days listening to the recording of Landman's voice, transcribing and editing until she had every nuance ready for her documentary. And, of course, she also had her date with Mrs Ruiters, who had called earlier to say that Whitney had to be moved somewhere safe. She had insisted Clare meet with her. She wanted her to record her statement, and she was too afraid to tell her over the phone.

Clare thought of that coming Sunday, her birthday – and hoped she and Riedwaan would spend it together. They would get coffee, sweet winter oranges, newspapers, and then return to the bed that held the mingled traces of their desires. They would read and doze and make love. They would do normal Sunday things together. They could maybe start again and this time she would make it work. She turned to him and fell asleep.

Clare was wide awake at five. Riedwaan was sprawled across

the bed: one hand at home on her hip, the other curled under her hair. He knew she couldn't sleep if the nape of her neck was exposed. At six she inched out of his embrace. The pull of Constance was irresistible, and so Clare chose her twin. She slipped out of bed. Riedwaan awoke while she was dressing in the dark, searching for her keys. He watched her in the darkness, saying nothing as she slipped out of the room. He held her pillow tight against his chest, but her warmth was already gone. Traces of her perfume taunted him. He got up and made coffee, taking it into the cold courtyard to watch the sun rise.

28

Across town, in a leafy, cloistered suburb, Cathy King sat cradling a phone, her shoulders bony under her cashmere cardigan. She drew up her knees, sharp beneath her fawn trousers, as she stared straight ahead. Her untouched teacup was dwarfed by the over-sized coffee table. It looked ridiculous. Much like she did on the enormous blue wave of a sofa. The French doors were open, the sage carpet blending with the luxurious sweep of lawn rolling down to the pool, its great, dead eye staring unblinkingly at the sunless sky. Cathy hated the swimming pool, and never swam in it. Neither did India.

The thought of her daughter was a knife twist where her most recently cracked rib was healing. Her doctor had raised an eyebrow when she went to him. 'Again, Mrs King? You must be more careful.'

Indeed, she must. Cathy stared dry-eyed at the swimming pool. It stared back. She had tried so hard to be careful with India. Last night she had waited up all night, pacing, pacing. The beautiful daughter, who she loved with an aching intensity, had not come home. Cathy knew she had failed her daughter – her broken rib told her that. So did the burn scars down the inside of her thighs. Despite her love, she had failed India. Now she forced herself to phone Brian to say that she was worried about India. He hadn't come home either. He never did on Saturdays. It was her one night of respite.

'You idiot,' he snarled at her. 'That little slut is probably fucking herself silly. Just like her dumb bitch of a mother would, given half a chance. Make sure you do nothing to embarrass me. I'll see she learns her lesson when she does come home. You don't fucking move. You hear me?'

'Yes, Brian,' she whispered. She kept from her voice the steel forming where her heart had once been. 'I won't.' And she waited humbly, as always, for him to cut the connection. Then she looked at the *Cape Times* she had pulled out of the recycling bin and keyed in the emergency number at the end of the article on Amore Hendricks.

It was light now. She closed her eyes and, gathering the remnants of her strength, she pressed 'call'.

'Faizal.' The voice was guarded, rough in her ear. She was quiet. 'Who is this?'

Cathy gritted her teeth, did not cower. 'My daughter is missing. This is Cathy King.'

Riedwaan felt the strap of tension tighten across his shoulders. 'Mrs King, why are you reporting this to me?'

'She looks like the girl in the newspaper. The one you found. Amore Hendricks.' Her voice was almost inaudible, as if the air had been sucked from her lungs. The terror she had held at bay all through the darkness overwhelmed her now. She heard his voice again. It sounded muffled, as if she were deep inside a well.

'Can you come to the station?' he was saying. 'Mrs King? Immediately? Can you bring a photo of her – a recent one? Shall I send a patrol car? Or is there someone who can bring you? Your husband?'

'No! Not my husband. He's not here. I'll come straight away.'

Cathy fetched her handbag and went upstairs to India's

room. Her school tights, left hanging on a chair, carried the outline of her slim legs, the grubby marks of her toes. She must have been walking somewhere with no shoes on. Just her lovely stockinged feet. Cathy picked up the tights and put them into her bag. A photo of India was propped next to the bed. Cathy slipped it into her bag, nestling it with the tights. She would not cry yet. She had to find her child. If she let go, even for a second, she would shatter finally. So she held the shards of herself together.

Downstairs, she took a second Valium. She checked her face in the hallway mirror. The skin was pale, smoothly sculpted over her cheekbones. She remembered to put on her lipstick, grateful that her face was unmarked this time. She went to the garage, hating the flashy little car Brian made her drive. She reversed and drove down the oak-lined road. The houses here were so far apart that no sound you made would ever carry to your neighbours. She took in nothing of the drive around the mountain to Sea Point.

The police station that Captain Faizal had directed her to was ugly, a squat face-brick building, the windows covered with anti-hand-grenade mesh. Riedwaan Faizal made her feel better. His face was hard, but the eyes had a vulnerability to them that comforted her. He escorted her to the untidy cubbyhole that served as an office.

She accepted the cup of milky tea he gave her, and then told him what she thought he needed to know. That India was sixteen. That she had gone to watch a friend at a theatre rehearsal. That the friend should have dropped her home at eleven. She did not tell him that none of India's friends ever came inside the house – why should she? She did tell him, though, that her daughter had not come home. That her daughter had not answered her calls. Yes, she had contacted her mother. She had SMS'd to say she was having a great time

162

and might be late. Cathy had been watching television then, so she had not heard the message come in. And yes. Here was the picture of India. Taken two months before when she and her friend Gemma had auditioned to be movie extras. Their role had been to mill around in a café in Long Street. They had loved the whole experience.

Riedwaan looked at the photo of the laughing girl. Her long mane of black hair was a blur, caught as she flung her head back, delighted by the photographer. She was holding her elegant hands up in a gesture of mock submission. High, rounded breasts were firmly held in place by the tight white T-shirt. A very beautiful girl.

'Can I keep this, Mrs King?' There was a feverish look in her eyes. He knew the look. He had seen it in Shazia's eyes when their daughter had vanished. He must have looked like that, too. Cathy King nodded.

'We need to take a formal statement and I need to get a list of her friends and activities,' he told her. She nodded again and handed him her daughter's address book. Then she made her formal, detailed statement, signed it, and handed it back to him.

'She would have had most of her numbers in her phone, I suppose.'

'We will do everything possible, Mrs King. If you think of anything, no matter how small, then call me. If anyone contacts you, any strange calls, let me know at once.'

She picked up the card he pushed across the table. 'I'll wait at home.'

'I'll be sending someone else to talk to you at home. She will want to look through India's room – maybe there will be something there.'

'Who will come, Captain Faizal?'

'Dr Clare Hart. She's been working on the investigation.'

'The profiler – the one I've read about in the newspapers?'

Riedwaan nodded. Cathy King's last vestige of hope drained away. She put her hand out, as if she was about to fall. But she didn't. She winced as she straightened her back.

'We will keep you informed, Mrs King. And we will do our utmost.' The words rang hollow.

'Goodbye, Inspector.' She turned and walked to her car.

She looked so alone. Riedwaan went to get some coffee, thinking of Mrs King. The wedding ring was conspicuous on her finger, so it was odd that she had come alone. Where was India's father? The anger that surged through him was intense. He deliberately turned his mind to the killer they were looking for. If they could just work out who he was. Or if the killer made a mistake, there would at least be a chance of finding India alive. That, to his chagrin, was the truth. He reached automatically for a cigarette, remembering that he had given up only when his hand found nothing there. He went out to bum a smoke, grabbing a cup of coffee on his way out. But he had made all his colleagues swear to refuse him a cigarette and they stuck to it: no one would give him even a drag. He tried to call Clare. There was no reply. She must have gone out of range or switched off her phone. Annoyed, he waited for the kettle to boil.

When he sat down again, he pulled out the two case files. Amore Hendricks. Charnay Swanepoel. He prayed that he would never label one India King. But he did not hold out much hope. They knew how these girls had died, how long it had taken for them to die, what they had last eaten. And yet nothing pointed them anywhere. There were no witnesses. The DNA they had didn't match any on record. It could be gang-related – some new initiation method. Or perhaps a coded warning to the increasing numbers of freelancers – Charnay certainly seemed to have been one – who were being pimped in the more upmarket areas. Kelvin Landman was an ideal candidate. The right profile. Sadistic, ruthless, meticulous about cleaning up after himself. No witness had ever testified against him. That could be the answer. But something niggled. He knew Clare suspected that Landman was a candidate. But she was not convinced of this. Riedwaan slipped the note Rita had left for Clare into the file. 'Only posh florists use that ribbon. See you Monday, R.'

Clare Hart's profile pointed her elsewhere. Landman, she argued, was cruel for a reason. That was where he did not fit the profile of a serial killer. With this particular killer, Clare contended – with nothing to back her but her intuition – the killings were an end in themselves. They were too staged, the symbolism was too obscure, to be a message to others. If someone was trying to scare prostitutes, then why Graaff's Pool? Why not Somerset Road? Riedwaan had worked with Clare often enough to know she was rarely wrong.

29

Clare ached with the heaviness of leaving Riedwaan, yet there was nothing to do but get into her car and drive up the lonely road curving between the coast and the green hills, soft in the morning light. There was no other traffic so early on a Sunday morning. Snow gleamed against the black cliffs of the jagged mountains in the distance. They seemed to march relentlessly north, only to peter out, though, defeated by the vast inland plains of the Karoo. Clare gripped the wheel, her knuckles white. She glanced at the skin on her hands, already starting to ridge and coarsen. Then she glimpsed her face in the rear-view mirror. The crow's feet furrowing the corners of her eyes lingered now, even when she was not laughing.

Like today: the birthday she shared with Constance. Her twin would have been pacing all night. Clare had given up trying to heal Constance, but she could not abandon her. The sun disappeared behind the clouds and a soft rain started falling. Clare listened to the hypnotic swish-swish of the windscreen wipers. It had been raining on their birthday twenty years before when Clare, desperate to be separate from Constance, had rid herself of her virginity.

The rain was coming down harder now. Clare slowed, remembering how the need to be independent had driven her out of the school boarding house and into Isaiah Jones's arms. She had had three hours of perfect freedom – abandoning herself to the pleasure Isaiah had skilfully coaxed from her inexperienced body.

Swish-swish-swish went the wipers.

Sometime after midnight, she'd worked out afterwards, when it was all over, Constance had realised she was fine, absolutely fine, on her own. She had followed Clare's secret path through the chapel window and into the shadowed park adjacent to the school. Constance had wanted to tell Clare that she was able to be alone, that she would let Clare come and go as she pleased – but Constance never made it.

Filled with dread, Clare had awoken suddenly from a sticky, satiated sleep. Isaiah had followed her into the night to look for her twin, not questioning Clare's intuition. They had found Constance barely alive in the park, the marks of the gang's brutal rite of passage indelibly written on her body.

Clare turned down the familiar nave of trees. The pale branches reached mournfully over the ribbon of road, brushing their tips against each other. She parked in her usual place, her breath a fine vapour hanging on the cold air. As she walked down the path to her sister's secluded house, a bright finger of sunshine broke free of the mountains in the east, illuminating the garden. She stepped onto the polished red stoep. It was very cold here where the sun was always absent. She sensed Constance standing on the other side of the heavy door, breathing with difficulty through her hammer-damaged nose.

'Constance,' said Clare. 'Open for me.'

The door opened a crack, and then wider. A white hand, like a plant too long in the darkness, reached out and drew her in.

'Our birthday, Clare.' She had assumed Clare would come. She always did. Constance held Clare to her, her nostrils flaring at the male smell clinging to her. Riedwaan's smell.

'You must bath. I must wash you. Come.' She led her sister down the passage to the bathroom. Here she ran the water hot. Constance removed Clare's clothes, throwing them away from her as if the smell on them might corrupt her too.

Constance stroked her sister's smooth, naked body. Her fingers traced the skin on Clare's breasts, stomach, thighs – and also her own scars. Clare turned away from her and stepped into the hot water. It was lovely, the warm, enveloping relief from the cold and tension. She lay back. Constance picked up a sponge and rubbed soap onto it. She picked up Clare's left arm and washed it carefully, as a cat would wash her kitten. Then the right arm. Then the feet, calves, thighs, and between her sister's legs. Clare submitted. She had managed to pare down the daily rituals to this annual birthday cleansing, which she did not have the heart to resist. She wondered if she might not also need it, this purging of the previous year. Constance moved behind Clare and soaped her smooth back, though seemingly lost in tracing the script that first one man, and then the next, had carved into her own back while they'd taken turns in sodomising her.

'What does it say, Constance?' Clare always asked her this question. 'What did they write on you?'

'Can't you read it?' she always replied. 'Don't you *feel* it?'

As Clare got out of the bath, Constance roughly wrapped the white dressing gown around her and pushed her feet into a pair of slippers. Clare was aware of her sister's anger, and tried to distract her from the violence of her memories.

'Let's get something to eat,' she quietly suggested, and walked ahead of Constance to the kitchen. The room was warm and orange-hued: the Aga was burning, as it did all through the winter, and the sun was filtering through the stained-glass windows. Clare opened the fridge, set out milk, cheese, yoghurt, the last remaining figs. She was desperate for coffee, but there wasn't any. She settled for rooibos tea and honey, a mug for her, and one for Constance. She made the toast and they ate in silence. Constance subsided into herself.

'Constance, won't you please paint whatever it is you always trace on my back?' Constance looked startled. Then Clare got up slowly and put a thick piece of paper in front of Constance. She fetched a brush and the blue tube of paint already open on her sister's easel. 'Paint it, Constance. Paint what you always draw on my back. Make me see it.' Constance just closed her eyes and remained perfectly still.

Clare's thoughts shifted to Riedwaan waking alone this morning. She wanted, needed to be free of the brutal calligraphy that had tethered her to Constance for two decades. But first she needed to understand. She looked up with surprise as Constance suddenly reached for a brush and dipped it into the paint. She began to draw: angles, loops, spirals. It was beautiful, but it meant nothing to Clare. Constance's back was just a welter of crude scars, her painting just random shapes.

Looking exhausted, she eventually gave the picture to Clare. 'Let's sleep now, Connie.' Constance followed Clare to the bedroom, where they lay down – spooned, just as they had slept as children. Clare fell asleep at once and woke hours later, with a sleeping Constance in her arms. Clare extricated herself and got dressed. Then she made tea and took a cup to Constance.

'I'm leaving now, it's past five already,' she said, smoothing her sister's hair from her eyes. Constance smiled and turned towards the wall again.

'There's something for you on the desk, Clare,' said Constance. Clare picked up the brown envelope. She could feel the familiar shape of the card inside. She pulled it out gingerly. The sixteenth card. The Tower. Two figures hurtled down, head first, towards the jagged rocks at the base of a citadel.

'What does it mean, Constance?'

'It's warning you of catastrophe.' Constance sat up. 'It's a warning about the face of evil. Take it with you.'

Clare put the card into her handbag. There was no arguing with Constance, she knew.

'You can also read it as illumination. Perhaps you are closer to understanding things than you think.'

'I wish I was. I'll see you soon.' Clare kissed her sister on the forehead and left, making sure that the door locked behind her. The sky was dreary and cold.

The remains of a lonely day stretched before her, but Clare turned eagerly to things there was still some hope of resolving. On her own way home, she drove past the Hendrickes' house. The murdered girl had lived in Mountain View, a bleak estate on a cold, windswept patch of denuded sand dunes. Serried ranks of dwarf houses bunkered down behind high walls, pinioned against their backyard braais by shiny new cars parked most precisely in front. Clare could see women moving back and forth behind the front windows, serving invisible dinners to invisible families – the television flicker making life just bearable.

In one house, otherwise indistinguishable from the rest, there was a candle in the front window. A small shrine. Clare drove past slowly, turned, parked, and was about to get out to meet the occupants, to ask some questions, to pry. She saw a man come out and bend down with a pleading expression to a woman in the garden who was sitting listlessly on a child's swing. The intimacy of their grief stopped her. She looked in the cubbyhole for copies of the interview tapes Riedwaan had given her. She found the one labelled 'Parents' and put it into the tape deck. Then she fast-forwarded past the opening preliminaries, to where Riedwaan began to probe the raw wound of a daughter's murder.

'When last did you see Amore, Mr Hendricks?' asked Riedwaan, his voice comforting, low, his accent exaggerated by the electronic device.

'Saturday afternoon, *nê skat*?' Mrs Hendricks must have nodded. '*Ja*, Inspector, Saturday at about three o'clock.'

'Where was that?'

'She was here, at home.'

'What were her plans?'

'She was going to the Canal Walk shopping centre. She's *mos* at that dance college there. They were all rehearsing for the winter dance festival. She was a very beautiful dancer, *jy weet*. Ballet, modern, even African. Look at all her eisteddfod certificates. There is her letter from the University of Cape Town telling her that she was invited to a final audition.' Here his voice cracked. 'It arrived on Thursday. I'm sorry,' he mumbled.

'Why, Inspector? Why our baby?' This was the first time that Mrs Hendricks had spoken. Riedwaan, Clare knew, would have had no answer to that question, knowing as he did that an innocent victim was a rare thing. He was silent for a while, perhaps waiting for Mr Hendricks to master his grief.

'How did she get to town?' he eventually asked.

'She got a lift with our neighbour. They were going to the movies.'

'Who is he?' Clare could hear a lilt of interest in Riedwaan's voice.

'Not he. She. Mrs Vermaas and her mother. They dropped her off and she went to her rehearsal.' Clare knew that her devastated dance teacher had corroborated this. The other dancers in her group had worked with Amore till six before dispersing in twos and threes for supper or home. There was

171

a long pause. Then Mr Hendricks continued. 'She SMS'd me at seven to say that she had a very exciting surprise for us later. That she would tell us when she saw us.' The tape crackled in the silence.

'That's the last we heard.' It was Mrs Hendricks who spoke eventually, with distilled pain.

'How was she planning to get home?'

'She was meant to meet my brother at ten-thirty. He has a taxi. He was going to drop her off at home, as usual.' Mr Hendricks's voice faded as he moved away from the microphone. Clare pictured him moving closer to his wife, holding her hand perhaps. 'But she never arrived. He phoned her and he says the phone was answered. He could hear Amore's voice. Heard her laughing. That he could hear glasses and music. He thought it was a bar or a restaurant. And then the phone went dead. Before he could speak to her. He tried to call again but her phone was switched off. And he couldn't find her.'

'What did he do then, your brother?'

'He alerted security – he knows those guys – and he put a call out to the radio taxis. Then he called us and told us to come. He also called the police. He had a very bad feeling because there was just no sign of her. Nothing. Nothing.'

'What time was that, Mr Hendricks?'

His wife answered. 'It was just past eleven. You see, the shift changes at ten-thirty. That is why he always comes home then. He brings the afternoon shift home and quite a lot of them live near here . . .'

Clare cut her off by jabbing the rewind button. The tape whined, forced back a few loops. '. . . the shift changes at ten-thirty.' That is what Mrs Hendricks said again, quite clearly. It would explain why Amore hadn't been seen. Each shift reported back to one of two security centres. It was here that they handed their two-way radios and their luminous bibs to the next shift, and then went home. If Amore Hendricks had gone somewhere then – willingly or not – none of the security guards would have seen her.

Clare watched the house. Behind the drawn curtains someone blew out the candle, snuffing out the last remaining light. Clare was chilled to the bone. She saw Mr Hendricks take his wife in his arms. She sagged against him, broken. Clare drove away. The swipe, swipe on her windscreen did not improve her visibility until she was back in Sea Point.

Clare knew she would have to explain her disappearance to Riedwaan, but she felt utterly drained. She poured herself a glass of wine instead and drank it, listening to one of the classical CDs that Riedwaan had bought on her last birthday. She poured herself another glass and left her cellphone off. She would face her life again on Monday.

30

Clare was up early. She came back from her run refreshed, prepared for the day. She'd scheduled a meeting for that morning, to work through the details of the profile and to strategise the next moves. Chief-Superintendent Phiri had the press breathing down his neck and the Minister for Community Safety about to break his balls. He was desperate for some meat to throw at them at the press conference scheduled for two o'clock. But Clare did not want the profile she was assembling to be released. She hoped that none of the forensic evidence would be passed anonymously to a journalist. That had happened once before, and a child murderer had walked free because of it.

Clare was sure the killer would be watching the press. He was an exhibitionist, the daring display of his corpses left no doubt of that, and he would delight in taunting the police. She switched her phone back on. There was only one message – from Riedwaan. He had been married so long that the intimate habits of obligation came easier to him than to her. It was her own weakness that had taken her to him on Saturday night. This had opened up the hurt for both of them again. Clare hoped that it was not going to derail their work on the case.

'I'd better listen to it now, and then phone and apologise.

Again!' she said to Fritz who was rubbing herself against Clare's legs, hoping for breakfast. Clare listened to the message. Riedwaan's voice was filled with an icy, impotent rage. 'Where the fuck are you? It's Sunday morning. There's another girl missing. Her name is India King. Our man is just getting into his swing and you're playing games with me. I hope you've got something very smart for me. Call me back. I'll have my phone on.'

Clare's legs went numb. She slid to the floor with her back to the wall and called Riedwaan – but there was no answer. She left a message that she would meet him as soon as he called. Then she called the station. Joe Zulu told her that Riedwaan wasn't there, but he gave her what meagre information there was about India King.

Clare showered and dressed in five minutes. She took her coffee to her desk to wait for Riedwaan to call her back. Her notes about the murders were strewn across her desk. She arranged them neatly before putting them to one side, so that her thoughts could sink down into the dark space where the killer lurked.

She sensed him, his implacable rage all the more frightening because he seemed to have plenty of resources. Firstly, a car – how else would he get the bodies where he left them? He had money too, or access to it. The clothes he decked his pathetic corpses in were absurdly expensive. He had control, too: the bound hands told her that. Or did they? Clare stared out of her window at the reddening sky. She picked up a pen and jotted some more notes:

He needs to exert control. Why?
The control he exercises over the girls is displaced – there must be some other place where he periodically loses control.

175

Sexual fetish.
No assault.
Money?
Murders: not cheap.

A text message pulled her back into the present. It was from Riedwaan. 'Meet me at the station. Eight-thirty.' Clare gathered her papers, finished her coffee and walked to the police station. Being outside calmed her enough to face what was coming. She opened the door of the caravan where their investigation was housed. Riedwaan had cleared a wall for India. All that was there were her name and a photograph. Her brown eyes sparkled at Clare across the room. Riedwaan's greeting was cold. He did not thank her for the file she handed him. Clare went out to get some more coffee, leaving him to read the profile she had written.

Soon afterwards, Clare went with Joe and Riedwaan to retrace India's movements before she'd disappeared. Nothing. Her friend had said goodbye after the rehearsal. India had said she was meeting someone.

'No,' said Gemma, her friend. She didn't know who or where. But she had been distracted so she hadn't really paid attention. 'Yes,' she said, they often split up, went their own way.

By the end of the day that was all they had: that India had gone to the Little Theatre on Long Street. That she had left at about nine-thirty – perhaps to meet someone, perhaps not – and that she had vanished. She had not been seen again. Not by a car guard or any of the sleepy bouncers Riedwaan had woken. She had simply vanished.

'Girls like her don't just vanish like that,' said Joe, shaking his head.

'Not unless she slipped into a car,' said Riedwaan. 'Well-dressed girl getting into an expensive car. Who would notice?'

Rita Mkhize sauntered in. 'Hey, Riedwaan. Your fax from ballistics.' She handed him the two pages. He skimmed them quickly.

'Confirmation that it was a scalpel. But not a type widely used here any more. More like the kind of blade widely used thirty years ago. Still deadly, though.' He read on.

'Now here's something interesting,' he said. 'The keys are duplicates. Both girls had their hands tied around copies of the same original.' He handed the fax back to her. 'Rita, won't you check out all the key duplicating places from Sea Point to Woodstock. Find out which have this particular mastering system.' He pointed out the section she needed. 'You and Joe might want to pay them a visit.'

'Okay,' said Rita. She turned to Joe. 'I'm going back to my office to put that list together.'

'Don't you like our palace?' asked Joe. Rita laughed as she made her way down the caravan's rickety steps. Joe watched her disappear into the main building.

'Those keys you can buy anywhere,' said Joe. 'It's a long shot.'

'What would you suggest, Joe? You got any aces up that designer sleeve of yours?'

'Cool it, Riedwaan,' said Joe. 'I'm just thinking about where we're putting our time.'

'There's another girl missing, Joe. Should I just sit here on my *gat*?'

'Well, we're not going to catch anything if we fight,' said Clare. 'Let's go over those statements again and see if there's something we've missed. Phiri needs something for the press this afternoon.'

Riedwaan turned back to the growing pile of folders on his desk, tension knotting his neck. 'Okay, let's get going.' He opened India's file – it was the slimmest one, just a missing-

177

person report – as if it would suddenly reveal the truth. It didn't. They worked through lunch, ordering pizza to keep them going.

Phiri came by just before two. He skimmed through Clare's report.

'I'm cancelling the press conference,' he said. 'There's nothing new here. These guys are after my blood and your profile.'

'What will you do, sir?' asked Riedwaan. 'The press won't be happy.'

'I'm going to issue a statement about India King's disappearance. I will advise young women to stay indoors or move with an escort.'

'That will make you very popular,' said Riedwaan.

'Thank you, Captain Faizal, your concern is noted.' Phiri slammed the caravan door.

'Sir,' Riedwaan called after Phiri through the small window, 'ask anyone who has been approached in a threatening way to come forward.'

Phiri nodded curtly and slipped in the back entrance, avoiding the gaggle of journalists at the front.

'That will go down like a ton of bricks,' said Clare.

'I'm going to join Rita and Joe. I want to see how they're getting on with those keys.' Riedwaan picked up his keys. 'I'll see you tomorrow?'

'Yes,' said Clare. 'I'm going to go through these old cases – see if I pick up anything similar to this.' She reached her hand towards him. He took it, and bent down and kissed her cheek.

'How do you get away with it?' he asked.

'See you,' Clare smiled as she turned back to the heap of unsolved cases in front of her. 'Get some rest.'

She worked till six. She had invited Marcus and Julie for a

belated birthday dinner, and dashed home to wash away the long hours she'd spent with Riedwaan and the rest of the team, glad that she hadn't cancelled. Clare set the table just inside the balcony doors and put the graceful arum lilies she had bought into a vase. She had ordered an elaborate array of sashimi from her favourite Japanese restaurant, which was delivered just as Marcus and Julie arrived. They sat and looked out over the sea towards Robben Island, washed pink by the dipping sun. A trick of the light made it seem close enough to touch.

'Hard to imagine it as either a prison or a leper colony,' said Marcus. 'I'm designing a new visitors' centre for the island where tourists will be able to order exactly what Mandela and his fellow prisoners had eaten. 'For two hundred rand you'll get a bowl of lumpy pap and a tin mug of tea,' said Marcus.

'I'll bet you'll be able to sleep in the cells soon. At five hundred a shot,' said Julie, shaking her head.

'You think you're joking!' said Marcus. 'That's phase two.'

It was a relief to be drinking wine and talking about ordinary things. Clare let the conversation wash over her, a balm after a brutal Monday. The food was superb. Clare marvelled at the precision with which each piece of moist, pink salmon was butterflied, each vegetable pared paper thin. Their talk ebbed and flowed pleasantly around Marcus's work, Julie's children. Beatrice's most recent misdemeanours were reported for Clare's amusement. And Imogen's school successes were listed for her praise. Clare managed to deflect the conversation from what she was working on until dessert.

'By the way, Clare. I found out who owns that building on Main Road,' said Marcus. 'The one where all the illegals live.'

Julie looked concerned. 'Are you all right, Clare?' she asked. 'You're so pale.'

'I'm fine. Just a lot on my plate at the moment. Thanks for doing that, Marcus. Who owns it?'

'Your friend, Otis Tohar,' Marcus replied.

'Oh,' said Clare. 'Did he buy it recently?'

'Apparently so. Flour months ago. Cash. But I heard that he had a cash-flow crisis, and Landman conveniently stepped in with the bridging finance. Two million. The pound of flesh Landman needed to bring his friend to heel.'

'Still, that's a lot of cash,' said Julie.

'My deep throat at the deeds office told me that it was not all Tohar's money. Apparently he had a little help from a friend,' said Marcus.

'Do you know who?' asked Clare.

'Your other friend. Kelvin Landman. He runs quite a few little sidelines.'

'What I want to know,' said Clare, 'is how you pay a loan like that back. A gangster like Landman is not likely to give easy credit. With such a huge cash loan, he must have Tohar right where he wants him.'

Clare had finished her dessert. Julie gathered the plates and stood up to clear the table. Then they stacked the dishwasher and switched it on.

'Coffee?' asked Julie.

They took their coffee cups through to the sitting room where Marcus had resuscitated the fire. An SMS from Imogen finally eventually summoned her parents home. Clare saw them out. Glad to be alone, she went out to the balcony and watched a ship drift across the night horizon.

31

The chef's assistant wiped the last sushi knife clean and flung his apron into the laundry basket. Exhausted, he scrubbed feebly, ineffectually, at the red stain on his trousers. He said goodnight to the stern Japanese chef, shrugged on his jacket, and hooded himself against the wind outside. He hurried over the road, shoulders hunched. Looking out for cars, he didn't notice the moonlight being lightly tossed by the waves close by. Glad for the shelter of the bus stop by the palm trees, for the kick of the longed-for joint, he slowly looked up at the sea, at the quiet wink of the lights across Table Bay.

The girl lay on the grassy bank between two palm trees. A flower among restless plastic bags, abandoned sticks, dog shit. Her black hair arrowed due west, her feet were splayed east – the left one naked, the right encased in a long, stilletto-heeled boot. Her bloodied hand, bound with a thin blue rope tied agonisingly tight, was partially obscured by a plastic bag that had drifted against her body. Her clothes were ripped, and the buttons of her blouse had popped open, exposing breasts feathered with stretch marks.

She lay there as if she were sunning her long legs. He called. Nothing – no response. He went over to her, thinking she was just another young clubber full of drugs. Her body was beautiful. It had been a long time since he'd touched a woman without having to pay for it. He bent down, cupping her breasts in his hands. They were as full as the moon. The wind lifted the scarf around her neck, the movement drawing his eyes towards her face. The exposed smile of her slit throat hurled him back towards the bus stop. Her throat had been cut with such savagery that a neck vertebra was visible, seeming to have been scored. Her eyes were open. She gazed blindly up at the heavy moon. His expensive white trainers imprinted their logo in blood on the pavement.

He saw a bus approaching. He controlled his breathing and got on.

Sat down.

Nobody saw her. Nobody looked.

She receded as the bus moved away. Then she was indistinguishable from the mounds of seaweed strewn across beach. He rubbed his hands together: they burned where he had touched her.

32

Clare went into the kitchen after Julie and Marcus had left. She rinsed the coffee cups with Fritz winding in and around her ankles, delighted to have Clare to herself again. She was tidying the cushions when the doorbell went.

Clare pressed the button immediately. 'Julie! Your pashmina's here. You didn't need to come up. I would have dropped it off for you.'

But there was no answering, guilty laugh, just the hush of an empty pavement. The hairs on the nape of Clare's neck rose. She went into the hallway. The knock on her door was insistent, unfamiliar. The wood looked very flimsy. Her hand sidled towards the panic button.

'Who is it?'

'It is me, Giscard.'

Clare had seen Giscard earlier, guarding cars in his usual spot. Clare opened the door as far as the security chain allowed. It embarrassed her to have to speak to him through the small gap.

She dropped her hand but she didn't open the door. 'What are you doing here? Are you all right?'

'I know it is late, Madame Clare, but I must tell you something about the girl in the newspaper. The one who is gone.'

Clare closed the door, then slid back the chain to open it. 'Come in,' she said. He followed her into the kitchen. 'What is it?'

'The girl everyone is looking for. India King,' he struggled with the unfamiliar name. 'I think I know where she is.'

Clare felt the strength drain from her legs. She sat down.

'How do you know? Where is she?'

'Somebody, a friend, told me he sees her there near the beach. At the Japanese restaurant past the lighthouse.'

She went cold. 'Sushi-Zen?'

'Yes, yes – that is the one. The man who saw her, my friend, he works there.'

'What do you mean, "saw her", Giscard? Where did he see her?' Giscard shifted in his chair.

'He saw her there on the grass. The moon is shining too bright. He sees her there. He think she is sleeping. But when he goes to her he sees she is dead.'

Questions skittered through Clare's mind as she reached for the phone and dialled the police station. 'Put me through to Riedwaan Faizal.' She had asked him to join her this evening, trying to make peace. To their mutual relief, though, he was on duty. The phone buzzed in her ear. She was about to put it down, try his cell number, when he picked up. 'Riedwaan. Someone has found India King.' She could hear him exhale.

'Where?' he asked. 'Who found her? When?'

'On the beach outside Sushi-Zen at about midnight. There is a bus stop there, two palm trees. She's there.' Clare could hear him scribbling it down. 'Giscard told me. It was his friend who found her – he works there.'

'I'll send Rita with a car to fetch Giscard. We will also have to find this friend of his.' He put down the phone.

Clare stood up. 'I'll make us some coffee. The police are on their way.'

Giscard looked longingly at the door.

'Giscard, you knew you would have to speak to them if you came to me.' She poured his coffee, handed him the sugar. 'Why did you do it?'

'Xavier, my friend, he stays with me because he is also from DRC. He came home tonight and he was very, very strange. He was talking about the dead girl, the dead girl. He keep saying he touch her. That it is wrong that he touch her because she is dead. But he say he did not know she is dead.' He stirred more sugar into the coffee, as if trying to make sense of Xavier's incoherence.

'What else?' asked Clare. She took the spoon from him. The sound of it scraping on the bottom of the cup was grating her nerves raw.

'He have blood on his new Nikes. I asked him how it got there but he say to me he did nothing. Just that he found her. He saw her when he was waiting for the bus.' He looked up at Clare. 'Please help me, Clare. I must come to you because he came on the bus. Maybe the driver sees the blood and tells the police. I say to him: come with me to the police. You must tell the truth or they will find you. I tell him that the police in South Africa will find you. It is not like DRC. They will want to find who killed this white girl. But he won't come. He is too afraid.'

'He won't be deported if he has his papers.'

Giscard stared at her. 'He is not afraid of them. He is afraid of her. Her body is warm when he touch her, like she is alive.'

They drank their coffee and waited for the car. Clare craved a cigarette as desperately as if she had given up yesterday, rather than five years before.

'The police will want to question Xavier,' said Clare. 'Is he at home now?'

185

'Is that necessary?' asked Giscard. 'I come to you already.'

Clare put her hand on his shoulder. 'He will have to make a statement. They will want to question him, find out what he was doing there. They will want to know what he knows of the other girls.'

'Why? He is innocent. He just found her there.'

The doorbell went and Clare buzzed in Rita Mkhize and a uniformed officer. 'They will take you to pick up Xavier,' said Clare.

Giscard stood up to follow the officers to the car, his shoulders slumped in defeat. 'I wish I not tell you this, Madame. Not good for me to do good thing.'

Clare had no comfort for him. She locked up, wondered how long it would be before he was deported. Then she drove down to join Riedwaan.

33

The scrappy stretch of beach was full of lights and people. A small crowd had gathered to watch from the other side of the police tape. The police photographer was busy. Clare looked up at the darkened restaurant where people had been chatting and eating and drinking just an hour before. Riedwaan came up to her, his eyes dark with anger.

'Come and look, Clare,' he said. He took her arm and walked her over, holding the tape up so that she could easily step under it.

'Due west,' said Clare, moving around the body. She had seen a photo of India while she was alive. In it, she was laughing, animated, her hands and hair a blur of enthusiasm. But this was a broken doll. The arrangement of the body was the same – the bound hand, the tarty clothes. Clare made herself look at the girl, keeping revulsion at bay, trying to pinpoint what was eluding her.

'It's the fury,' said Riedwaan. 'He slashed her throat to the bone. Either the fantasy is not working out right. Or something else rattled him. Or she fought too hard.'

'He needs co-operation. Or some semblance of participation,' said Clare. 'He believes, I would imagine, that these girls want to be part of his game.'

'Look here,' said Riedwaan. Clare knelt beside him. The grass on the slope below the girl's body gleamed in the moonlight. Clare put out her finger. Touched it. It was sticky with blood. India King's throat gaped like a sacrificial lamb's where it had been cut in full view of the road, of the restaurant, of the block of flats over the road.

Clare turned away and was unexpectedly and violently sick. Riedwaan stood by, knowing her well enough to let her purge herself and regain control.

'I can't believe that nobody in the restaurant saw anything,' said Clare.

'Let's go and check what you can see from up there,' said Riedwaan.

They crossed the road and made their way to the entrance. The restaurant was closed but Riedwaan's badge convinced the security guard let them in. It was very quiet, with just a murmur of voices in the kitchen. Riedwaan went in search of the owner. Clare walked over to a table by the sliding doors and looked out. She could not see anything other than a snarl of black rocks, the ocean and the island in the distance. She moved to another table. The same view. The balcony blocked the view of the road. The grassy slope and the beach were invisible, something you would know only if you had been inside the restaurant. Clare slid open the glass doors. It was very cold on the balcony. It had been so all evening, and the tables there had not been laid. Now they were chained together in a corner.

She looked down again. Even from here, it would have been difficult to see anything happening on the beach below. She looked up at the apartment block. Nefertiti Heights was new and unoccupied. There was nobody there either to have witnessed anything. Clare looked back down at the beach. India's face had at last been covered and her body strapped to a gurney. The paramedics, barely older than India had been, were carrying her corpse to the waiting ambulance. Clare's eyes filled with tears. The beach was empty, except for one wakeful gull circling overhead. She watched it trace a silver arc against the night sky, white feathers glinting in the moonlight. The bird landed in front of a huge storm-water drain, a dark maw leading under the road into the belly of the city. The ambulance flashed its light and pulled away, heading for the morgue. There would be no peace for India yet, thought Clare grimly. Dr Mouton would spend hours tomorrow carefully puzzling over how she had died and when.

Riedwaan came up to her. 'Just that little patch is hidden from view.'

'I can't help thinking that he must have known that. Can we borrow their booking list?'

'I've already asked the owner for it. We'll get it as we go out.' He turned to leave. Clare stayed him with a touch to his arm, but she felt the heat of him through his jacket, and pulled her hand away.

'The display of the bodies is contradictory,' said Clare. 'Very public, but no witnesses.'

'What do you mean?'

'Well, the first one you would have expected to show up on the CCTV, but that camera was false. Could have been a fluke, but I don't think so,' said Clare. She paced up and down the balcony, speaking more to herself than to Riedwaan. 'The second girl was dumped at Graaff's Pool. There are no cameras there, although there are a few on the pathway that leads down to the beach. But the killer could have used the old tunnel under Beach Road.'

'There is no physical evidence to support that,' said Riedwaan.

'No,' said Clare. 'But I'm sure that's what he did. A boat

would have been impossible to land that night and the cameras would have picked him up going there.'

'Here he knew exactly the spot where the body wouldn't be seen. Even though when she was found, it appeared so shockingly public.'

Clare stopped and looked thoughtfully across at the busy police scene. 'He's playing with us. But I don't think he wants to be caught. At first I thought he was asking to be caught, to be stopped. That's not unusual, a killer wanting to be stopped, convinced that he's killing because the police aren't doing their job. But I don't think that is the case with this one. I think he knows exactly what he's doing, that he feels justified in doing it and that he wants to continue.'

'He wouldn't have been seen if he'd parked there and then dumped her. Watch this.' A police car appeared where Riedwaan was pointing below – just a moment before, the car had been completely obscured by a clump of bushes beyond the bus shelter. Riedwaan lit another cigarette. 'If he'd parked there, no one would have seen him. I'll get Rita to check it out.' He called her and they watched Rita and Joe move behind the bushes to check for evidence.

They made their way downstairs. Riedwaan had the booking list under his arm. 'What did the chef say about Xavier?' asked Clare.

'Nothing much. He started here five months ago. He's from the DRC, claimed to have cooked for Laurent Kabila while he was still alive. Did his work well, was good at it, always alone, always on time. No girlfriends. No drugs. No trouble. Especially good with knives, excellent at carving vegetable sculptures. Had papers, but they never looked too deeply into any of them. Said goodbye as usual and left just before twelve.'

'When will you talk to him?' asked Clare.

'I'm going to talk to your friend Giscard now,' said

Riedwaan. 'I hope I can persuade him to tell me where to find Xavier. I had an SMS from Rita to say that they couldn't find him. I'd be very interested in having a little chat with him about what he's been doing since he got here.'

'I'll be surprised if it's him. How is an illegal chef who shares a flat with five other illegal immigrants going to find somewhere to keep a girl captive? Also, the restaurant was very busy. How was he going to move her body while carving roses out of carrots for ten sushi platters an hour?'

'Those are questions I look forward to asking,' said Riedwaan. 'If Giscard's dates are correct, these killings started just after Xavier arrived in Cape Town.'

Riedwaan walked Clare to her car. 'I'll bring you the preliminary autopsy report as soon as I have it.'

'No chance of me coming to the autopsy?'

'You know Piet and his rules,' said Riedwaan. 'He's not going to make an exception.'

'Okay. Call me the minute you get it?' asked Clare. 'I get the feeling that this killer is either overconfident or unravelling. That means that the killings will accelerate. It also means that he will make a mistake. That's when we catch him.'

'*I* will,' said Riedwaan emphatically. He tucked her hair behind her ear. 'Goodnight, Clare.' Then he walked back towards the taped area.

She started the car and indicated to do the U-turn that would take her home again. 'Hey!' It was the police photographer. 'Don't you want these, gorgeous?' He was holding a bunch of irises in his hands.

Clare wound down her window. 'Where did you find those?' she asked.

'Lying there.' He pointed towards the lighthouse. 'I went up there to have a smoke and there they were, lying on one of the benches. It seemed like such a waste. And then I saw you looking fab as always. And Riedwaan not paying you the attention he should. I thought maybe I could get a look in.'

'Fuck off, Riaan,' she said. 'Don't you ever give up? Bag them and give them to Rita.' The irises were tied with the same twist of gold ribbon as the flowers found near Amore Hendricks's body at Graaff's Pool.

Clare closed her window and drove home. She fell into bed and immediately fell asleep. When she woke up, her skin filmed with the icy sweat of a nightmare, she went through to the kitchen and put on the kettle for tea. It would soon be dawn so there was no point in trying to go to sleep again. There was not much she could do until she had the pathologist's report. Clare knew that Mouton and Riedwaan would be busy there now. She paced for a while and then picked up her phone. Two rings and it was answered.

'Mouton here.' His voice was muffled as if he was holding the phone between his shoulder and his ear. Clare did not like to imagine what he was doing with his hands.

'Dr Mouton, this is Clare Hart.'

'*Ja*, Doc?' He would be looking at Riedwaan, eyebrows raised, Clare suspected.

'The autopsy, what's it telling you?'

'We'll be busy for a while still. But it's safe to say the pattern is the same. We have some body fluid samples, so we can see if it's a copycat killing or not.'

'What's different?' asked Clare.

'This girl's eyes were also cut. But this time I'd say it was after death. There's almost no bleeding.'

'Odd,' said Clare. 'Maybe he was disturbed.'

'India King put up one hell of a fight,' said Dr Mouton. 'I think we'll be able to get the knife identified. The way she's been cut, has to be someone who knows about knives.'

'A chef?' asked Clare.

'Maybe,' said Mouton. 'Or someone medical.'

'A doctor?'

'Not necessarily, but someone who knows a bit about anatomy.'

'You sure it's the same weapon each time?' asked Clare.

'I'm sure. I can't prove it, but I think that this time he was rattled – cut too deep, so there's a good blade mark on the vertebra. That'll make those ballistics okes very happy. Go get some more sleep in the meantime. Riedwaan's not going to be up for much today – or tonight, for that matter.'

'Thanks for that, Piet. We'll speak later.' Clare didn't go back to bed. She watched the sun rise slowly over the mountains. The light did not bring her any clarity, but a visit or two later on to some of the more upmarket florists would do the trick. She emailed Rita, asking her to get onto it as soon as she got into the office.

34

Clare went in to the station early. Rita Mkhize was already there, phoning florists.

'Hi, Clare. Thanks.' She took the take-away cappuccino gratefully. 'Guess who was meant to be at Sushi-Zen last night?'

'Who?' asked Clare.

'Brian King. India's stepfather. He had a booking for nine. But he didn't pitch.'

'I wonder what changed his mind?' Clare stirred her coffee. 'Did you get anywhere with the florists yet?'

'Nowhere. None of them open before nine-thirty. And we didn't find anything on the road. If there were tracks, they were lost because of the police van that parked there.'

Riedwaan arrived with Piet Mouton's autopsy report.

'This attack was certainly frenzied,' said Riedwaan. He flicked past Mouton's meticulous illustrations of the corpse. 'Look here. India had a contusion on the back of her head and, unlike the other two, there are signs of sexual assault.'

'Any body fluids?' asked Clare.

'No semen. Mouton thinks that she was assaulted with a blunt wooden object. There were splinters in the vagina. Those are being tested now.'

'Any blood?' asked Rita, perching on Riedwaan's desk.

'Some under her nails. The inside of her mouth is torn. The face bruised. It looks as if she died of asphyxiation. She put up a fight before she died, though.'

'Time of death?' asked Clare.

'An hour max before she was found. Piet thinks she was killed somewhere else and that that her throat was cut after she died. But the killer must have moved very quickly, because there was blood where the body was found.'

'He kept her somewhere close to where he dumped her,' said Rita.

'That is what we have to figure out before another girl dies,' said Riedwaan. 'Mkhize, you come with me. I want to have another chat to Luis Da Cunha. Might be worth finding out where he was last night.'

'You're clutching at straws, Riedwaan,' said Clare.

'Any other suggestions? Or shall I just sit here and watch you think?'

Clare shook her head, pulling the autopsy report to her. She compared the three murders, putting everything she had up on the poster boards she had bought. Charnay had disappeared from the Waterfront, Amore from Canal Walk, India from Long Street. All on busy weekend nights. Piet Mouton had worked out how they were killed. She knew where they had been found. There was the similarity in age, hair colour – but, other than that, the only link between the girls was their killer.

Why were they killed? Clare went to make herself another nauseating cup of instant coffee, thinking of the key each girl had clutched in her bound hand. Cheap keys, untraceable, bought in any supermarket. She sipped, looking out onto the dirty strip of sand behind the caravan.

'What are you thinking, Clare?' She had not heard Riedwaan return.

'What happened with Da Cunha?' she asked.

'He's away. Whole family went to a wedding in Portugal last week.' That's him out of the picture.' He lit a cigarette.

'Give me a drag,' said Clare. The nicotine rush was wonderful. 'I'm missing something. He takes them to a place close by. A place that people probably pass every day. There's no link between these girls. Charnay did freelance sex work, but I think that was coincidental. He doesn't fit the profile of a mission killer – out to purge prostitutes. Those girls were out alone. But the last two, we presume, were trying to get home. Charnay – that we don't know – but she was pretty enough and young enough to be selective. I guess she would have gone willingly with a customer, particularly if it wasn't someone who had used her before.'

Riedwaan came and stood behind her. 'We've checked everything in her diary,' said Riedwaan. 'It shows when she worked, but not who her clients were.'

'Do you think we should pull that nasty little brother of hers in?' asked Clare.

'Rita and Joe have already interviewed him again. Here.' Riedwaan fetched the notes from his desk. 'His alibi is watertight. You'll be interested that there are two assault charges against him.'

'From the rugby match?'

'One, yes. The other charge is recent. A girl in his class laid a sexual assault charge against him.'

'A violent assault?'

'No,' said Riedwaan. 'He's accused of putting a webcam in the girls' change room. And posting it on the web.'

'Charming,' said Clare.

Rita walked in the door, and Riedwaan asked, 'You checked on the Isis website for her picture?'

'I did. No sign of her there. Charnay must have chickened out in the end.'

'Her friend Cornelle is hostessing there,' Clare observed.

'Yes, I spoke to her,' said Rita. 'But it's nothing more than that. She's not doing movies.'

'What about Amore Hendricks? She left her friends after the movie ended at nine forty-five. She was meant to meet her uncle at ten-thirty at the taxi rank,' Clare asked.

'We don't even know for sure that she was abducted from Canal Walk. She could have gone anywhere,' said Rita.

'She must have met someone en route. It had to be someone she knew,' Clare persisted.

'Okay. Then what about the phone call? The one her uncle made at ten forty-five?'

'He didn't actually speak to her, remember. My guess is that she stopped somewhere, probably in an outside area.' Clare checked in her notes. 'Look here. It was pretty busy that evening. She would have been very easy to get into a car if someone had spiked her drink.'

Riedwaan picked up India's autopsy report. The smell of the laboratory still clung to it. 'This poor girl got one *moer* of a *klap* on the head. Piet Mouton is pretty certain it was with an iron bar.'

'I'm surprised he didn't kill her,' said Clare.

'Look here.' Riedwaan held out two photographs. 'Piet thinks that she sensed him, saw him maybe, and that she ducked. 'Look at the bruises here on her arm. He would have caught her there and then hit her as she tried to get away.'

'What are all these microfibre reports from the wound?'

'He must have held her to him and then picked her up or put her into a car. Piet thinks that the fibres are from an overcoat, black cashmere most probably.'

'An expensive dresser,' said Clare. 'That would put our little chef out of the picture.'

Riedwaan turned the page. 'Read this: bits of acrylic carpet. Most likely from the boot of a car.'

'You can't tell the make?'

'They're working on it but I don't think so. There will be blood traces on that carpet if they find the car.'

'That's all you've got?'

'That's it. Apart from a cellphone call that India made at nine-thirty. She called her friend Gemma after the rehearsal to say she'd left her scarf in her bag and that she'd come round and get it the next day.'

'She didn't say how she was getting home, did she?' asked Clare.

'She didn't, but Gemma had the impression that she was walking while she was talking to her.'

'And that was on Long Street?'

'That's what the cellphone records say. There was also a free concert at the Pool Bar. Gemma thought she might have been going there. The DJ was at school with them.'

'Did you speak to him?'

'Her, actually. Yes, we did. India had said that she would pop in, but the DJ never saw her. Nor did the doorman,' said Riedwaan.

'Any other sightings of her?'

'The only person who says he saw her is the security guard at the 7–Eleven. He saw her walk past the Long Street Baths.'

'No one else?'

'Nobody. She seems to have vanished. The easiest place, I suppose, would be Keerom Street. That takes you back to Wale Street and there's no one to see you there.'

'No vagrants saw her?

'Nothing. We've checked with the regulars. Not a word until her mother called me after . . .' he stopped.

'I couldn't let Constance down,' Clare muttered at him.

'You won't let her go,' he replied in a low voice. 'You're afraid to let her go,' Riedwaan's anger flared for just a moment. '*Ag*, I'm sorry too. I was looking forward to spoiling you a bit.' He touched her hand and she curled her fingers around his. Then he exposed the nape of Clare's neck and kissed it. Rita coughed as she bent over the desk and straightened the paperwork.

Shivering at the sudden pleasure that rippled across her skin, Clare pulled her shoulders back hard and asked, 'Shall I go and see the family again?'

'*Ja*, check it out. Talk to her mother and find out what Brian King was doing while he was not at the restaurant,' Riedwaan suggested. 'I'm going to check out valet services. See if anyone has brought in a car with a dirty carpet recently.'

'Okay.'

Riedwaan went out, closing the door behind him. Clare pressed her hands to her temples to stop the drumbeat of why, why, why.

'Go home,' said Rita. 'It's not easy.'

'The case or the man?' asked Clare.

'Both, *sisi*. Both.'

199

35

It was drizzling when Clare got home. She made a sandwich, fetched her duvet, and settled in to watch an old black and white movie. Its gentle tedium lulled Clare to sleep within an hour. The telephone's insistent ringing roused her, but when she picked up the phone there was only silence.

'Who is this?'

Faint breathing was the only reply.

'Whitney? Where are you?'

'Clare?'

There was silence. 'Tell me, Whitney. It's safe.' As Clare waited for Whitney's voice, she picked up the tape on her desk. She had pencilled *Interview: Florrie Ruiters: Local Trafficking* on the spine. Mrs Ruiters had phoned Clare and they had met in a nondescript café in Wynberg. Smoking her way through half a pack of cigarettes, Florrie Ruiters told Clare how it had taken three days to coax her fragile child outside the house again. For it was there, while she'd sat in the sun in the front yard, that Landman's men had taunted Whitney. Florrie, her fear banished by fury, went on to tell Clare that the price exacted by Kelvin Landman and his gangsters escalated as his stranglehold on the community tightened.

'It makes no difference, Dr Hart,' Florrie had said when Clare urged her to press charges. 'If they get convicted – and it is a

200

big "if" – a lost docket costs them just a couple of hundred rands, you see. *If* they get convicted they just run things from inside. This government gives amnesties left, right and centre. And heaven help you when they get released.'

'Can you come?' Whitney pleaded at the other end of the line, pulling Clare back into the present. 'I'm at my aunt's house in Mitchell's Plain.'

Clare looked at her watch and sighed.

'Please fetch me now.' The girl's terror had settled like a stone in her throat, making it difficult for her to speak. 'You promised.'

'What's happened?' asked Clare. 'Who has threatened you?'

'My cousin says they know where I am. Will you come?'

'I'll come,' said Clare. She picked up a pen. 'Tell me exactly where you are. I'll come as soon as I can. Don't go anywhere.' Clare wrote down the address. Then she made a call. It did not take her long to arrange what Whitney needed.

Clare wove her way through clogged evening traffic until she reached the highway, then she pulled into the taxi lane. The turnoff came sooner than she expected and Clare easily found the street. She pulled over at the modest little house. It was ice-cream pink, in defiance of the grey sand that seemed to have seeped in all over the area. Whitney opened the door as she heard the car door slam. Her small bag was packed. Her coat was on, a beanie pulled low over her forehead.

'Hello, Whitney.' The girl hurtled down the path. Clare opened the car door and Whitney collapsed into the seat. She looked back at the house. A grimy net curtain swung back into place in the front room.

'What happened?' Clare asked. Whitney stared straight ahead as Clare started the car and drove back to the highway.

'They kept asking me,' said Whitney. 'They kept asking me what they did to me. They wanted to know the details. And then they would discuss what they did to me, whether I had got HIV.' Her voice drifted off into silence. The street lights had come on. They cast a ghostly orange light that flickered rhythmically across their faces as Clare drove. Whitney did not move a hand to wipe the tears that glistened on her cheeks. Clare turned back onto the highway, away from Cape Town.

'Where are you taking me?' asked Whitney.

'I know a woman on an apple farm up near Elgin. I phoned her and she said you could stay. You'll be safer there. And they don't know what happened to you,' said Clare.

They drove in silence for a long time. Clare decided not to ask Whitney why she had not gone back to see the counsellor after the first session. The charges that she had reluctantly laid – at her mother's insistence – had been withdrawn, and Whitney had refused to speak to Rita Mkhize when she'd arrived to follow up.

'There was somebody else there the first night.' Whitney's voice was just audible above the car's engine. Clare turned to look at her. The girl was staring straight ahead. Her jaw was clenched with the effort of memory, the effort of speech. 'He watched.' She turned briefly to face Clare. 'He watched what they did.' Again, Whitney looked into the black night. Cape Town had receded into the distance. They started to climb the steep pass that would take them over the peaks that bordered False Bay.

'He told them what to do. Sometimes he told them to do the things again. Then again.'

Clare said nothing, afraid that any word from her would dam the flow of Whitney's thoughts.

'He filmed it. He had a camera. I think two cameras. One I saw when they first brought me in. I saw myself reflected in its eye: it stood there on a tripod. Like another one of them. First they made me put on some boots – very high, I couldn't stand properly in them. And then it all started. But the other man, I saw him come out of the corner of the room where it was dark. He had another camera in his hands.' She stopped speaking. It was very dark now that the mountains hid the carpet of city lights.

'I thought he would help me.' Whitney laughed bitterly.

'Who was he?' Clare asked.

'He was a director. That's what they called him. He was telling them what to do. To me. He came right close to my face when they . . .' She put her hand to her mouth, took it away again. 'When they hurt me. He liked to watch my face. Then he would make them do it again – what they were doing to me – so he could film that too.'

Cutaways, thought Clare. Always make sure that when you shoot you have enough cutaways. She gripped the wheel and kept her eyes on the broken white line marking the centre of the road. She counted the sections. One. Two. Three. Four. Five. That kept her calm enough. 'Did you see him?'

'I see him all the time. He's the one I see all the time.' Whitney's fury erupted. Then she slumped back in her seat. 'But I didn't see his face. He was wearing a hood. A blue hood with holes for the eyes and his mouth.' She was quiet for so long that Clare wondered if she had closed in on herself.

'What was it for, Clare? Why did they do it? Why did they film it? That's what makes me feel sick. That they did that to me and now it's there for anyone to watch. It feels as if what happened is happening over and over and over. I can never stop it now because it's there on their tape.'

For a long while, Clare could not think of anything to say. She turned onto the rutted farm road, slowing down so that she didn't miss the turnoff. The twin lights from the front windows of the cottage glowed, warm and sudden, in the dark.

'You'll be safe here, Whitney. The woman who lives here

203

will take care of you. And she'll leave you in peace. If you stay indoors until everyone has gone to the orchards, nobody will know you're here.' Whitney did not respond. The effort of delving into the horror she had endured had sapped her. She clutched her bag to her chest.

There, outlined under the cheap, pink fabric, was Clare's book. She reached over, traced the spine. 'Did you read it?' she asked. Whitney nodded but offered nothing more. They arrived. Clare parked under the enormous oak that dwarfed the whitewashed labourer's cottage. The door opened, releasing warm yellow light into the blackness.

Dinah de Wet stood broad in the doorway, her shoulders strong from years of picking and pruning and carrying other people's children. Her body was soft as she hugged Clare. She turned to Whitney. The girl sank further into her seat.

'*Kom binne, my kind.*' Her guttural voice was gentle, its tone one she used for a nervous puppy or a fretful baby. She took Whitney's hand. 'Come. I'll show you your room.'

Whitney was unable to extricate herself from the situation, so she capitulated and followed Dinah inside. Clare followed. Dinah's single plate and cup were neatly stacked in the sink. The fire welcomed them. Dinah took Whitney into a small room that led off the living room.

'You sleep in here, my girlie. I sleep in there.' She pointed back to the lounge. 'If you are cold you can come in with me.'

Whitney surveyed her room. The single bed was covered with a crocheted blue and pink coverlet. A teddy bear clutching a red satin heart was perched on the pillow. A candle stood next to the bed. Nails on the walls had empty hangers on them for clothes that Whitney had not brought. On the windowsill was a vase with a bunch of purple-flowered fynbos.

'Whose room is this?' asked Whitney.

'It was my daughter's,' said Dinah. Her face was in shadow. 'But you are welcome to it as long as you need it.'

Whitney set her bag on the bed and sat down next to it. She had no idea of how to continue.

'I'll get you some tea,' said Dinah. 'Come with me, Clare.' They went through to the kitchen. Dinah set out cups, poured water.

Clare took some notes from her wallet. 'This is for food, or whatever.'

Dinah took the money. 'Whatever happened to the child?' she asked, tucking the notes into her bra.

'Maybe she'll tell you if she trusts you. I promised her that nobody would know she was here.' She picked up a cup of tea and took it to Whitney. She was in bed with all the blankets pulled close around her. She did not acknowledge the tea that Clare put on her bedside table. Her eyes were closed tight, arms around her knees. Her back was a tight, defensive curve.

'Bye, Whitney. Stay here, you'll be safe. Phone me if you need anything. Dinah has a cellphone.' Clare was about to close the door when Whitney spoke.

'Where is Constance now?'

'She's safe now.'

'Where is she?' Whitney sat up, her eyes feverish.

'On a farm. Like you. She lives there now. She never leaves it.'

'Tell me the name.'

'Serenity Farm. It's near Malmesbury.'

Whitney said nothing more, so Clare closed the door. She said goodbye to Dinah and drove back to Cape Town. Clare could not get the film Whitney had told her about to stop playing – the unseen images were like circling vultures in her head.

36

Clare needed her map to find the Kings' house. It was positioned discreetly at the end of a three-kilometre cul-de-sac that traced the crest of a wooded ridge. The avenue was lined with stately oaks that obscured the palatial houses set far back from the road. Security guards, stupefied with boredom, sat at the gateways. The King mansion was a sparkling white jewel set in an acre of emerald lawn. Clare rang the doorbell. A well-trained maid asked who she was, what she wanted. The gate glided open at the mention of India's name. Clare parked behind the garages and crunched across the gravel to the unwelcoming front door. The same maid, generously built, her broad face kind above the black and white uniform, let her in.

'I'm Dr Clare Hart.' Clare held out her hand. The woman looked surprised, but she shook it.

'I'm Portia,' she replied.

'And your surname, Portia?'

'Qaba,' she volunteered, again with some surprise, and continued, 'The master is not yet home. And Madam is in her room. She is not well.'

Clare had not made an appointment. Riedwaan had told her that he found the King home unsettling, so she had thought it best to visit unannounced.

'I am part of the team investigating India's murder,' said Clare. 'Perhaps I could have a look at India's room while I wait for Mr King.'

'This way, Dr Hart.' Clare followed her up the curved staircase. India had had the whole eastern wing of the house to herself. Portia opened the heavy curtains. The bedroom windows faced north and east, giving her a view of the undulating Constantia valley. No expense had been spared on India's room. It was tastefully feminine, all expensive French quilts and imported furniture, but it was soulless, like a room in a boutique hotel. Its intimacy could have wrapped itself around any anonymous occupant. Clare tested the bolt on the inside of the door. It was clear that an amateur handyman had installed it. Or an unpractised girl.

She moved round to the neat desk. There was a maths book open, and a half-completed algebra exercise next to it. Clare picked up the books, put them down again. They were as impersonal as the room. She opened the top drawer. India's homework diary lay there. Clare flicked through it. Notices about hockey matches, tests, letters from the head of the exclusive school India had attended. These admonished against piercings, tattoos, highlights. Clare put it back, pushed the drawer closed. She felt it stick. So she felt along the back of it. A small pencil case had wedged there. Clare unzipped it. Inside was a half-finished package of contraceptive pills. India had taken the last one on Friday. The day before she had disappeared.

'It's for her skin,' said Portia. 'She doesn't have a boyfriend.'

'You sound very sure,' said Clare. She replaced the contraceptives. India had obviously meant to be home that night.

'I was her nanny since she was born,' said Portia, her voice cracking. 'She told me everything. Sometimes she would come and sleep with me, if she was afraid.'

'Where was she going that evening?' asked Clare.

'She went to her rehearsal, for the theatre. Then she said she wanted to go to Long Street. Her friend was there. She told me she would come back with a taxi.' Portia wiped her eyes with her apron. 'She never came back. I waited for her. Her mum waited for her. She never came back.'

The crunch of a car on the gravel broke the quiet. 'It is Master,' said Portia. 'Come with me. I will take you to his office.'

She hurried Clare out of India's room and led her downstairs, ushering her into a large study. It looked precisely as the study of a wealthy man should. Clare walked over to the bookshelves. A decorator must have chosen the expensively bound books. The collection was incoherent, revealing neither taste nor education. Clare ran her hand along the virgin spines. Not a single book had been opened. She pressed her hand against the smooth back of *The Collected Works of Shakespeare*. To her surprise, the entire shelf swung away. Behind it were four shelves of neatly stacked videotapes. The alphabetically arranged titles revealed Mr King's taste for the more extreme forms of discipline, the finer forms of bondage and fear. The tapes on the bottom shelf were pushed right back. Clare bent down to look at them. Each bore the deep-blue Isis logo, though they seemed to be copies. There was a single cassette lying across the top of them.

Clare heard voices at the bottom of the stairs, the man's filled with irritation, Portia's placating. On impulse, she picked up the loose tape and dropped it into her bag before quickly closing the concealed shelf again. She turned to find Brian King at the door. He greeted her urbanely enough. Clare recognised his face, but she couldn't place where she had seen him before.

'I'm Clare Hart.'

'Yes, I know who you are, Dr Hart. I'm sorry I wasn't at home when you arrived. But I didn't know you were coming. How can I help? I thought we had been over everything with the police already.' He shrugged off his overcoat and hung it on a coat rack.

'I'm sorry to disturb you, Mr King, and I'm so sorry for what has happened.' Clare sat down and he took the chair opposite hers. 'I am developing a profile of the man who killed India. I was hoping to discuss India with you. Who her friends were, what she did, what her interests were. I know this is painful, but the more we know about her, the more likely it is that we can find whoever killed her.'

'I can't tell you much more about her than is in my statement. That is her mother's domain. This is most upsetting, most unnecessary. I warned Cathy so often that the girl was not disciplined enough. That she gave her too much leeway.' Clare kept quiet, waited for the anger just below the surface to bubble over. 'India was cheeky, dressed like a tart. They all do, don't they?' Clare's incredulity must have shown, because he caught himself. He avoided Clare's gaze, running his fingers through his hair. His wedding band glinted in the subdued light.

'Did she bring her friends home? Did you know them?' Clare stood. She walked to the bookshelf and looked at the single photograph displayed there. It showed Brian King with his arms draped over his wife and daughter.

'No, none of them. I work long hours, you know. And she was not very sociable. Recently, I think she went out more. But other than that, I can't tell you much else.'

'India was interested in acting. She went to a drama school in town, didn't she? Did you ever see any of her shows?' asked Clare.

'No. No, I didn't.' He stood up. 'I am upset, as you can see.

I'm not myself. And with all the funeral arrangements . . .' He walked over to the desk and picked up a sheet of paper. 'Her school wants a memorial service. Some march against violence against women. Most unfortunate.' He paused again. 'It's so difficult for me to deal with. My wife, of course, is hopeless. Has completely collapsed. Not that I blame her, of course.'

'Can I see Mrs King?'

'Not now. She is devastated, and our doctor has had to sedate her. Now, if you wouldn't mind . . .' taking her cue, Clare stood up, too '. . . I have several things to attend to.' He held the study door open for her. 'Mr King,' said Clare, 'do you have any idea why India installed a bolt on the inside of her bedroom door?'

'I have no idea. I never went to her room. What were you doing there? Do you have a search warrant?'

'Oh, I didn't search. I just wanted to get a sense of her.' Clare stepped past him. She saw Portia slip away. 'I'll find my way out, thanks.' Clare held her hand out to him. He shook it, his grip unnecessarily hard, hurting her.

'I hope you find him. The police are not known for their competence, are they?'

Clare did not rise to this. 'Please contact me if you think of anything. Or anyone that India met recently.'

'I will. Goodbye, Dr Hart.' She turned to leave. 'Oh, by the way, I enjoyed your documentary on the DRC immensely. The one about the women. Excellent.' His tone sent a shiver down Clare's spine.

'Thank you,' she said politely, and turned round again. 'There's one more thing I'd like to ask you.'

'Yes?' he said, looking at his watch.

'Where were you on the night India disappeared?'

'Why?'

'We need to check everything,' said Clare.

'I've already spoken to your colleague. Rizza – or something like that.'

Riedwaan Faizal?' asked Clare.

'Something like that. Rather a chip on his shoulder, I thought.' Clare did not respond. 'I told him I was having a celebratory dinner with some business associates.'

'All night?' said Clare.

'Well, you know what business is like – we had overseas clients, from the East, and that's how they do things.'

'How do they do things, Mr King?'

'They expect to be entertained.'

'So I hear,' said Clare. 'I presume that they will corroborate?'

'If it's absolutely necessary, I'm sure it can be arranged.' His face had purpled with rage. 'Your colleague asked me the same question. I supplied him with the name of the business manager. I hope he'll be discreet.'

'Oh, I'm sure he'll be as discreet as he needs to be. You will remember, I'm sure, that we are investigating a murder case. You had a booking at Sushi-Zen that night. The restaurant where India's body was found. Any reason why you didn't make it?'

A vein pulsed in King's temple. 'Dr Hart, I am her father. Surely you can't be so crass as to interrogate me when I have just endured the most tragic loss.'

'Where were you, Mr King?'

'We changed our minds and went to the Isis Club instead. Nothing sinister. Just a change of mind.'

'Oh,' said Clare. 'And what was the reason for this celebratory dinner?'

'Just a potential property deal. Really, Dr Hart, I do find this most intrusive.'

'Who were your companions?' persisted Clare.

211

'Our Asian investors. Two fellow directors. The City Manager, Hermanus Fipaza, and two local investors.'

Clare looked up from her notebook. 'And who are these investors?' she asked.

'Otis Tohar and Kelvin Landman.'

'Surely the Isis is a bit noisy to discuss business. A bit distracting?' asked Clare. She brushed against King's luxurious coat hanging near the door.

'You are naive, Dr Hart,' said King.

'What time did you say your dinner was?' asked Clare, ignoring his derision. She closed her left hand over the smooth black fibres she had pulled from the sleeve of King's coat.

'I didn't,' said King. 'But we ate at ten, ten-thirty. Landman and Tohar were a bit late.'

'Did they say why?' Clare asked, facing him.

'We have mutual interests, that is all. I did not consider it appropriate to pry.'

'You will be asked to come and make a formal statement.'

'Is that necessary?' asked King.

'Mr King, this is a triple murder investigation. One of those is your own daughter.'

'One cannot forget, can one?' King hurriedly ushered Clare through the door, closing it before she could say anything more. She walked rapidly to her car, relieved when the side of the house hid her from his view. Then she slammed her door shut and rested her head on the steering-wheel. With trembling hands, she pulled an envelope from her bag and dropped the threads of black cashmere into it. Clare jumped at the quiet knock on her window. It was Portia.

'Hello, Portia,' she said, opening the window and wiping away tears she had been unaware of shedding.

'He is not her father, Dr Hart,' said Portia. Her gentle face was twisted by fear and fierce anger. 'He hates her. Hated her.'

'What do you mean, Portia?'

'The reason her mother couldn't speak to you is he beat her.' She spat. 'He beat her because her baby was murdered. He married Cathy. Yes. When she already had India. He just married her to punish her. You find who killed that baby girl.'

'Where did she go that night, Portia? Who did she go with?'

'She went to town. Her mummy dropped her to meet her friend. But she never came back. Cathy waited all night but she never came back. Mr King never came either. In the morning Cathy was more afraid for her baby than she was afraid of her husband. That is when she went to the police. To the inspector who came here.'

'Where was King?'

'I don't know. He is never here on weekends. I think he has other women somewhere. It gives Cathy some peace at least.'

'There wasn't anyone India was seeing?' Portia shook her head, and Clare continued, 'Her friend said they had no plans to meet on Saturday. That she was at home working for exams.'

'I don't know, but I hope she had a boyfriend who loved her. She was a very unhappy girl, her heart was breaking,' said Portia.

'Will you tell Mrs King that she should phone me? I would like to talk to her too. Tell her I'll meet her somewhere else. And please give me your phone number, Portia – I may need to get hold of you.'

'I'll tell her,' said Portia. 'You remember you asked about that lock?'

'Yes,' said Clare.

'I put it there for her. So she can be safe.'

Clare looked up at the house. Security beams were discreetly positioned everywhere. Portia shook her head.

'The danger in this house – it is right inside.' She stepped back into the shadow of the garage as Clare started her car.

There were only two lights on in the enormous house. One was in King's study. It had a blue television flicker. The other was in a bedroom upstairs. The curtains parted slightly as Clare drove back up the lane. Behind them, Cathy King pressed her swollen cheek against the wall as she watched Clare's headlights flicker past the trees. The coolness relieved the pain of her bruised face. She watched the lights until they were gone. Then she counted the pills that lay in a neat row in front of her. Soon there would be enough.

37

Clare had two calls to make. She pulled over once she was out of the driveway. The first call was to a number she had saved to her phone but never used. She scrolled through until she found it, then dialled.

'Landman.' The voice was harsh.

'Mr Landman, this is Clare Hart.' There was silence. 'I wanted to ask you a few more questions.'

'Clare.' He sounded flattered. 'You did have me for longer than most women get. Do you want to know about my new career prospects?'

'No,' said Clare. 'I wanted to ask you about the deaths of three girls.'

Clare could hear his breathing. 'You listen to me,' he said. The charm was gone, his accent raw. 'I explained to you clearly. I'm a fucking businessman. Willing buyer, willing seller. Why do you think I would know anything about those girls? From a business perspective it would be stupid to waste stock like that, even if it had been mine in the first place. You've been to my clubs, you've spoken to my girls. You know it's a fair deal. They're safer with me than they are on the streets. Why would I risk my investment by killing girls who will then attract a big investigation? Why would I kill them, anyway? Dead girls make me no money. Live ones do. Even you should understand that.'

'Two of the girls who died had your blue calling card,' said Clare.

'Well, maybe they were auditioning. I run a corporation. I have managers, scouts, recruiters, like anybody else running a business.' He paused and breathed in, calming himself. 'They're no use to me dead.'

'It depends how they die, Mr Landman. It depends where they die. And why. I've heard that there is a nice little sideline in real live action.'

'Don't start that shit about snuff movies, Clare. They're all staged. Nobody dies in them. Even if they did, why would anybody be so stupid as to distribute them?'

'The first girl, Charnay, she'd been tattooed with your – what shall I call it? – trademark. The same one as your Isis girls have.'

'Maybe she freelanced. So what? She was old enough. She needed the money. She had expensive tastes.'

'So you knew her?'

'She came to the bar. Christ, what does it matter?'

'You saw her that evening, Mr Landman. She was at the same bar that you were at the night she disappeared. Why did she die?'

'Who the fuck knows? Who the fuck cares? One cunt less, what difference does it make to anybody?'

Clare thought about Charnay's mother rocking herself back and forth, arms clutched around a hollow womb. She didn't answer.

'I hear from Brian King that you two had dinner together the night India King's body was found. With Otis Tohar and the City Manager. You were meant to have dinner at the restaurant near where her body was found. Just a coincidence that you didn't arrive for that dinner?'

'I think you should listen to me, Dr Hart: I'm warning you to stay right away. I have helped you with your film, explained things to you about my business. People like sex. They like pornography. If they are prepared to pay, let them have it. But you be very fucking careful about what you say and who you talk to.'

'Are you threatening me, Mr Landman?' Clare asked.

'I hear you've got a pretty little niece, Dr Hart? Nice tits she's got. I think I might even have seen where she goes to school.'

'You stay away from her, Landman. I'm warning you.'

'You stay away from my girls too, then. And Dr Hart . . .'

'What?'

'While I do my job, you do yours. Catch your killer. This whole business is fucking up my trade. Figure out who he is, and you've done us both a favour. Then I can get on with my business in peace. And that washed-up alky boyfriend of yours will look good too.' He leered. 'Maybe he'll be able to keep it up long enough to make you happy.'

Clare killed the connection, unable to shake the conviction that he was telling at least half the truth. 'Which half?' she muttered to herself as she jerked her car into gear and onto the road that would take her back into the city.

'Bastard,' said Clare as a driver cut in front of her.

She made her second call while she was driving, keeping an eye open all the while for a highway patrol car.

'Mouton.'

'Hello, Piet. It's Clare. Can I bring a sample over?' she asked. She could sense his reluctance. A warm dinner would be waiting at home for him. So would Mrs Mouton. 'I'll be quick. I've got something I need you to match urgently.'

'Okay,' he said, his professional curiosity piqued. 'Call me when you get here and I'll let you in.'

'Thanks, Piet.' Clare drove quickly to the lab, grateful to

have missed the afternoon gridlock. Piet let her in. He seemed surprised that she was alone.

'So, what have you got?'

'Fibres from a black cashmere coat. India King's father's.' Clare handed him the envelope. Mouton shook the fibres carefully onto a slide and slipped it under a microscope.

'You won't be able to use this as evidence, you know that.'

'I know,' said Clare. 'But can you check anyway?'

'I'll check for you. But I'll have to let you know. It might take me a bit of time.' He scrabbled at the pile of folders on his desk and pulled out the one containing India King's autopsy. 'I'll check back on the other two as well.'

'Thanks, Piet. I appreciate that.'

He walked her to the exit. 'Don't give Riedwaan too much of a hard time.' He closed her door behind her. 'He's not so bad.'

Clare sighed. 'I'm the problem, not him.'

Piet patted her hand. 'You're not so bad either, Clare.'

'See you, Piet.'

As Clare headed westwards along the freeway, her thoughts returned to Brian King. She could not place where she had seen him before. The memory was there, on the outer periphery of her thoughts, but each time she directed her mind at it, the detail vanished. She gave up, and relaxed into the curving sweep of De Waal Drive where it hugged Devil's Peak. Where, where, where? The swish of the wheels on the wet road mocked her. She turned down Loop Street and drove past Jakes's studio. Then she braked sharply. The party. Of course. Tohar's party that she'd gone to with Jakes. She parked, hazard lights flashing, and pushed Jakes's buzzer.

'Who's missing me?' came his voice.

'Don't be a moron, Jakes. It's me.' The door opened immediately and she took the lift up to his floor. Jakes was waiting for her. He kissed her cheek.

'Hello, darling. This is a surprise.'

'Hi, Jakes.' She followed him into the flat. There was a white sofa, a shaggy carpet near the fire, and a bottle of red wine with two glasses – only one used so far – on the low table. 'Am I interrupting you?'

'Not yet, not yet. And you wouldn't care if you were, would you?' He took her coat. 'Can I give you a glass of wine?'

'Thanks,' she said, craving a drink. 'I stopped on the off-chance that you'd have the photos from that Osiris launch party we went to. Do you?'

'Yes. I do have them. I've just developed the last lot. They're here.'

Clare picked up her glass and followed him to the studio. The old picture of her was still there at the end of the passage: he had caught her off-guard, her face turned towards him at the moment he had called, her mouth just open, eyes unguarded, her naked body twisted beneath the long curtain of her hair. He had taken the photo soon after they had become lovers – the year Clare had gone to university. The year Constance had immured herself on Serenity Farm. Jakes had taken it to show Clare that she was beautiful, that her body was whole, unblemished, that he loved it. It had made his reputation when he exhibited it as 'The Victim's Sister'.

The darkroom was an ordered muddle, and Jakes ferreted around among a pile of pictures. He pulled out the contact sheets Clare wanted and handed them to her. They were pungent with chemicals. Clare flicked through them. With his practised, cynical eye, Jakes had captured the party's slide into decadence.

'Thanks, Jakes,' said Clare. 'I'll bring them back in a day or so.'

'Oh, keep them,' said Jakes. 'I have the negatives and I've already chosen the ones I want to enlarge.' He pointed to a picture of Kelvin Landman standing next to Otis Tohar. Landman's arm was around Tohar's shoulders, his veined hand resting on Tohar's chest, casually malignant. Tohar was a big man, but in this photograph he was diminished by Landman's proprietary grip. The doorbell chimed and Jakes twitched in anticipation.

'I'm on my way,' Clare said.

He walked with her to the door. 'You don't want to stay for another glass of wine?' Jakes asked as they waited for the lift. It opened, spilling out a blonde confection of hair and legs, high heels and cigarette smoke.

'Some other time, Jakes.' Then, 'Hello,' she said to the girl, stepping around her to get into the lift.

'Hi,' said the girl to Jakes, proffering her face for a kiss, winding his arm around her bare waist.

'I'll see you, Clare.'

The lift closed on them and returned Clare to the street. She sat behind the wheel, switched on the light, and went through the pictures Jakes had given her. She found him on the third sheet. King – sitting at one of the card tables. Playing with Tohar and two other men. One she did not recognise, the other was a member of Landman's entourage whom she had met at the Isis Club. There was an apparent ease between them, a camaraderie. Clare looked up. The street was empty except for a couple of vagrants listlessly begging from the last of the evening stragglers.

Clare had a fleeting vision of India lying cold in the morgue, her lovely body stitched together again after the post-mortem in readiness for the funeral. There was no privacy in death. She would be stacked on one of the metal tiers that held Cape Town's dead – among those who had died in suspicious circumstances. A street child banged at her window, his outstretched hands demanding money. Clare shook her head and started her car, wincing at the thud of his fist on the boot as she pulled away.

38

It was already very dark when Clare got home. She dispelled the feeling of neglect in the flat by switching on lights and closing curtains. She took the dead flowers from the hall and dumped them in the bin. She was expecting Riedwaan at eight. They'd be going through the case again – they were still missing something vital. She looked into the fridge: a lone cauliflower, which had bloomed black fungus. Mister Delivery would be bringing dinner. Clare made a pot of tea and took it through into the lounge. Then she took the cassette she had taken from Brian King's study and pushed it into the video machine. With Fritz on her lap, she curled up on her couch and pressed 'play'. The television screen flickered into life.

The opening shot was a close-up of a woman driving. Then the camera pulled back, revealing an oak-lined drive. It had clearly been shot from inside the house – every now and then the hand-held camera wobbled, inadvertently including curtains and the side of a window. The camera's hidden eye swept down again when the woman parked. It did not bother with her face; rather it zoomed in obscenely on her breasts, then her buttocks, as she leaned into her boot to pick up her shopping. The woman's obliviousness imbued the ordinary scene with menace. The camera panned as she turned. Clare sat bolt upright, spilling scalding tea onto an incensed Fritz.

The house and garden that came into view was the one she had been in that afternoon.

The screen went dark, then flooded with light as the woman opened the door and was briefly silhouetted against the sun, keys in hand. She set her bags down and closed the door behind her. Then strangely, suddenly, she was looking directly at the camera, her face frozen in horror. She was uncannily like India. The woman's body sank down, as if the weight of what she saw crushed her. A man stepped into the screen. He was hooded, but the wedding band on his hand was unmistakable. It was Brian King. He took the woman's wrist and twisted a piece of blue rope around it, viciously tightening it. Clare watched, waiting for the woman – it could only be Mrs King – to struggle, to protest. But she did neither. She held up her other hand, cowering like a dog that hopes its punishment will soon be over.

Her husband twisted the rope round her hand, forcing her to her knees. He ordered her to strip, but she shook her head mutely. Stupidly. King jerked her to her feet and dragged her down the passage towards the study where Clare had sat that very afternoon. He pushed her towards a door behind his desk and made her open it. The camera followed her, then stopped to pan across the three men in the room. They all wore hoods. Cathy King's knees buckled, and her husband kicked her over the threshold.

'Now you are going to be useful, bitch.'

His voice hissed with revulsion towards the woman grovelling at his feet. He clicked his fingers and one of the men stepped forward. He raised the horsewhip in his hand and brought it down hard on her back. The thin fabric of her silk shirt parted immediately, revealing the tattoo – two vertical lines bisected with an X – and delicate red beads of blood.

Clare pressed 'stop'. The film, for all its hand-held feel, had been professionally shot and edited. The shots were tight and the sound clear. It had a layered, Hitchcock feel. Kelvin Landman had said that you could make as much money out of celluloid girls as you could out of live ones. Apparently, Brian King shared the same idea.

Clare put down the remote and picked up her tea again. She would wait for Riedwaan before she watched the rest. She dug around in her bag, remembering that King had given her his business card. There it was, tucked into her wallet: *King and De Lupo: Wolf Media, Director*. Brian King would certainly know how to get a video shot and edited. Yet Clare knew that the police would do nothing unless Mrs King pressed charges. Somehow, Clare doubted that she would.

The phone rang, startling her. She picked it up.

'Clare? It's Riedwaan. I thought you'd forgotten. I've been ringing your doorbell for the past five minutes.' He was irritated.

'Sorry. It can't be working.' She buzzed him in and went to the front door to welcome him. He had two Woolworths bags – one with dinner, one with two bottles of wine. Under his arm were three folders. Charnay, Amore and India. Their three dinner companions. Clare's appetite drained away, though she was glad of the wine that Riedwaan poured her.

They went back to the lounge and Clare lit the fire while Riedwaan cleared space for the three files. He put the photographs on the table and laid the final autopsy reports next to each one. The wood crackled, domesticating the room and drawing Fritz away from the couch and next to the fireplace.

Clare went through to her study and brought her own photographs and notes. She laid these down next to Riedwaan's files. 'This is the stuff I've been gathering for my film about trafficking. At the heart of it all is Kelvin Landman,' said Clare. 'I know you want to focus on the killer of the girls, but I'm convinced that the two things are linked. Landman's tentacles spread everywhere. He's like a cancer, corrupting everything he touches.'

'You've been working hard.' Riedwaan reached out, tentatively massaging Clare's tense neck. The presence of the three dead girls neatly filed on her table seemed to cool the warmth of his hand. She didn't relax – but she didn't pull away, either. Over her shoulder, he read the profile she had been working on. 'Looks like one person. Although he could have an accomplice. Targets his victims. They look similar, similar age. Out alone, hence vulnerable. Some indication that he set it up a rendezvous beforehand. Presume that the first two went willingly. Third one not. Has a car. Extreme need for control. Very precise planning needed for the fantasy to work.'

'This describes Landman exactly, Clare. But he doesn't like to get his hands dirty. He'd have someone to work with him.'

'It could also describe Brian King or that rent boy's client, Da Cunha,' she suggested.

'We've got a DNA sample from India, a good one. There was semen on the body, and that's been analysed. It matches the sample of that girl who was raped in Johannesburg. The suicide.'

'God, Riedwaan, how did you get the lab galvanised? They usually don't do anything unless the case is going to court.'

'Let's just say I had a favour or two to call in and somehow this got itself to the front of the queue.'

'Have you been able to match it with anyone?'

'Nothing. None of the fuckers we have on file.'

'We have to keep on looking, then,' said Clare. 'Do you have any DNA for Landman?'

'None. But the two different groups – that points to two men.'

'We could bring King in for questioning. He could do some explaining,' said Clare. 'It could just as easily be one person – about twenty per cent of men are a different blood group to that indicated by their semen.'

'But he was at the Isis – like he said he was,' said Riedwaan. 'I also checked up on the girl he spent the night with. I don't like him, but so far there's no chink in his alibi.'

'I took a very nasty video from his house,' Clare revealed. 'A film of him orchestrating the gang rape of his wife.'

'Did she lay charges?' asked Riedwaan.

'I doubt it,' said Clare.

'There's not much to be done until she does.' Clare reached for the remote. 'Don't show it to me,' said Riedwaan. He pulled her away from the video machine. 'I've had enough for today.' He traced the underside of her jaw, down the soft curve of her neck. Clare leaned into the enclosure of his arms.

'Are you going to stay?' she asked

'I am.' Riedwaan pulled her to her feet. 'For a while. Let's go to bed. I'm too tired to eat.'

He was asleep by the time Clare was out of the bathroom. She slid in next to him, unused to moving so quietly in her own bedroom. He reached for her without waking. With someone breathing beside her, it was so much easier to relinquish her body to sleep.

39

It was just past four when Clare awoke, drenched in cold sweat. She had dreamt that she'd stumbled into a vast hall of mirrors. She stared back at herself in each mirror, her eyes wide open, each image reflected to infinity in every mirror. The shattered repetition of herself was dizzying. She hunted desperately for the door where she had entered, but it was gone. She tried to calm herself within the slow horror-time of the nightmare by staring down her own reflection. She was naked, suffused with shame at her body exposed and slug-like in the harsh light. As she tried to cover herself she realised that her hands were bound with blue rope. She tried to cry out but no sound came. When she opened her mouth, she saw that she had no tongue.

Clare sat up, switched on her bedside light, and calmed her breathing. She delved back into the nightmare as it receded. There had been a ghost with her in the mirrors. Hovering over her image had been the outline of a man with a camera, filming her shame and terror. Her hands had been painfully bound. She flexed her fingers and then smoothed out the bed where Riedwaan had lain. The indentation of his body was already cold. She curled up under her duvet. The touch of his hands lingered on her body, but she was glad to be alone.

'They make a picture of me. Like a dog I must beg for them to hurt me,' Natalie Mwanga had told her.

Clare pushed the duvet off and went to the lounge. The video she had taken from King was still in the machine. She pressed 'play' and watched it through to its bitter, humiliating end. Chilled, Clare went back to bed. 'He was a director ... he was telling them what to do ... when they hurt me ... he would make them do it again.' Whitney's soft voice whispered to Clare in the dark, 'Why?' Clare had no answers. She got back into bed and drifted into a troubled sleep just before dawn broke.

40

Whitney waited, fully dressed and wide awake, for the siren to blast across the valley. It came, summoning Dinah de Wet from the saggy warmth of her bed. Whitney lay under her blankets listening to Dinah cough. The kettle boiled for Dinah's tea. The toaster browned her single slice of white bread, the door banged shut. A tractor roared into life, taking everyone to work. Whitney heard the muffled morning shouts receding towards the orchard.

With the return of silence, she was up. She made herself some coffee for now, and jam sandwiches for later. She thought about writing a note. *'Dankie, Tannie Dinah, vir alles . . .'* is what she would have liked to say. But she didn't. Instead, she picked up her packed rucksack and headed for the door before it got any lighter. There was nobody around. She slipped between the houses and found the path that curved around the dam. A ghostly swathe of white arum lilies guided her to the farm road. Here she walked faster, hands deep inside her pockets, head down against the wind. There was snow somewhere, it was that cold.

Three kilometres later, the dirt road met the tar. She turned towards the west, trusting that her heart would guide her. The sun was up behind her now. It shone bleakly, not warming her at all. She crossed the N2, taking a road that skirted Cape Town. She had worked out her route by studying the old school atlas Dinah's daughter had left behind. After she'd walked for more than an hour, a truck pulled over. Whitney looked at it warily. There was a man in it, alone.

'Where you going, girlie?' He smiled. He seemed nice. A farmer, she guessed.

'To near Malmesbury,' she answered, standing close to the passenger window he had leaned over to open.

'Come, *meisiekind*. It's blerrie freezing outside. I'll give you a lift.' He opened the door. Whitney looked down the road ahead of her. It was a long way to walk. She slipped her rucksack around in front of her and climbed in.

'I'm Johan,' he said, turning the radio on.

'Hi,' she said. 'Thanks.' The warmth of the heated car enveloped her immediately. She didn't want to tell him her name, and he didn't ask.

They drove through the awakening farmlands and the small satellite towns that were spilling cars into Cape Town. Just before Atlantis, they joined the N7. Whitney had nearly fallen asleep when she saw the sign. She sat up. 'Can I get out just after the turnoff, please?' she asked.

'Where exactly are you going?' asked Johan.

Whitney decided to tell the truth. 'I'm looking for a place called Serenity Farm,' said Whitney. Her hands traced the outline of Clare's book beneath the fabric of her bag. 'Do you know it?'

'*Ja*, I've seen the turnoff just past Atlantis. It's *mos* that farm for mad people. Larney loonies, hey?' Whitney didn't say anything. 'Why are you going there?' he asked.

'I've got a friend,' she said. 'She lives there.'

'Oh.' He glanced at her but he didn't say anything more. They drove on in silence until he pulled over. The small wooden sign pointed up the dark avenue of trees. 'Good luck, hey,' he said.

229

'Thanks,' she said as she got out.

'You should smile more, you're a pretty girl when you smile. You could give me a blow job for the petrol?' Whitney froze. Her hand crept towards her rucksack. 'Hey, relax. I was only asking. You never know when you'll get lucky. See you.'

Whitney did smile as she walked between the welcoming trees. She had slung her rucksack onto her back again. The gun nestled against her. She had hidden it below the book, right at the bottom. She pictured it, calm and grey and smooth. It had been waiting for her in the farmhouse when she had gone with Dinah to do the cleaning yesterday. It had beckoned her from the farmer's cupboard, gleaming among socks and condoms and small change. It had fitted so snugly into her hoodie's deep pocket. And now here it was, giving her courage as she walked along the endless lane of trees.

Clare's book had told her things – things that Clare had not known she was disclosing about Constance. It had told Whitney things that she thought only she knew. Whitney knew where to find Constance. She had to find her. She walked down the path, the sound of her footsteps loud in the quiet of the dawn, towards the sequestered cottage. She knocked quietly. The door opened as if someone had been expecting her. Constance stared at Whitney, startled but not afraid. Whitney took the older woman's thin shoulders and turned her around. She pulled down Constance's white shift, exposing the lumpy mass of scar tissue across the width of her back. Whitney wet her finger on her tongue and traced the marks like an artist tracing a pattern she knew by heart.

'You can read it?' asked Constance. Whitney nodded. Constance's breath was warm on her neck as she leaned forward to kiss the scars. She took her hand and drew the girl inside, locking the door behind them.

41

The sun was high in the sky when Clare eventually awoke.
She pulled on her dressing gown and fetched the *Cape Times*
from outside her door. She wondered where Riedwaan was.

'Woke and couldn't fall asleep again. Speak to you in the
morning. Riedwaan.' She found the note propped on the
counter when she went to make coffee. Clare crumpled it in
her hand and waited for the kettle to boil. The phone rang
as she was going back to her bedroom.

'Yes?' She balanced her cup as she climbed back into bed.
'If this is a game, then we're quits now.'

'Clare? It's Piet,' was the bemused reply. 'I've got those
results for you.'

Clare was glad he couldn't see her blush. 'Sorry, Piet, I
thought you were someone else.'

'Apparently. So, do you want them?'

'Yes, of course I want them. What did you find? Did they
match the fibres you found on India?'

'That's what's odd,' said Piet. 'They didn't match. But I ran
a second check and I found that some of the fibres did match
what I found on India's shirt. There are a few that are
identical.'

'How can you tell?' asked Clare, noticing the business section
of the newspaper, which had slipped to the floor. There was

a banner headline announcing the end of the property boom.

'The fibres are very similar, both cashmere. But the dyes are different. One is a synthetic dye, the other is a much more expensive natural dye.'

'Which ones matched the fibres I brought you?' asked Clare. She was sitting on the edge of her bed, oblivious to the cold.

'The synthetic ones. There were only a few of them. The ones I'd found were under the naturally dyed ones.'

'Where did you find the synthetic ones? Where on her body, I mean,' asked Clare.

'They were around the shoulders, a sprinkling on the nape of her neck. Where you would expect, if someone put an arm around your neck to hug you,' said Piet.

'But definitely traces of two people?'

'Definitely.'

'Thanks, Piet.' She disconnected and dialled Riedwaan's number immediately.

'Clare, I'm sorry,' he said.

'It doesn't matter, Riedwaan. Piet Mouton just called me about those fibres I dropped off with him. They match some of those on India. They're the ones I took from King's coat when I was there.'

'And the others?'

'Don't know,' said Clare. 'Different dye, according to Piet.'

'It could just mean that he gave his daughter a hug before she went out.'

'A girl with a bolt on the inside of her bedroom door is going to hug her stepfather before she goes out?'

'You've got a point there,' said Riedwaan. 'Maybe I'll pay him another courtesy call and check when he saw her for the last time.'

'Let me know how it goes,' said Clare.

'You want to come with me?' asked Riedwaan.

'Thanks, but I think I'll pay our friend Otis Tohar a visit instead.' She folded the newspaper up thoughtfully. 'I think he might be a little stressed.' She slipped it into her bag.

'Oh?'

'Just a feeling. Landman and him are all over each other like a rash. And I saw some pictures of Brian King at that launch party. Their shared interest in films might be worth exploring a little more.'

'Where did you see the pictures?' asked Riedwaan.

'Jakes took them.'

'I didn't know you'd been seeing him,' said Riedwaan.

'I'm not. Don't be paranoid,' said Clare. 'I stopped by there because something niggled and he showed me the pictures he took at Tohar's party.'

'Was this before I saw you?'

'Yes. Riedwaan, why are you interrogating me? Are you jealous?'

'No. I'm just asking.'

'Well, don't. It's not your business anyway.'

'I'll speak to you later.' Riedwaan cut the connection. Irritated, Clare pulled on her running gear,. She had to get out. It was a bright morning, with the sun reflecting in the pooled rain. She lost herself temporarily to the steady pounding of her feet on the paving, and got home with her head much clearer. It was already nine o'clock when she phoned Tohar to arrange a meeting. She showered and dressed quickly and was there by ten. She pressed the intercom and waited. Eventually a voice asked what she wanted. 'It's Clare Hart. I've come about the interview.'

The door clicked open and she was inside. The mirrored elevator was waiting for her. Within seconds it had delivered her safely to the penthouse apartment. Looking svelte in a tailored suit, Tohar's PA was waiting for Clare.

'Hello. I'm Janet Green,' she said.

Clare put out her hand. 'Hi, I'm Clare Hart.'

'Mr Tohar said he'd be in shortly.'

'Do you mind showing me around while we wait for Mr Tohar to arrive?'

'Absolutely. Come this way.'

Clare followed her from the hall into the sitting room. It was immense and luxuriously furnished. The art was original, expensive: vast abstract canvasses that picked up the colours of the sofas. It was a perfect room, but cold, with not a single photograph or book in sight.

'Can I bring coffee?'

'Thanks,' said Clare. She sat on a large blue sofa by the window, the sweep of the bay in front of her. She pulled the newspaper out of her bag. In the margin of an inside page was a tiny story warning that the big developers who had bought too much and not sold on fast enough were facing a big crunch. The article singled out the Osiris Group as having over-extended itself and run into problems. Its bankers were reluctant to increase their lending and were considering calling in their debts as the group's cost spiralled and prices levelled out. Osiris had apparently found one or two anonymous investors, but with the sudden dip in prices and a strong local currency, even this investment was looking dicey. There were also allegations of black economic empowerment fronting. Already, the liquidators were circling on the periphery.

Clare put down the paper and looked out at the graceful curve of the bay. Otis Tohar was in a very vulnerable position, though he must have accessed cash from somewhere to have kept going. Clare thought about Landman's proprietary air. She grimaced. She'd certainly not like to be owing Landman money, and be unable to pay him back when he demanded.

Janet Green came back with the coffee and poured it. It was very strong. 'How long have you worked for Mr Tohar?' asked Clare.

'I started with him about six months ago. I was working for one of the hotels before. This seemed like an interesting opportunity.'

'And has it been?'

'It is challenging,' said Janet.

'What do you do, exactly?'

'I manage Mr Tohar's publicity. I also manage his social diary, and I've been involved in re-branding the Isis Clubs.' Janet stood up before Clare could ask her any more questions. 'Shall I show you around now?'

'Thanks,' said Clare, putting down her coffee and following the PA. The apartment had been converted from the original old hotel rooms. Enormous sums of money had been spent on it. Janet gave her detailed descriptions of the furnishings and artworks in each room.

'Would you like to see anything else?' asked Janet.

'Yes, I would like to see the home cinema. I hear that it's state of the art.' said Clare. Janet paused to answer her phone and Clare walked ahead down the passage. She opened the first door on the left. Instead of seeing the edit suite she had expected, she stepped into what looked like a dungeon. There was an array of whips and manacles and other props on the walls. There were cables and plugs on the floor and lighting tracks on the roof. Just then, Janet Green came up behind Clare and closed the door.

'Come this way. Please.' She opened the next door. There was the edit suite that Clare had seen before. The cinema was on the other side of the perspex window.

'What sort of movies do you make here, Janet?'

'What do you think?' She picked up a tape and gave it to

Clare. 'What does it matter if people like it and they pay? There's nothing illegal in that.'

Clare looked at the tape. On the cover was a woman in a black mask, thigh-high boots and a corset. She was standing holding a whip over some girls dressed as glamorous galley slaves in what looked like a stone boathouse. 'Who does the filming?'

'Mr Tohar is good. He does some. Otherwise we hire a cameraman,' said Janet.

'And who acts?'

'Some of the Isis girls. This is easy money for them.'

'What is your role, Janet?'

'Admin, finding locations, production management.'

Clare put her hand out, touched the bruises that twined up Janet's slim, white arms. 'Is this part of the deal?'

Janet pulled her arm away. 'That's nothing. I had an accident.'

There was a noise – the front door opening. 'Come. He's back.' She hurried Clare out of the suite and down the passage.

Otis Tohar was in the sitting room. 'Bring us fresh coffee,' he demanded.

Janet disappeared into the kitchen. 'So, Clare. I was surprised to hear you were coming. I can't see how I can help you with your investigation. Do you like what we've done here?'

'Your renovations are stunning. But I had a couple of things I wanted to ask you.'

'Yes, Janet told me. Did she show you around?'

'She did, thank you.'

Janet returned with the coffee. She put it on the table next to Tohar. 'Why don't you go and get your things ready, Janet?' said Tohar. 'We have that lunchtime meeting at La Traviata.' But he pulled her towards him, his fingers closing very precisely over the bruises on her arm. 'She's been looking after you?'

'She has, thank you,' said Clare.

'So, how can I help you?' asked Tohar. He let Janet go.

'I was curious about your relationship with Brian King,' she asked.

'Purely business,' said Tohar, voice smooth, hands steady. He took a delicate sip of coffee. 'We looked at a development together. It wasn't feasible, unfortunately. So tragic about his daughter.'

'Yes, it is,' said Clare. 'Did you know her?'

'No. Never met her.'

'You didn't know the other two girls, did you?'

'No. Why would I?' He placed his cup on the tray. 'What a peculiar question.'

'One of the girls auditioned at the Isis Club.'

'We have very high standards. I presume she wasn't up to them.' Tohar stood up abruptly and handed Clare her jacket. The interview was over. Clare went to the door.

'Just one more thing I wanted to ask you,' she said. He took his hand from the door handle.

'What was that?' he asked.

'How is your company dealing with all the financial pressure? There's such a squeeze on developers at the moment, especially high-end apartments.'

A muscle pulsed in Tohar's throat. 'My investors are wealthy men. We can weather a bumpy ride. It's a matter of managing your cash flow and keeping costs strictly under control.'

'I imagine it's a strain, especially if you have cash investors who want quick returns.'

'It could be, but information flows help. Keeping people informed.'

Clare held out her hand. Tohar took it, his palm slippery

with sweat. 'Your sideline, if it's not just a hobby, must be lucrative,' she said.

'What do you mean?' asked Tohar.

Clare took a wild chance, 'Your films – how shall I put it? – starring these girls . . . there's clearly more to it all than meets the eye.'

Tohar withdrew his hand. 'Janet. See Dr Hart out. I have things to attend to.'

Clare walked to her car, parked out of sight in a side street. She tried to phone Mrs King but there was no answer on either her cellphone or the home phone. She was about to call Riedwaan when a basement garage door opened. Otis Tohar's Jaguar accelerated down the narrow street. On impulse Clare turned her car to follow him. He made his way down to Beach Road and then turned left into the parking lot above Three Anchor Bay. Clare followed, keeping her distance and pulling over on the other side of the road. Tohar climbed out of his car and walked rapidly to the slipway that led to the boathouses and the beach. Then he turned back, seemingly at a loss, patting his pockets. The conversation, when he found his phone in his breast pocket, was brief and punctuated with agitated hand movements. He was facing Clare. His face was congested with fury. He snapped the phone closed and wrenched the car door open. The car lurched forward and he turned back in the direction he had just come from, just missing a woman crossing the road with a pram.

Clare got out of her car and went across to the steps that led down to the grimy bay. The tide had come up high and the stench of rotting seaweed was nauseating. There were people down on the beach, cleaning their kayaks. Ropes and buckets had been stacked in the sun and two women were industriously sweeping the boathouses. Clare went down and had a look into the closest one. It was carved like a crypt out of the rock, and only the roof sections were bricked.

'Spooky, hey,' said one of the women who was sweeping. 'You should see all the tunnels around here. It's like a whole underground city.'

'I'd love to. I live just over there,' Clare pointed, 'and I've often wondered how this promenade works.'

'I'll show you. We've got a map inside.' Clare followed her into the boathouse. The air was dank. The woman showed her a map of the promenade, and the tunnels below it and Main Road.

'This is all reclaimed land, isn't it?' said Clare.

'It is. The council issued these when there was a flood a couple of years ago. They had to go and find all the old Victorian maps to get to the problem. I love old maps, so I bought a couple.'

Clare leaned closer, tracing the tunnels. 'They look like spidery veins. It's fascinating.'

'I'm sure there's another map somewhere.' The girl ferreted through a pile of paper. 'Here it is.' She held it up in triumph. 'Would you like it?'

'I would! Thank you,' said Clare. She followed the woman out, glad to be in the sun again.

'How often do you clean up?' asked Clare.

'Oh, only once a year. We always do it on the same day. We all just pitch in together and get it done.'

'We did it last year,' said a man, carefully folding old sails, 'and the next day there was that huge storm – do you remember it?' Clare nodded. 'That storm broke the doors down the day after our spring-clean, can you believe it. So we're keeping our fingers crossed that it won't happen again.'

Clare looked out to the west. The sky was clear, the sea sparkled. 'Doesn't look like it. Who owns these boathouses?'

'The council does,' said the same man. 'Our families have rented them for years and years. It's kind of hereditary.'

'They're thinking of charging us more, though – I know that. As if we don't pay enough rates in Sea Point.'

Clare walked to the end of the small beach. She could still hear the group arguing about whether their rates were too high or not. The sea wall bulged broadly before it flattened towards the lighthouse. There were several large openings on the edge of the curve. They studded the sea wall like blind eyes. Clare pulled her coat around herself. It was very exposed where she was standing, and the wind was biting cold.

42

The clock said five-thirty when Theresa Angelo finished her voice-over.

'I need a break,' said Sam Napoli. 'You want to get a cappuccino?'

'No, thanks, Sam.' Theresa blushed. Coffee made her jittery and it felt strange having coffee with someone who was nearly as old as her dad. Not that Sam flirted with her. He didn't at all. But he was rather sexy – even though his shoulders were getting that stiff look peculiar to men over forty, no matter how often they went to gym.

'Come on,' said Sam. 'You've worked hard. And you were brilliant, as always.'

'I've got to meet my mom,' said Theresa. 'We're going to see a movie. We always do on a Friday.'

'I'm going to have a word with your mother,' said Sam, looking her up and down. 'You're turning into quite a knock-out. She's going to have to keep you locked up at home to keep you safe!'

Theresa giggled. 'It's just my new haircut.'

'And a brand-new figure, too.'

'I'll see you next week?' asked Theresa.

'See you then. We need a couple more hours. And be good!' Sam called after her.

'I will. See you then.' Theresa picked up her bag from the security guard.

'You need an escort, *sisi*?' he asked. 'It's a bit dark now.'

'No, thanks. I'll be fine. I'm meeting my mom at the Waterfront. I'll see you Tuesday.'

'Okay, *sisi*, nice weekend.'

Theresa crossed the road and ducked under the boom at the exit to the Waterfront Marina apartments. Theresa was glad of the voice-over work. She was planning to take her mother away to a spa in the mountains. She had the brochure in her bag. Maybe that would make her happy again. Maybe a break would help her mother face the fact that Theresa's father had left her – finally and for good. For the better, was what Theresa thought. He had etched lines of sadness into her mother's soft face and slowly turned the corners of her smiling mouth downwards.

The wind off the sea was cold and damp. Theresa walked faster, to escape her thoughts and to warm herself up. She had two hours, still, before meeting her mother for a movie and a pizza. She walked along the marina and looked at the yachts, avoiding the people thronging across the drawbridge towards the Waterfront.

Floodlights glimmered on the black water where the boats rocked to and fro. Theresa was cold, her jeans useless against the wind which was starting to pick up. Beyond the slipway, light spilled from the small windows of The Blue Room. She went into the bar feeling very grown up. It was quiet, empty except for the barman polishing glasses. She made her way to a table away from the draughty doorway and sat down, dropping her bag at her feet. The barman came over to her.

'Cute bag,' he said. 'Can I get you something?' He was very good looking – dark hair, eyes shiny black.

'Thanks,' she said. 'I'll have a decaf café latte please. With

242

a glass of water.' Theresa calculated how much money she had in her purse. Should be enough. Theresa did not drink, but she was pleased that he hadn't asked her for ID.

'Okay. Ice and lemon?' He gave the table a superfluous wipe.

'Just plain tap water.'

'You waiting for someone?'

'Not here. I'm going to the movies later. I'm a bit early, that's all.'

He went behind the bar and rattled the coffee machine, steaming her milk into perfect frothiness.

'Here you are.' With a flourish, he put down the latte, and next to it a glass of iced water. There was a tiny biscuit with the coffee. Theresa was disappointed to see that a bit of the liquid had spilled and made it soggy.

She smiled up at him. 'Thank you. It's very quiet here this evening.'

He looked at his watch. 'It'll start getting busy soon. It usually fills up at about seven, seven-thirty. All the yachties come in then.'

'I love those yachts,' said Theresa. She watched the masts through the window, streaks of silver, magical against the night sky.

'You should have a look at them. There are some real beauties in at the moment.'

'I will when I'm a bit warmer,' said Theresa.

'What's your name?' he asked.

'Theresa. And yours?'

'Tyrone.'

She took a sip of her coffee. 'This is delicious.'

He flashed a smile. 'Like you, Theresa.'

Theresa blushed to the roots of her hair, but he did not notice. The barman had turned to welcome new customers. The three men moved in an unsmiling pack towards a table

243

by the window. Theresa was glad that they sat far away from her. She had not liked the way that one of them had looked at her and passed his tongue slowly across his lips. She zipped up her hoodie, finished her coffee and went over to the bar.

'Something else?' asked the barman.

'No, thanks,' said Theresa. 'Just the bill.' He handed her the slip of paper. She had just enough money.

'You take care, now,' he told her. She smiled at him and then she went out into the night. It was now completely dark. She could just make out a couple of people walking with their heads down towards The Blue Room. She had an hour to kill, so she wandered down the jetty to look at the yachts. It seemed unfair to have tethered them here. They were like restless horses, streamlined curves designed for movement, for freedom. The last yacht was the most beautiful, a gleaming dark blue with stainless-steel trim. She admired it as she leaned against the small barrier at the end of the jetty. The wind slapped the tightly furled sails against the mast.

There was a man on board. Theresa watched him stride up and down inside the cabin. He was tall, and the ceiling seemed too low for him. His phone was clamped to his ear and he was speaking in short bursts. The bright cabin lights were reflected in the sweaty sheen on his forehead. He turned and caught sight of Theresa watching. His gaze pinioned her, moving languidly down her curves, then back to her face. A slow smile of recognition spread across his face – handsome, like one of the old movie stars whose pictures hung in the Film Fusion studios. Theresa smiled back. She walked to the end of the jetty, but it was too cold to linger. It was time to meet her mother anyway, so she walked back. The man was no longer in the cabin, even though the lights were on. She burrowed her hands deeper into her pockets.

On her way, she paused at The Blue Room. It was filling

up, and the good-looking barman was busy, but he didn't see her. A raucous group of men were coming down the stairway. Theresa didn't feel like enduring the predictable moment of mock-threat before they let her pass, so she turned to walk between the ornamental trees lining the wheelchair access to the car park. It was much darker than she had thought it would be, and she walked nervously towards the gleaming cars. She relaxed when she saw movement, the comforting sound of someone chatting, loading their boot with suitcases.

'Hello.' The smooth, educated voice startled Theresa. But she relaxed when the man she had seen on the yacht stepped out from behind the open boot.

'Oh, hi,' she said.

'I see you like yachts,' he said. Theresa nodded. He stepped away from her, sensing that he had made her uncomfortable by trapping her in the narrow space between the cars. 'I'm sorry,' he said. 'I didn't mean to frighten you. But I was wondering if you could help me. My wife is just fetching more luggage, can you believe it, and I can't seem to get this bag into my boot.'

'Oh, sure,' said Theresa, embarrassed that she might have seemed rude. He stood back to let her pass. She put her bag down beside the wheel. Then she bent down, taking hold of the one side of his bag – it was not heavy, just large.

'Okay, I'm ready.' She looked up, wondering why the man wasn't lifting his side. She saw the hammer in his hand reflected in the polished car, but he brought it down too fast for her to move out of the way. The blow caught her across the back of her head, its force carefully calculated to defer her death. The man lifted her and dumped her into the boot of the car. Her hip bruised against the hard rim of the spare tyre. He then bundled her into the bag that she had helped him to lift. She tried to fight but her limbs would not obey.

He slammed the boot shut. Theresa put her hands to her head. Blood seeped between her fingers. She was furious. She had washed her hair with such care that afternoon. She fought to stay conscious, thinking of her mother parking right then, walking to meet her, bringing her a chocolate, or a fresh flower. Would her mother find her? She had long ago, the time Theresa had wandered away in the supermarket when she was only four. Theresa felt that same panic now, only infinitely worse.

The car started, jerking into reverse, and then moving smoothly forward. She heard a muffled conversation and a laugh. The guard at the boom? The car moved forward again. Then Theresa lost the battle against pain and fear, and slipped into the darkness.

43

Theresa Angelo lay on her back, legs splayed, arms flung out like a sleeping child. Her long hair was matted around her head, tumbling onto the stone floor. There were rat droppings between the coiled ropes that supported the naked mattress she lay on. Her coat had slipped to the floor. Her exposed skin was mottled, puckered with gooseflesh. Her wrists were bruised. There was bloody skin under the nails of her right hand. The contusion under her thick black hair had seeped blood all night. It was very cold, even though the sun had hoisted itself as high as it could, so deep into the winter.

Her shallow breath misted the air above her bruised mouth just regularly enough to show she was alive. Then the noise that had penetrated her unconscious mind started up again. The mournful bellow of the foghorn vibrated deep into the recesses of her mind. It sought out and found crevices of consciousness beyond the drug that had held her inert for hours. It penetrated the most hidden places of her mind and activated again the basic impulse to stay alive. Slowly, the insistent rhythm of the foghorn summoned her to consciousness, cell by cell. A pulse jumped at the base of her throat, she shivered as her body fought to keep itself warm. The fog momentarily released a ray of sun. It shot through the small barred window, striking her face.

She would not have seen it, even if she had opened her eyes, but on the shelf above her head was a twist of blue rope and a key. There was no knife – but that anyone might have at hand.

44

Clare awoke, anxiety gnawing, early on Saturday morning. She went for a run, buying milk on her way home. Fritz meowed in delight at the sound of her key in the lock, wrapping herself around Clare's legs as she opened the door. Clare noticed the envelope wedged behind the hall table when she bent down to pick up the cat.

Constance again. Clare's hands were suddenly clammy. She slit it open. A single Tarot card, grinning, enigmatic, fell out onto the floor.

The Hanged Man.

There was a slip of paper in the envelope. On one side – brushed in black ink – were two sure, familiar verticals, cut through the half X. On the other, Constance had written a reading. For rebirth: a sacrifice. From death: sometimes change. Clare's blood ran cold. She jumped when her phone rang, putting the Hanged Man with the other three cards Constance had sent her.

'Yes?' she said.

'Clare, another girl has gone missing.'

'When?' she asked. 'Where?'

'Last night. Her mother reported it immediately to Caledon Square. Somebody there thought it would be best if they handled it. They didn't see the link apparently between this girl going missing and the three dead girls.'

Clare heard the incredulous rage in Riedwaan's voice.

'It only came through to me now. And already there had been one *moer* of a *gedoente* about who gets what and why their officer can't investigate. We might have found her already if that fucking moron's ego hadn't tripped him up.'

Riedwaan had had hours of investigation time stolen from him. Clare knew as well as he did that it was those few hours after an abduction that were the most likely to return the person – if not unscathed, then at least still alive. 'Who is she?' asked Clare. 'What happened?

'Her name is Theresa Angelo. Lives in Gardens with her mother. Sixteen years old. Earns some extra money doing voice-overs. Apparently she had finished one at Film Fusion at the Waterfront, then left to meet her mother. She spoke to her mother at five-thirty. The mother was still at work and they arranged to meet for the eight o'clock movie. Her mother was there on time, but Theresa didn't arrive. She called her. The phone rang, but there was no answer. Mrs Angelo then phoned Film Fusion. The sound guy was still there, tweaking things. He said that Theresa had left straight after their session.'

'Have you been down there?'

'Of course. But those Caledon fuckers didn't go last night. They took it into their thick heads that she must have met a boyfriend and decided to go with him. So twelve precious hours and one beautiful girl gone.'

'Have you interviewed the sound man yet?'

'Sam Napoli? Not yet. Do you want to come with me?'

'I'll come,' said Clare. 'Will you pick me up? Half an hour?'

'See you now.'

Clare slumped down at her desk. The profile she had drawn up of the killer was there in front of her. What was she missing? She put her hands into her hair and pulled until her eyes watered from the pain. The pieces of the puzzle were there. But no matter how she shuffled them, no clear picture emerged. Clare went to the bathroom, retching again and again. Then she prepared herself for the day, and waited for Riedwaan.

45

Riedwaan picked Clare up twenty minutes later. He drove to the Film Fusion studios, his anger filling the car. 'What did she look like?' asked Clare. Riedwaan threw a picture of the missing girl onto Clare's lap. It was a posed school photo. Theresa Angelo looked demure in her blue dress with its silly white Peter Pan collar. The face was broad, a sweep of cheekbones promising beauty in adulthood. Her dark eyes were intelligent, challenging; her body sturdy, strong. Certainly not like the ethereal girls this killer had taken before. Had he made a mistake? Had something panicked him? Could they move fast enough to find him? To find Theresa alive? Clare felt a glimmer of hope.

'I've got to do a fucking press conference this afternoon. What am I going to say? Those sharks are going to be on a feeding frenzy. Why haven't you got this killer? What's wrong with the police? When I know and you know that the longer he's on the loose the more papers they sell. Bastards.' Riedwaan's rage boiled over.

'What do you have, Riedwaan?' Clare asked, wincing as he cut in front of a car, the driver hooting furiously. 'Does she fit the pattern?'

'I don't know. She's an only child. Father is a doctor on an oil rig. He's being flown in this morning. Goes to a private school in town. Gifted child, talented actress, well-behaved mommy's girl.' He hooted viciously as an old lady swerved across the lane.

'What happened last night?'

'Apparently they do voice-overs at Film Fusion if there's any spare time in the studio. Theresa makes some pocket money if they have a gap and she's free. She caught a taxi to the Waterfront because her mother was working. Got to Film Fusion just before four and went to work. Her mother could only meet her at eight so she was going to do some shopping and then meet her.'

'Why so much later?'

'Mrs Angelo has a catering business. She was doing a birthday tea so would only be free at seven-thirty. She came straight down and waited for Theresa – who never arrived. Phiri is baying for my sautéed balls on a plate. And the MEC for security is rabbiting on about community trust in the police force. Load of shit, they are going to crucify me, Muslim or not.' Riedwaan turned into Film Fusion's studio and parked.

'We'll get him.'

'When, Clare? Fucking when? You're meant to be the miracle worker. What have I got? A description of what he might wear? A list of psychological problems that this poor motherfucker might have had? My mother *donnered* the shit out of me when I was a kid. Do you see me killing anybody?' Riedwaan turned away. Clare ignored the tremor in his voice.

'We lose, Riedwaan, if we fight. You know that.' Clare got out of the car. Riedwaan lit a cigarette, then dragged on it like a drowning man sucking in a pocket of air. She waited. Clare sensed Theresa's presence, it was there like the scent of a woman who has just left a room. She reined in her thoughts, turning mind sharply to the facts. The killer kept the girls alive for some time before he killed them. If Theresa had been abducted last night there was a good chance that she was still alive. Panic coiled tightly in Clare's belly. He had kept the bodies of the first two for twenty-four hours before dumping them.

Riedwaan slammed the door of his car, startling her. He put his hand on the back of her neck and rubbed it. She took it as the peace offering it was and relaxed into his touch. Then they went inside and waited for the sound man. Clare checked the desk register. Theresa Angelo had printed her cellphone number in clear rounded letters at three fifty-five the previous afternoon. Clare jotted the number down in her notebook just as Sam Napoli arrived.

He shook hands with both of them. 'Come upstairs, please.' His tanned face was ashen. He took them into his studio and they sat down. Sam had tears in his eyes.

'I've worked with Theresa since she was ten,' he said. 'I can't believe this. That you guys are here looking for her.'

'Take us through what happened yesterday. Everything. Smallest details,' said Clare.

'She came to do a voice-over for a car ad. She was so excited about the job – it was the first time she had got an adult role. She had a fantastic voice – husky and alive.' He turned towards the console and twiddled a few of its vast array of knobs. 'Here, listen.'

'Hello, there.' Theresa Angelo's voice filled the room. Clare's flesh crawled at the uncanniness of it. 'I'm a Maserati girl myself. I deserve it. How about you?'

Sam switched the tape off again. 'She was so happy when she left. We had been joking about this dumb Maserati ad. You know Rod Stewart's immortal lines: "She was tall, thin and tarty and she drove a Maserati." Theresa was saying if she could write so brilliantly, then she'd be a millionaire too. Anyway, we finished early and she left – singing "Sailing". She has appalling taste in music.'

'What time did she leave?' asked Riedwaan.

'It must have been about five-thirty.' He turned back to his computer. 'Let me just check. Every job is logged here.' He called up the previous day's entries. '*Ja*, here it is. Five thirty-two I logged off. So she must have left about five minutes later.'

'Was there anything else you noticed?'

'There was something. It was a small thing. But she was wearing blue nail polish. I remember thinking that it looked odd – it made her hands look unnatural. She laughed when I said that – she said it was just a fashion. Must be true. My wife and my daughter are both wearing it. It told them it looks weird, but they don't care.'

'Anything else?' asked Riedwaan, 'Was she nervous? Different in any way?'

'No, just happy. She said goodbye and she was gone.'

Riedwaan closed his notebook. 'Thanks, Mr Napoli. I'll have this typed and then you can sign the statement. Can you come into the police station?'

'Sure, sure,' said Sam, getting up and walking with Riedwaan towards the door. 'I saw her again, you know.'

Tension whipped through Riedwaan's body. He opened his notebook. The paper crackled loudly in the sudden quiet.

'Where?' he asked.

'It was a little later. I was meant to be cleaning up the sound but there was some glitch with the machine. I went out onto the balcony for a smoke and I saw her. She was walking towards the Waterfront but she hadn't gone the usual way. She must have cut through those fancy apartments. I thought maybe she was going in there because I saw her wave. I didn't see who she was waving at. And then she disappeared for a while. I thought she must have gone in. I was about to go in when I saw her again. She was really looking great. I thought, There is our little Theresa, all grown up.'

'Was there anyone with her? Following her?' asked Clare.

'If there was, he must have stuck right close to the shadow because I didn't see anyone. She turned the corner then, so I couldn't see her any more.'

'Can you point out where she went?' asked Riedwaan.

'Sure,' said Sam. 'Come this way.' He led them through the coffee bar and onto the wooden deck. Each table had an ashtray filled to the brim with ash and stompies. 'That is where she went.' He pointed towards a narrow stretch of garden that snaked through the apartment buildings. It led down towards the Waterfront via the yachting marina. The delicate masts patterned the blue sky.

'I wonder if she went to The Blue Room?' said Clare. 'I would imagine that it's time for us to pay another visit. I'm sure you'll need a whiskey after your press conference. Do you want to meet me there later?'

Riedwaan looked at his watch. 'Shit, I'm going to be late. I'll meet you there in an hour. Cheers.'

Clare turned to Sam. 'Thanks, Sam.'

He was staring at the empty place where Theresa had been just half a day earlier. 'I've got a daughter just her age,' he said. 'What does one do?'

Clare put her hand on his arm. 'You wait. It's all you can do.'

46

Clare retraced Theresa Angelo's steps. She walked over to the security gate of the apartment complex. The guard was inside his hut, his radio blasting a soccer game at the road. He did not see her as she slipped under the boom. She looked back at the Film Fusion balcony. Sam had gone inside. Fifty metres down the road was a rank of municipal dustbins screened by some reeds. She looked up at the apartments. Not one window faced her way.

She walked towards the marina. At the other end of the service road there was a metal gate, with a hidden release mechanism Clare soon discovered on the inside. She pressed it, and the gate jumped open onto the small parking lot that served the yachting marina. Clare walked down the slipway, uneasy with the sense that Theresa had so recently walked this way. Then she made her way to The Blue Room. The barman was absorbed in the task of polishing a glass. It took him a few seconds to register Clare's presence.

'Can I help?' His voice was clipped, neutral. 'We aren't open for another half an hour.'

'Hello, Tyrone. I'm not here for a drink. I wanted to ask you a couple of questions.'

He paled, recognising her. 'What about? I wasn't on duty last night. I can't help you.'

'So you know I'm looking for someone?'

'I heard it on the news. That another girl is missing.' He put the glass down. 'And then I saw you, so I thought you'd be looking for her.'

'Why did you think I would look here, Tyrone?'

He turned to pack away the clean glasses. 'I can't help you. I was at home last night.'

'Who was here, then?'

He looked down at the glass in his hand and polished it again.

'One girl is missing, Tyrone. Three are dead. Information is the only thing that will help us catch him.' She put one of her cards on the bar counter. 'You call me.' He said nothing, did not pick up the card.

'We'll be checking your alibi,' she said, turning as she reached the door. Her card had gone, she noticed. Then she walked out briskly and settled herself on a nearby bench to wait for Riedwaan.

Sam Napoli had said that Theresa had been wearing blue nail polish. He had noticed it, commented on it because it was out of character and it had looked odd. Clare opened her phone and pressed Piet Mouton's cell number.

'Ja?'

'Piet? Clare here. Can you check a detail for me?'

'Those girls?' aksed Piet. 'I hear you've got another one.'

'Not yet, Piet. You keep yourself busy in your lab so long.'

'So what do you want me to check?'

'Did you note down if those girls had nail polish on?' She waited as Mouton shuffled through the organised chaos that was his desk.

'Okay, here they are. Charnay, yes. Amore, yes. India, yes.' Clare imagined him running his fat sausage of a finger down his pages of minutely detailed notes. 'Ja, they all were. India was wearing nail polish, but it was scratched. Like she had tried to get it off with something sharp. There were a few small cuts on the side of the nail bed. There were fragments under her nail, too. Why?'

'Just checking, Piet. This Theresa Angelo who disappeared last night was wearing blue nail polish. The last person to see her commented on it because it didn't fit with her.'

'Theresa Angelo. A dead angel. Tabloid heaven.'

'Thanks, Piet,' she said wryly. Any of the other tests in yet?'

'Not yet. I'll let you know.'

'Okay. bye, Piet.' Clare watched the inky-black water lapping at the sheer stone sides of the marina. She remembered a bottle of blue nail polish in India's immaculate bathroom that looked as if it had been used only once. She watched a seal waddle along a wooden jetty and dive in, gracefully transformed as soon as it hit the water. The phone's shrill ring startled her out of her reverie. She was surprised to see the number.

'Piet,' said Clare.

'I've just got one result in from the tests on the fibres we found on India. They were rope fibres. What is interesting is that there are traces of bird shit on it. I got my friend at the ornithology institute to run some tests. He said it's from a seagull – one that scavenges on human waste. An urban seagull.'

'Thanks, Piet.'

'Another thing, Clare. You remember the marks we found on Charnay's toes and fingers? Those were definitely gnaw marks. From rats. Your man keeps their bodies inside somewhere. We often find bodies that have been scavenged. But if those girls had been outside it would have been dogs, maybe cats. If it's rats, then it must be inside somewhere, somewhere quiet.'

Clare was silent. She was trying not to see the malignant gleam of rat eyes in the dark, moving closer, closer. Then biting, gnawing.

'You there?' asked Piet.

'*Ja*, I'm here.'

'I thought maybe somewhere at the docks. Maybe a warehouse or something?'

'Piet, are we looking for one man or two?' asked Clare.

'There were the two different blood groups on Charnay – one in the semen, one in the blood. But that's not conclusive. Eighty per cent of people express their blood group in other body fluids. So you can have mucosa, semen that has a different DNA structure to the rest. It throws you. You can't conclusively say you're not looking for two men.'

'But I'm so sure it is one man. It's so obsessive. Those keys he puts in their hands. What are they for?'

'A diversion?' asked Piet.

'I don't think so,' said Clare. She watched the raucous seagulls wheeling, diving, scavenging. Clare snapped her phone shut. Find her, find her, the gulls taunted. She watched one snatch food from the beak of another, smaller gull and then land on the mast of one of the yachts rocking in the tamed water.

She phoned Riedwaan and left him a message that she would be walking home, so not to worry to fetch her. Clare walked through the Waterfront and on to the newly built sea walls. Dwarfed by the massive chunks of granite that held the sea back, she let her thoughts go, willing them to find their way to where Theresa was. She was convinced Theresa had been taken by the same person, but that he had acted in a rush this time. Her thoughts wandered to Natalie, to Whitney, to their aching shame at being filmed. Were these girls being abducted to feed the growing snuff-movie market? It was rumoured that South African products were popular internationally. The only prosecution so far – in Johannesburg – had failed. All three accused had been acquitted.

Clare walked past the littered lawn in front of Sushi-Zen. There was a small white cross where India King's body had lain. Clare read the inscription. It said, very simply, 'With Love, Grade 12'.

The inscription made her think of India's debauched stepfather. Clare leaned against the sea wall, thinking that a bit more detail about him would be useful. She also thought it was time to discuss the nasty King and nasty Landman's nasty little home movie with its pathetic star, Cathy King. She tried the Kings' home number. No reply. And Cathy King was not answering her cellphone, either. But Clare did manage to get Portia Qaba on her cellphone; she promised to tell Mrs King to call when she got back from her weekend off. Not ideal, but it would have to do for now. She and Riedwaan would then arrange to see Cathy King together.

Clare's thoughts circled back to Landman. He was a killer, she felt sure, and absolutely ruthless. He was the type who would procure even child for a regular paying client. Clare did not doubt that he would torture and kill anyone for a fee, without compunction. Especially if there was a way of extending the profit. It should be him, but Landman, for all his absence of conscience, was now a businessman. He would kill only for a reason – for profit or expediency – and not simply for the pleasure of it. No, there was a different kind of zealot behind these murders. For now, though, there was nothing to be done except wait. Think and worry and wait.

Clare went to join Riedwaan later that afternoon. He was working alone in the caravan, grey with stress.

'I spoke to Piet,' she said, giving him the coffee she had picked up on the way.

'And?'

'Nothing new.'

'Why is it not falling into place?' Riedwaan slammed his fist onto the rickety desk, spilling coffee over his files. Clare handed him a grimy towel. He dabbed at the puddle of coffee. 'Shit!'

'Predatory criminals are the hardest to catch. Strangers with nothing to connect them with the victim. This one doesn't want to be caught. He shows off, but he's very careful. I think the body fluids on the first body were a mistake. He'd have seen the report in the press, so he's rectified that little error. We've had no witnesses – or none who have come forward. Nothing to link anyone to the crime.'

'We have to work it out. *You* have to work it out, Clare.' He looked at her. 'The chief is on my back. Phiri released that chef – his DNA doesn't match, and he was in the holding cells when Theresa disappeared. The press are on Phiri's back and the poor child's mother is demented with worry.'

Clare went to her desk and picked up the files. 'I think we should pull Brian King in for questioning.'

'Do you want me to arrest him?' snapped Riedwaan. 'On what grounds?'

'Just a feeling.'

Riedwaan didn't respond.

'I'm doing what I can. We're doing what we can,' said Clare. 'I'm going home now. Call me.'

'I'll call you. And I'll check up on King again. I did when we heard Theresa was missing. Good alibi – he was playing golf. With four other people.'

'Okay, but let's try him again. I'll see you.'

Clare laid the files out on her kitchen table when she got home. She had been over them so often that the details, the specifics of each case, were blurring into the others. She poured herself a glass of wine and then searched for a cigarette. She found a stale pack on top of the fridge and smoked one, even though it made her feel sick. She drank one large glass of wine, and then another, falling asleep with her clothes on.

47

Cathy King went upstairs to her daughter's bedroom. She had been sleeping in India's bed ever since they'd found her body. She had given Portia the weekend off. Brian would not be back for a long time. She was alone. She put the tape she had brought with her into her dead daughter's video machine and took the remote to the bed with her. If she pushed her face deep enough into the pillow there still was the faintest trace of the smell of India. Underneath the scented cleanliness traces of India lingered, a once-grubby, sunshine-warm child.

Cathy wrapped one thin, scarred arm around the pillow, pulling it against her breast. She looked at the bolt on the inside of her daughter's door, suffused with shame at her own weakness. Cathy opened the bottle of pills. This she could do. She tapped the pills into her open right hand. They looked like sweets. She dropped them into her mouth, washing the bitterness away with lemonade.

The phone rang deep inside the house. She ignored it as the pills started to dissolve, making her feel ill. She swallowed her nausea. It would take an hour, at most, to free her of the terror and guilt she had endured since marrying Brian King. Cathy lay quietly, remembering her phone call to the pathologist who had done India's post-mortem. Dr Mouton had gently reassured her that all suspicious deaths – car accidents, suicide, murder – came to him, and that the bodies were kept together in one place. He had answered her questions patiently, as if he sensed her need to find out, to know all she could as a way of coping with her bereavement. What Piet Mouton told her that day had made Cathy eager for the end. And she felt especially eager now, even as her body rebelled against the pills she had swallowed. At least she knew that her own body would be taken in a van to the mortuary where India lay. India would no longer be alone among the alphabetically ordered rows of corpses, their naked feet flopped outwards, as if napping. Cathy would be there to watch over her. This time, she would not fail her daughter.

The house phone stopped and her cellphone started bleating. Cathy King waited until it stopped, too, before she pressed 'play'. She did not hear either of Clare's desperate messages. She settled herself back into her daughter's bed and watched the film in which she starred, with her husband directing her gang rape. Here in her home. She recognised Kelvin Landman as she watched him twist and rip her clothes. He had been for dinner here earlier. She had served a perfect rack of lamb that night, she remembered. She watched as he used his beautiful knife to carve his initials delicately into her back, her hand reaching instinctively to touch the scar. It was when the credits rolled that she saw the other name. She pressed 'pause', understanding quite clearly now who had killed her daughter. Cathy reached for her phone, but the barbiturates tightened their lethal grip on her body. She slid bitterly towards death, the phone falling uselessly to the floor.

48

Clare woke up feeling cold. The wine had left her with a headache and her duvet had slipped off. She got up, the taste of a nightmare bitter in her mouth. She stripped off the shirt and slacks she'd gone to bed in and showered. Then she pulled on her thick winter gown and wrapped a towel around her wet hair. Fritz badgered her until she fed her – the smell of the fish making Clare gag. She sat down at the kitchen table again, staring at what was left of three young girls – photographs, DNA tests, ballistics reports, interview transcripts. The fourth file was the slimmest, just a missing-person's report at this stage. Clare prayed it would stay that way.

She stretched, her body stiff from too little sleep. Gathering the papers into her arms – Charnay, Amore, India – she carried them tenderly into her study. The walls there were blank. She pulled out a roll of masking tape from her top drawer and picked up the envelope of Tarot cards.

'I'll try it your way, Constance,' she muttered to herself. She stuck the first card, the Female Pope, on the eastern wall. That was the direction that Charnay Swanepoel's head had pointed when they'd found her. She placed Charnay's smiling school photo next to the Tarot card. Clare arranged the photographs and Piet Mouton's reports in a halo around the picture.

On the western wall, she placed the photo of Amore Hendricks next to the grinning orange devil. Clare gave pride of place to the expensive DNA tests paid for by Amore's bereft father. The card of self-imposed shackles, the bonds around this girl's body, were not of her choosing.

South was India King, her laughing, sunlit photograph next to the most catastrophic of cards – the Tower, showing a man and woman hurtling towards the ground. This card indicated the sudden bolt of understanding. Clare stuck what she had around the photo of India King. Her stepfather should be able to help with more information, thought Clare. She looked back at Charnay's chart – King could have met her through Landman. Or through the Isis Club. She could see no link with Amore Hendricks, but that did not mean there wasn't one.

Clare turned north. On this side of the room there was nothing but glass. She picked up the last card, the Hanged Man, and taped it to the glass. She looked past the taunting smile of the inverted figure. The sea was calm, with the first light beginning to dance on the breaking waves. Clare turned her back to the dawn and looked at the chilling images of death stuck to her walls. The answer was just beyond her – like a movement glimpsed in the corner of the eye, vanishing the moment she looked at it head on. Tears of impotent rage welled up hot and slid down her cheeks. 'What am I not seeing?' Clare fretted. 'What can't *I* see that these girls were blinded for seeing?'

Patience was what she needed. And time. The two things she did not have.

The thunk of the morning newspaper being delivered broke Clare's reverie. The paper was splashed with pictures of the missing girl and a re-run of all the ghoulish details of the dead ones.

Clare felt a strong urge to go for a run. She pulled on her

tracksuit, glad that she could leave off her rain jacket today. The air was crisp as she stretched against the sea wall. It lifted her spirits. She ran fast in the direction of the Waterfront. The morning sea was flat, the massive swell that had battered the shore for days exhausted. She turned back after three kilometres, enjoying the trickle of sweat between her breasts and down her back. The sun had swung up above the mountains, pearling the water. A single fishing boat broke the surface, leaving a trail of shattered colour in its wake. Clare absorbed the stillness of the moment. She would need it in the tumult of the day ahead of her.

Her heart contracted as she rounded Three Anchor Bay. A small group of people clustered around the railings. 'Please not.' Her words hung with the mist of her breath on the cold morning air. Clare slowed down as she neared the group.

'What is it?' she asked.

'Somebody thought they saw a whale,' an old woman explained.

'I don't think it was a whale,' said her wiry companion. 'I'm sure it was that elephant seal. Remember, he was here last year.' The huge animal had wintered here the year before, wallowing on the beach and bellowing mournfully for his lost females. After three lonely weeks he had slipped back into the water and headed back to Marion Island, thousands of miles south-east of Cape Town.

'It would be something if he came back again,' said Clare. The elephant seal had become quite an attraction, and nature conservation had posted a guard to protect him. Clare looked at the smooth surface of the sea, but saw nothing. Just some rubbish bobbing in the little breakers around the rocks.

She went home and downloaded her email. There was a deluge of increasingly frantic messages from her London producer. Clare opened the last one. 'Where is my next batch of footage?' it berated her. 'When will it be here? I have two slots with international broadcasters so where the fuck is it, darling?'

Clare clicked 'reply'. 'It's coming, don't panic, don't panic. Am pursuing a home-grown pornography link, so hang in there. C.' She packed up her interview tapes – with Natalie, with the barmaid from the Isis, as well as two spontaneous ones she'd done later with some of the dancers. And the formal interview with Kelvin Landman. She looked at the tape of her interview with Whitney's mother, Florrie Ruiters, explaining the metastasising hold of the gangs; how easily they picked up young women and worked them. She hesitated for a second and then threw that in too. Not quite as straightforward as Natalie's story, but more common in its murkiness because Whitney and her family were helpless in the face of the expanding predations of the gangs.

Clare was rummaging through her cupboard, deciding what to wear, when the doorbell rang.

'Hello.' Clare pressed the intercom, expecting Riedwaan's voice to reply.

'Hi. It's Tyrone.'

'Who?'

'The barman. From The Blue Room at the Waterfront.' Hope flickered as Clare pressed the intercom.

'Come up.' She phoned Riedwaan. 'The barman from the Waterfront is here. Come over.' She snapped her phone shut as he knocked on her front door. Clare held the door open for him. 'Can I get you something to drink?'

Tyrone followed her into the kitchen. 'Some coffee would be nice.' He was holding a pink rucksack. He put it down on the table, pulling his hand away as if it was dangerous. 'I found this,' he said. He looked down at his hands. The nails were bitten, the nail beds raw, bleeding in places.

'When?' Clare asked.

When I was going home. It's her bag. Theresa's.'

Clare was holding the kettle, about to pour water over the coffee. She repressed an overwhelming urge to hurl the boiling water into his face.

'So you lied to me – you were on duty that Friday night, Tyrone. And why are you only bringing it in now? This is crucial evidence that you've had since Friday night. The night she disappeared. It's now Sunday morning.' Clare stepped very close to him. The smell of too many cigarettes was rank on his breath. 'Do you know how long that has been for Theresa? Can you imagine what has been happening to her? While you worried about whether to hand it over or not, you useless little fuck!'

'I'm sorry. I was afraid. But I've brought it now. Maybe it can help her still?'

Clare turned away, ashamed of her outburst. She poured him coffee, handed him sugar and milk. 'Sit down,' she said. 'Tell me how you found it.'

'It wasn't that busy that night,' he said. 'I closed earlier than usual, about eleven-thirty, when the last customers left. I went up to have a smoke and wait for my lift. I was sitting up on that bench near the drawbridge. There were no cars around. It was so quiet, I could think a little bit.'

'So what happened, Tyrone? While you were thinking?' He sipped the coffee, wishing there was something stronger in it. 'I got up and walked around the parking lot. It's more sheltered there – it was really cold that night. I bumped my foot into this. It was in the shadow next to an empty parking bay.' He made himself touch the bag, pushed it over to Clare. The 'Hello Kitty' cartoon gave its silly, mocking wave.

'I remembered it from when she was in earlier.' There were tears in his eyes when he looked at her. 'She was so friendly. So pretty.'

270

Clare did not touch the bag. There was still the smallest chance that forensics would find something.

'Did you find anything else?' Clare was sure that he had looked.

Tyrone shook his head. 'He was there again. I saw him.'

'Who, Tyrone?' asked Clare. Tyrone put a finger into his mouth. He tore at a strip of skin next to the nail. Blood oozed.

'Landman. Kelvin Landman.' His voice was a whisper. 'He came in just as Theresa was leaving.' He shuddered. 'I saw him look at her. You don't want him to look at you like that if you are a girl.'

'Explain, Tyrone.' Clare's voice was urgent. She wished that Riedwaan would come. Tyrone drew a deep breath, squared his slender shoulders. 'You remember Charnay? And her friend Cornelle? You know they worked for him? Or better to say it like this: he worked them for himself. To death.' His voice was bitter. 'All this trouble with the police now, with the murders. They're everywhere. Some of the local customers are nervous, I think. All the South Africans are careful, even the Jo'burg guys. It has been affecting his business, I think.'

'Hang on. That will be Riedwaan,' she said, responding to the doorbell. Clare let him in and handed him a cup of coffee. Riedwaan shook hands with an anxious-looking Tyrone, then sat down.

'Carry on, Tyrone,' said Clare. 'You'll have to make a statement to the police anyway, so you may as well do it now with Inspector Faizal here.'

Tyrone was trapped, a rabbit in the headlights. 'Theresa came in first, like I told you.'

'Had you seen her before?' asked Riedwaan.

'No. She had never been in before, not while I have worked there. I asked her what her name was when I brought her order. It wasn't busy, so I chatted. She said she was meeting

271

her mom. Just as she was leaving, Kelvin Landman came in with those guys who are always with him.' Tyrone swallowed with difficulty, his throat suddenly dry.

'Did they speak to Theresa?' asked Clare.

'No, like I told you, they just checked her out. I don't think she liked it because she pulled her coat tight around her when she saw them. They are not people you mess with.'

'Then what?' asked Clare.

'Theresa left and I went outside to check if there was anyone else. There wasn't, but I did see Theresa at the end of the jetty where all the yachts are moored. I waved to her, but I don't think she saw me. When I came in, Landman was *vloeking* into his phone. They left quite soon after that. I was glad. I don't think the other customers like them much.'

'Who was Landman with?' asked Riedwaan.

'The only one I knew was Kenny McKenzie,' said Tyrone. 'He grew up near me. I stayed right out of his way.'

'I don't blame you,' said Clare.

'Did you see Theresa again?' asked Riedwaan.

'I didn't. I found her bag much later. At about half past eleven, like I told you.' He put out his hand as if to stroke the bag, but then thought better of it and his hand dropped back into his lap.

'Why did you only come forward now?' asked Riedwaan. 'Why didn't you call the police immediately, when you knew she was missing?'

Tyrone looked sullenly at Riedwaan. 'I know those gangsters, Inspector.' There was disdain in his voice. 'Like you know them. You know what happens if you split.'

'So why are you telling us at all?'

Tyrone twisted his fingers. He looked very young. 'She was a nice girl. But I think I must go now. Thanks for the coffee.' Tyrone stood up.

'Wait,' said Riedwaan, 'I want you to take me to exactly where you found the bag.' Riedwaan called Piet Mouton. He wanted the bag combed for hair and fibres. The pathologist cleared his schedule.

Tyrone watched Clare put on her coat and pick up her bag. Then he said, 'Landman's connection came back.' His voice was thin, exhausted, now that he had unburdened himself of his secret.

'Kenny McKenzie?' asked Clare.

'Not McKenzie, I don't know his name, but he came back at about half past nine. Maybe ten. I didn't serve him. The other barman did because I was busy. He had a scratch on his hand and he asked me for a *lappie*.'

Clare felt her blood chill in her veins. 'Did you give him one?'

'*Ja*, I had a clean cloth in my hand so I gave him that.'

'What did it look like? The scratch?'

'I don't know. Like he'd caught his hand on a bush. Or a cat had scratched him,' said Tyrone. 'He didn't stay long – just had his whiskey and then he was gone again. It was like he was looking for someone. Or something, maybe. I saw him drive away some time later when I was bringing in the outside tables. I don't know where he was in between.'

'What did he look like?' asked Clare.

'Dark hair. Tall,' said Tyrone. 'He looked rich.'

Riedwaan came out of the bathroom, drying his hands.

'Have you done any checks on Otis Tohar?' she asked.

'No. I know the organised crime boys are keeping an eye on him. Nothing, so far.'

'You go ahead. There's something I want to check. Go and meet Piet. I'll catch you later,' said Clare.

She closed the front door behind Riedwaan before he could say anything and turned on her computer, typing in her search

273

question, her body taut with excitement. 'Come, come, come,' she whispered. The French news site she was waiting for flickered to life. She checked on Lebanon first. Not even a blip, apart from a litany of unpunished honour killings. Clare felt her shoulders slump. She had been so sure. Then she tried Sierra Leone, without any real hope. But there was – an endless list of mutilations and amputations. She scrolled through them swiftly.

There it was, what she had been looking for: 'Another young woman murdered', she translated aloud. A French journalist posted to Sierra Leone to witness the evacuation of families of French troops had written the story. The girl's death was bizarre even in the midst of the routine slaughter of a civil war. She was beautiful, despite the grainy distortion of the digital image. Clare was transfixed by the detail of her death. There was a picture of the girl's broken body, the hands bound, the eyes mutilated, the legs grotesquely splayed. Clare manipulated the image, enlarging it as much as possible. Clutched between the girl's hands was a rectangular box. Clare stared at it. A video cassette and a small, silver key.

The shrill summons of her cellphone brought Clare to her feet. 'Hello?' she said sharply.

'Clare, its Rita here.'

'Hi, did you get hold of Cathy King? Will you arrange an interview with her as soon as possible? Get hold of Riedwaan, he's just left. We'll have to see her later.'

'I am with her now, *sisi*, but no one is going to be talking to her again.'

The strength drained out of Clare's legs. 'What do you mean?' she whispered.

'Portia Qaba, her housekeeper, called here. I tried to get Riedwaan, but his phone was off. So me and Joe Zulu came out here. Cathy King is dead. It looks like she took an overdose. Joe thinks it's suicide. So does the pathologist – he is busy with her now.'

'Poor woman,' said Clare. 'Where did you find her?'

'In India's room, on her bed. She must have been watching a video.'

Clare's blood ran cold. 'What was she watching?' asked Clare, sure that she knew the answer.

'It's horrible, Clare. It was a film with her in it. Her with Landman and her husband. Very brutal, very abusive. But there's something very strange.' Rita hesitated, uncertain about her intuition.

'What?'

'The tape was paused in mid-frame. It looked like she had paused it – you see, the remote was right by her hand. And then I looked again. More closely, at the image . . .'

'What did you see?' asked Clare, itching with impatience.

'There's another man there. He must be holding the camera. But you can see him reflected in the window, right at the end. I think I've seen him before, but I don't know his name. Can I bring you the tape now? I just got this feeling that maybe you should talk to him too. About India. It's so terrible, what they did to her eyes.'

'I've seen that tape,' breathed Clare. 'Thank you, Rita, thank you.'

Clare was already in the lounge, scrabbling through the videos on top of her television. She quickly found the one she had taken from India King's house. She pushed the cassette in, fast forwarding through the agonising humiliation of Cathy King. Yes, there it was, right at the end. The man with the camera was mirrored briefly in the plate-glass windows, his mouth slack as he watched, and filmed – mesmerised as the woman was efficiently bound. The camera moved inexorably in until the screen was filled with her face, then only her eyes. Her pupils were dilated with terror. And then, visible for the merest second, and only if you really looked, was a special effect done in post-production: a red flash, then a trickle of fluid as the blue irises were sliced through.

Clare called Riedwaan but he did not pick up. She had to move if anyone was to see Theresa Angelo alive again. Warrants and procedures would create nothing but a lethal delay, so she didn't call the station. Clare grabbed keys and a warm jacket. She manoeuvred her car around the growing knot of people who had come to look at the elephant seal, then made her way down to Beach Road. She looked up hopefully at the penthouse suite of the old Sea Point Tower: Tohar had to be in his apartment – and Theresa *had* to be alive.

49

Clare was out of her car before the security guard had even stood up from the chair in his warm booth. 'I'm meeting Mr Tohar.' She thrust a card into the perplexed guard's hand. Looking past him into the garage, she noticed that Tohar's car was gone. 'It doesn't matter if he's out. I'll see Tatiana.'

He called upstairs and then nodded to Clare, 'She's there.' The guard keyed in the code and the lift delivered Clare to Tohar's flat. Clare stepped onto the plush carpet. The place was silent, apart from a faint sound down the passage.

The door was open just a crack, but Clare could see a woman moving rapidly from the cupboard to the bed and back again. She packed with the efficiency of someone used to moving out quickly and carrying their life away with them in one bag.

Clare knocked. The woman dropped a pile of shirts, her face white.

'Tatiana?' said Clare. She picked up a fine silk scarf and ran it between her fingers. 'Are you going somewhere?'

'No,' she whispered.

Clare touched the beautiful face, its contours blurred, swollen. 'What happened to you?' she asked.

'Nothing. It is nothing. I must finish my packing.'

'Maybe I can help you.' Clare wrote down a phone number

and an address. 'I have the feeling there are not many places where you feel safe,' she said, handing Tatiana the piece of paper. 'Go to Shazneem. She'll help you without any questions.'

Tatiana turned, closed her suitcase. 'What are you looking for?' she asked Clare, slipping the address into her pocket.

'Your husband,' Clare ventured. 'What is your cellphone number? I might need to contact you.'

'I don't know where he is. I am sorry. I have to go.' Tatiana wrote the number down. She picked up the suitcase and walked towards the lift door. She pressed the button to summon it, her hand shaking. She turned to Clare. 'I know why you want to see him.' Clare put her foot between the lift doors, preventing them from closing. 'You think he make those girls disappear, no?' asked Tatiana.

'What do you think?' asked Clare.

'It does not matter what I think,' said Tatiana. 'I don't have papers here so I have nothing to say.'

'Who are you afraid of?' asked Clare. 'Your husband?'

'He is not my husband.'

'Why are you here, then?'

'I am here because I was sent here. Mr Landman send me as a present to Mr Tohar.'

'Did you want to come here?'

Tatiana laughed. 'What could I say? Mr Landman bring me to this country, I must do what he say. I owe him lot of money for my ticket so I must work where he tells me.' She pressed the button for the basement. Clare stepped into the lift.

'And now?' asked Clare. 'Where are you going? Back to Landman?'

'No. I cannot,' said Tatiana. 'Better I die than go back.'

'Let's find you a taxi to take you to the shelter. Shazneem will take you in. I'll call her.'

278

Clare took Tatiana's arm and walked her briskly past the suspicious guard. He was on the phone as soon as they got into Clare's car. She drove to the taxi rank and negotiated a price with a driver. Tatiana got into the back seat and clutched her bag against her slim body. She put her hand into her coat pocket and handed Clare a small bottle. It rattled as Clare took it. Pills. Clare opened the cap and shook a couple onto her hand.

'What are they?' asked Clare. There was a small R in the middle of each tablet.

'Rohypnol,' said Tatiana.

'The rape drug,' said Clare. 'Who is it for?'

Tatiana looked down at her long painted nails. 'Mr Landman used them for the young girls.' Her voice was very quiet. 'It makes it easier when they first start.'

'Young girls where?' asked Clare. She tried to keep the revulsion out of her voice.

Tatiana lifted her head. 'At the Isis Club. Where I work before I come here.' She looked away, was quiet. Then she added, so softly that Clare almost didn't hear her, 'Also when they make the movies.'

'Where did you find them?' asked Clare.

'I find them in Mr Tohar's coat. He come home very late. I do not see him. I just hear him. But I got up early. I find his coat lying in the sitting room. So I pick it up because he hates a mess. And those fell out.'

'When was that?' asked Clare.

'Two nights ago.' She leaned forward and tapped the driver's shoulder. 'We go now?'

Clare stepped back onto the pavement. Two nights ago Theresa Angelo had disappeared.

Six in the morning. Charnay Swanepoel on the promenade had been first.

Six in the evening. The time they had found Amore's body at Graaff's Pool.

Midnight had produced India King.

Like clockwork, one after the other. Clare immediately dialled Tatiana's number, watching as she lifted the phone to her ear. The taxi was only a hundred metres down the road.

'What kind of coat does Tohar wear?' she asked.

'A black one,' said Tatiana. 'Is cashmere. Very expensive from Italy.'

'Thank you.' Clare watched the taxi disappear behind a bus. Theresa Angelo's broken body would turn up when the sun reached its zenith tomorrow – unless Clare got to her before anything terrible happened.

50

Clare called Riedwaan on her way home, willing him to answer. She needed him for back-up. She snapped her phone shut, killing his voice asking her to please leave a message. There was a bad taste in her mouth, and her body ached with tension that she decided to walk off on the promenade. Heavy fog had rolled in from the south-west, and the Green Point foghorn blared anxiously at passing ships. Skeletal fingers of mist were swirling off the sea, making it difficult to see more than a few metres ahead. 'Where is she? Where is she? Where is she?' was the percussion of Clare's stride. She stopped to call Riedwaan again. Then cursed his voicemail and walked on along the promenade, all the way to Clifton and back again.

It was almost dark as she heard the raised voices cut through the evening silence. The fog was disorientating, but the argument sounded as if it was coming from Three Anchor Bay, where the elephant seal, exhausted by his thousand-mile swim, had heaved himself up to rest. Clare walked towards the glow of a fire that the animal's guard had made to keep himself warm. She could see the outline of a man, beside himself with agitation. He lunged at the guard, grabbing him by the front of his jacket and pulling him off his feet.

'Hey!' shouted Clare, running towards them. She went up to the guard, who had fallen back against the railing.

'Are you okay?' she asked him, helping him back on his feet. His attacker was swallowed by the dense fog.

'I'm okay. I'm okay. What is his problem?' The guard was enraged. 'He wants to go now to the boathouse. But nobody can sail out in that swell.'

'Who is he?' asked Clare.

'I don't know. He's a crazy man. He came earlier and he wanted to go to the boathouse. The other people who have boats also wanted to go. So I explained to them that no one can go while the elephant seal is there. Nobody. They don't mind at all. They are happy. Except him. He says he must go. It is his right. I say rubbish. That big seal came thousands of miles to visit here. He can have some peace now until he goes back home.' The guard poured himself some tea from his flask, added four soothing spoons of sugar and drank it down. 'That man tells me he will phone the mayor. I point to the sign and I tell him that the mayor ordered that we close the beach for the seal. Hah!' the guard spat, still furious.

'When was that?' asked Clare.

'That was this afternoon. Then he came back now. First he tried to give me money. I said no. He asked me if I wanted more money. I said no again. I tell him he must go away. That is when he started shouting at me, saying I must let him in. He grabbed me here,' he said, pointing to the front of his jacket.

Clare went to the railing and looked down. There were three boathouses below, the doors bolted against the weather. In the gloom on the other side of the beach was a slipway that dipped under the promenade and came out at the high-water mark on the beach. Here, there was another bolted door in the granite sea wall that curved around to the lighthouse about three hundred metres away. The great animal lay inert on the beach, its large eyes blinking whenever the lights of a car disturbed it. The slipway had been blocked off since the arrival of the seal

She turned to the guard. 'Do you have binoculars?' she asked, her heart beating faster.

He ducked into his booth and handed her his glasses. Clare looked down at the seal. She could make out the bristles around his stubby nose. She lifted the glasses up to the door. It was tightly locked, but there were tracks on the sand. Slowly, she swung the glasses around the sea wall. The granite was pitted and scarred by the sea. There was a glimmer of light about fifty metres away where the sea wall dipped into the next inlet. She focused carefully. It seemed to emanate from the stone itself, then vanished. She handed the glasses back to the guard.

'Thank you,' she said, light-headed with hope. She snapped open her phone. Two rings, and he answered.

'Riedwaan,' she whispered. 'Where are you?'

'I'm in Bellville. With Dr. Death.'

'Riedwaan, I think I've found her. How soon can you get here?'

'Give me half an hour. I'll be with you. Where are you?'

'I'm above the Three Anchor Bay boathouses. She's here, I'm sure of it.'

'How can you be so sure?' he asked.

'I went to see Otis Tohar.'

'Tohar?' asked Riedwaan. 'How is he connected?'

'I'm not sure, Riedwaan. But I'm going to find out.'

'What are you going to do now?'

'I'm going after her, Riedwaan.'

'I'll be there as soon as I can. I'll get Joe and Rita to organise back-up for you.'

'Be quick.'

'Don't ever tell Phiri that we had this conversation. He'll have my balls for breakfast.'

'What good would that do me?'

Clare closed her phone and went back to her flat for a torch. She could not wait for Riedwaan, there was no time. She unlocked the drawer beside her bed. The cold stillness of the gun was comforting. She picked it up, checked it was loaded and slipped it into the inside pocket of her trousers. It was like holding an old lover, the familiar shape snug against her thigh.

She looked through the untidy heap of paper on her desk. The map was not there. It wasn't in the kitchen either. Clare looked next to her bed. Nothing. She was sure she had kept the map of the underground tunnels. She looked next to her bed again. It had slipped behind the headboard. She coaxed it out, trying not to tear the thin paper.

Clare spread the map of the old drainage system in front of her. On it, she marked the places where the bodies had been found. It was the one near Sushi-Zen that interested her most. The storm-water drain opened right onto the patch of lawn where Xavier had found India's body.

She traced the route of the tunnel. It ran under the lighthouse and then snaked back towards the promenade wall. Here it branched, and a second, narrower, tunnel seemed to lead to the slipway at Three Anchor Bay. There must surely be an entrance nearby, leading to the boathouse. If these girls had been held there, then that would be the way in. Or, for the killer, a way of getting them out. There was plenty of space to hide someone there and, with a genuine boathouse in front, to deflect suspicion.

Clare sprinted to the storm-water drain near Sushi-Zen. The entrance stank of human excrement. She held her breath and stepped over the filth. The darkness closed in on her. She switched on her torch. A rat, its eyes gleaming red, scuttled past her. She forced herself to keep going, bearing right all the while, towards the boathouses. And praying her instinct was right.

51

Theresa's head ached. She remembered helping the man and then the excruciating pain of the blow. The wound oozed if she moved, and warm blood matted her hair. She breathed in deeply, trying to order her jumbled thoughts. If she had even a chance of survival she would have to make sense of this. Of him. He had bound her hands and feet tightly. Blood had trickled into her eyes, but she forced them open, pushing away the agony in her head. Theresa had no idea how long she had been unconscious. The man had parked his car. She had heard his footsteps as he came round to open the boot. The air was fetid. Her skin had crawled at the exploratory touch of his hands, smooth and clammy – it was like being touched by something dead. The man hoisted Theresa over his shoulder, but she kept her body limp. He grunted. She was heavier than he had bargained for.

Theresa was not the sort of girl to blow over in the wind, her father always teased her. The thought of her father made her weak with hopelessness. How would he find her? Theresa opened her eyes. The car was parked underneath a stone shelter. The man pulled a heavy wooden door open and carried her into a darkness so dense it almost seemed solid. He dumped Theresa onto something lumpy and hard. Pain shot through her shoulders that had been twisted backwards. She heard him breathing deeply, satisfied. Theresa did not move.

Then he was gone, slamming the door shut. The key grated in the lock. He shot two bolts across. They were obviously stiff, but the door was too thick to hear if he swore or not. Like runnels, tears ran through the blood on Theresa's face and into her hair. She shifted her weight off her arms, relieving the pain in her shoulders and neck. She was barely able to move – he had tied her expertly.

It was not only dark but also cold where she lay. She spread her fingers out wide, trying to feel what it was she was lying on. The fibres were tight, hard, pressing into her hips and her shoulders. Rope, thought Theresa, a great coiled-up rope. She listened to the muffled thudding.

'The sea. Where?' Her voice in the darkness startled her. It sounded cracked, as if it belonged to someone else, someone old. She thought about the girls she'd read about who had been found dead on the promenade. Their killer had not yet been caught. Panic rippled through her. Theresa breathed in and out carefully, forcing herself to keep calm. She turned away from the wave of horror bearing down on her.

'Work it out. Work it out.' The darkness was filling with tiny sounds. She focused on them, distracting herself by trying to work out what they were.

She thought of the promenade, where she and her mother sometimes went for walks. They parked at the swimming pool and walked from there, enjoying the whoosh of air that the skaters dragged behind them, the nannies with their over-dressed charges on the swings. She retraced the grey ribbon of stone from memory, counting benches, deciding whether they were yellow or blue, placing orange dustbins, cracked paving, snatches of overheard conversation. Theresa reached the turning point of her imaginary walk just as she saw the boathouses at Three Anchor Bay. The man would have driven his car down the slipway and unloaded her there. No one would hear her here. There would have been no one to see her, either. No one would remark on an expensive car parked on the slipway. If anyone saw a man get out of the car with a girl they would look away. At night it was only street prostitutes who brought their clients here – rich men, sailors with shore leave, whoever was paying. A woman's scream would attract no attention – even if it was heard.

Theresa turned her face to the wall. Dread overwhelmed her. She closed her eyes and let herself slip back into oblivion. She did not hear the skritch, skritch in the recesses of her cell. The rats – fattened of late, and replete – waited for their moment.

Theresa surfaced despite herself, awoken by the resistance of the rusted bolts, her throat burning with thirst. She listened to his approaching footsteps. She couldn't bear to die this thirsty. She kept her eyes shut. She would fight to stay alive. She couldn't bear the thought of dying at all.

The man was close now. She had to buy herself some time, recover from the blow to her head, force herself to think. His smell, pungent with adrenaline, assaulted her nostrils. His breath brushed her cheek, moved over her lips. She did not flinch. The man's warm breath moved down her throat and neck, followed by a hand that traced the outline of her body without quite touching it. A low moan escaped him, thick with desire and relief. Theresa's skin burnt when he held his hand over her breast. She flinched, unable to contain the revulsion. He must have looked at her face again, because she felt his breath on her throat once more and then it was gone. She felt his hands at her ankles. He was untying the ropes there. The blood rushed painfully back into her feet. He pushed her over and released her hands.

Every fibre of her being recoiled, but she willed herself to

287

stay limp, silencing the scream burning in her throat. His hands moved over her body. Purposeful, this time. He removed her shoes with practised dexterity. Her jeans went next. Her top was more difficult, but he slipped first one arm then the other out, like a mother undressing an infant. Then he jerked it over her head. The cord of the hood scraped her face. She felt the cold blade on her skin as he sliced off her bra and panties. The trickle of blood where the scalpel nicked her was hot. He traced the hips bracketing her hollowed stomach. His fingers passed over the mound of dark hair and lingered on the small mole on her thigh. Theresa wondered if being a virgin made her feel worse.

The man bent close, burying his nose in the hollow of her throat. Slowly he moved up towards her ear, breathing her in, sniffing for the essence of her. His wet lips left a trail of slime on her skin. Nausea pressed at the base of her tongue. He knew she was ready for him. He put his lips close to her ear and stroked her eyelids with infinite softness.

'Wake up, beautiful. We're going to have some fun together.' The ordinariness of his voice pressed the air from her lungs. She had to look this nightmare in the face. She opened her eyes.

He smiled at her. His face was familiar, nice-looking, the man who had waved at her from the yacht. Friendly lines crinkled the corners of his eyes. He was so close, she could see his thick eyelashes. They were very long – like a girl's.

'How is your head?'

He was so solicitous that, before she could help it, she replied, 'It hurts.'

'Here, sit up. Have something to drink.' He helped her up and gave her some water.

'Who are you?' she asked him. 'Why have you brought me here?'

'Do you like movies?' he asked, as if she had not spoken at all.

'Yes,' Theresa said. She would try something else. 'I'm cold,' she said. 'Do you think I could have my clothes back?'

He looked at her naked body. But Theresa's question had shifted something. Very briefly, he lost the power to direct the interaction. Theresa felt the movement deep within the chrysalis of hope she was holding fast.

'My clothes are there,' she said, pointing as well as she could to the pile of garments hurled into the corner.

'No, no,' he said. 'I have something much better for you. Something for a girl of mine.'

He reached behind a chair and pulled out two shopping bags. Theresa recognised the exclusive labels.

'Put these on.'

He pulled out a very short skirt and a transparent top. The underwear was sleazy and uncomfortable to wear. She put it on, biting back her repugnance as she slipped the blue garter onto her thigh. The boots were blue suede. They came halfway up her thighs. The boots and the clothes were tight. The man must have had someone smaller in mind when he'd bought them. When she was dressed she stood up straight, turning slowly for him.

'How do I look?' she asked, marvelling at her ability to summon a coquette out of her terror. She might survive if she kept her wits about her. If she kept talking. It seemed to throw the man off track. If she lost it, then her clothes would stay in the pile in the corner. Her skin crawled. Her clothes would be covered by somebody else's in a month or two, just as her jeans and hoodie were covering someone else's now.

'Is this where you brought the other girls?' she asked. Her voice was so light it bounced off the heavy stone walls.

'It is. Cosy, isn't it?'

'Yes,' said Theresa. 'Did you watch TV together?'

He patted the large set. A video machine was balanced precariously on top of it. 'We did. We watched TV and we made a bit of TV too. Just a little home movie. That's what we are going to do, too.'

'That's what the costume is for?' He nodded. 'You must have known I was an actress, then.'

'All women are actresses,' he said. 'Born to it.' He stood up. The focus was back in his eyes. Theresa felt very afraid. The fragment of power that she had imagined she had held was gone. 'Stand up,' he ordered. 'We have a lot to do.'

Theresa stood up. 'My name is Theresa,' she said. 'Theresa Angelo. I want to go home. Let me go now and no one needs to know anything.'

She did not see his hand pull back before it caught her across the jaw. The blow knocked her against the wall with dizzying force. She slid down, wedged behind the bed of ropes.

'You dirty little bitch. You don't speak again unless I tell you.' He leaned over and yanked her back to her feet. He held her fast while he rearranged her clothes and hair to his liking. Then he took her left hand. Her bones crackled as he folded her fingers tightly around a small silver key. He took a length of blue rope from his pocket and wound it with great speed around the hand, trapping the key inside. It cut into her palm. Blood trickled between her fingers, but she did not moan or pull back. Then he kissed her on the cheek.

'Don't worry. It'll be fun. I'm sure you'll put your talent to excellent use in just a minute.' He pulled a metal stool forward. 'Sit here. We're going to watch a movie together.'

There was no way she was able to sit on the stool, so Theresa perched. The skirt he had made her wear rode up her bottom. The heels of the boots were too high, and her toes were pinched. Her flesh was purpling with cold.

'Who's in it?' she asked.

He stopped and looked at her, working out what would be the best light angle. 'I'm not sure you'd know them. Some girls I entertained here. You'll see. They were fast learners.' He leaned over and tucked her hair behind her ear. 'Smile now,' he ordered.

She made herself smile into the camera that he had set up on the tripod. It was a professional camera. Small, light, digital. Used for making the best quality documentaries. She concentrated on the camera's make, on what else was in the room, on the man's actions. He inserted a tape. That gave her some hope. She still had two hours.

He was setting up lights, plugging things in, when his cellphone rang. The sound ricocheted through the space. The man scrabbled in his pockets, swearing to himself. He looked at the screen – it was clearly a call he couldn't ignore.

'Hello.' Theresa's heart contracted. Why was an ordinary person, a person who other people phoned, doing this to her?

'What do you want?' he said into the phone. There was a clear note of fear in his voice. 'No, I've told you. I'm working on it. These deals take time.' The man started to pace, a caged animal in the small space. He was quiet, listening to whoever had called him. 'You know that you will get all your money and more. I just can't give it to you now. There is no risk for you. Or your partners.' Theresa's legs started to cramp where the tops of the boots cut into her calves. She stood up awkwardly, trying to get the blood to flow again.

'Okay, I'll come. I'll see you in . . .' He looked at his watch. 'In half an hour.' He was standing right next to Theresa, apparently oblivious of her presence, when she screamed out for help.

Enraged, he snapped his phone shut and kicked her. She scrambled as she fell onto the ropes. 'No one is going to come.

Nobody. It's just us here.' Then, taking a length of rope, he hobbled her. He giggled as she stumbled and sent a stone skidding under the stool, almost knocking it over. Blood welled from under Theresa's torn toenail, staining the blue boot. She bit her lip to stop herself from crying out.

'Like a little filly,' he sneered, 'a filthy little filly. Have fun. There are lots of movies here for you to watch. That's the key to them.' He pointed to the key in her hand. You take that and open that cabinet over there – everything you've ever wanted to watch is inside it.'

He leaned over and kissed her on the cheek before he left. His footfalls receded. She heard the slam of the heavy doors, the bolts crashing into place. Theresa breathed in steadily, then out again. She would not give in to the sobs filling her chest to bursting point. She would find a way out. She stood up. The hobble made it difficult to walk, and her leg hurt where he had kicked her. She tested it, and was relieved when it took her weight as she limped over to the television and put the key on top of it. Her face also ached where he had hit her, and there was blood and a piece of broken tooth in her mouth. She spat it out on the floor. She looked around her prison cell and prayed that it would not be her grave.

52

Though cold and afraid, Theresa eventually fell asleep, and when she woke up she could hear the sweep of the sea. The ocean heaved mutinously against the retreating tide. Slowly, she stood up, trying not to fall as she felt the slender strips of blue rope pull tightly at her ankles.

She shuffled around her prison, the rope cutting into her tender flesh. She discovered another small room adjacent to the room she had been dumped in. There was only one door. It was made of very heavy wood covered with a protective sheet of steel. She stood next to it, resting her head against the cold stone. No sound at all penetrated from the outside.

'Help me,' she called. 'Help me.' Her voice, harsh with yearning for her mother, would not be heard on the other side. Theresa took her hoodie from the pile of clothes on the floor and pulled it over her head. She knew that the man would be back, and every cell in her body contracted in horror at the thought of his return. But if he didn't come back, she would die here of starvation. His return, she realised, was her only hope. Feeling sick at the meagreness of that hope, she put her palms together in a reflex of prayer.

She remembered the key, fetched it and inserted it into the cheap padlock on the cupboard next to the television set. The door swung open. It contained seven video cassettes. 'Alice in Wonderland' was written on the first. The others were untitled. Each one had been packed into a red heart-shaped box – the kind often used for wedding videos. Each box swung from a chain attached to a small hook. There was a twist of hair in the small plastic holder where the bride's name should have been inserted. At the end of the row of boxes was an empty hook. Theresa's heart pounded. *Her* hook.

The sharp crack of bolts being shot back startled Theresa. She closed the cupboard and sat down on the coil of ropes. The door opened and the man came in, bringing with him the dankness of the slipway and the muffled sounds beyond the boathouse walls. Theresa braced herself. She knew instinctively what was in those videos. There was going to be no rehearsal for her. She doubted that there had been one for any of the other girls. There would be just this one performance. Her life hung from the slender thread of her intelligence and luck.

The man was wearing a heavy black overcoat. He placed the medical bag and the irises he was carrying on the table against the wall. This time he did not look at Theresa. He opened the bag and brought out a scalpel, holding it up. The blade gleamed in the dimness. The man licked his lips as he set it down precisely. He checked the camera.

Only then did he look at Theresa. He was displeased. He turned around and picked up the scalpel again. He inserted his finger at the neck of her hoodie, his knuckle sharp under her throat. Then he yanked hard, slicing the blade through the material. Her top fell open, exposing her to the cold. Tears splashed down her cheeks, hot and uncontrollable. He smiled, pleased with her now. He pushed her down onto the stool, swinging her around so that she faced the television. He switched on the camera, focused it on her. Leaning forward, he lifted her hair from her face and adjusted the focus again.

'I have such a show for you. You are a lucky girl.'

'My name is Theresa,' she said stubbornly. 'Who is in these films?'

His shoulders twitched. 'You'll see. You'll see. You'll like it, I know, because they all did. And then it will be your turn.' He reached for the remote and switched on the television. Then he ducked behind his camera and started the tape rolling.

'Why don't you use your key?' he asked, his voice seductive, soothing. He had pointed to the cupboard. 'We're going to make our own little wedding video.' Theresa did not move. Her body prickled with cold sweat. 'Open it,' he snarled. 'I know you've already looked in there.'

'No,' said Theresa. 'I won't watch.'

He leaned close to her, his breath hot on her face. 'Yes, you will. And it will be the last thing you see.' His nose crinkled at the smell of her fear. 'You choose the tape. That means you have a say in your own ending. Otherwise I choose it all for you.'

Theresa felt time slipping away from her. The spark of hope she had coaxed into life died. She opened the cupboard and chose a tape. She ran her finger over the lock of hair fastened to the cover.

'Who is this one about?' she asked.

'You'll see now,' he said. 'Just give it to me.'

'Tell me about her. I want to know who she is, what her name is. Tell me.' Theresa demanded. 'I want to know who it is. I want to know why you have me here. I want you to let me go home.'

This enraged him. She wasn't doing things properly. She wasn't obedient like the other girls. She was making the sequence of the film in his head go awry. He grabbed the cassette from Theresa's hand and shoved it into the video machine. Theresa scrambled backwards and wedged herself behind the pile of rope against the wall. The man had her cornered. He struck her twice across the face. Her head cracked into the wall behind her. He grabbed her arms and she bit him, her teeth breaking the skin. The taste of his blood made her gag as she spat it out.

He laughed. 'Just do as I say and you'll be fine. Now you're really going to look a mess for your star role.' He dragged her up, grazing her skin on the ropes, and positioned her on the stool again. Theresa was limp with exhaustion. She had stopped resisting. But he held her by the hair and punched her in the stomach anyway. Theresa clenched her teeth so that she didn't cry out. She did not want to provoke him into doing it again – did not want to give him the pleasure of hearing her moan. He stood in front of her, his face relaxed, now that she was under control. He shoved a knee between her thighs and splayed her legs. Then he wedged the irises under her arm, almost toppling her from the stool.

The tape wasn't rolling yet. Theresa had clawed several minutes of her life back from him. She wanted more.

'Let's make love first,' she whispered through her cracked lips. 'Let's make love and then watch your film.'

'You little piece of filth. I have you to do with as *I* please. You watch this now. You'll see quite soon enough that you will have all the time in the world to indulge every little fantasy you've ever had.' He flicked 'play' and the screen flickered to life, bringing its ghostly violence into the room.

Theresa could see that the film had been through post-production. Someone had watched it before her, had seen whatever she was going to see, had edited and tweaked it. Theresa wouldn't be here if this person had said something, done something. The thought sent a surge of rage through her pain-racked body.

The camera was fixed on a girl huddled in the centre of a

room. She was alone, her arms wound tight around her knees. Her bone-thin shoulders shook occasionally. Theresa could see that the hand she cradled protectively had bled, staining the skin on her knee. The images sucked the sound from the room, and soon the girl's ragged breathing filled the dank boathouse. Theresa looked over at the man. The wet, pink tip of his tongue had crept out of his parted lips. She watched in revulsion as it glistened its way from one corner of his mouth to the other, knowing, anticipating what was coming on the screen.

The sudden click of a door opening jolted Theresa's attention back to the television. The girl's head had shot up at the same sound. Her large black eyes were glazed over in horror at what she could see off-camera. The camera moved in close until her eyes filled the screen. Theresa heard the faintest click and looked over to the source of the sound. The man had trained the camera directly onto her face. She knew instantly that he would have her in the same terrible close-up as the girl cowering on the screen. Then he panned to include Theresa, as well as the film she was watching.

She saw the four men prowl around the cowering girl like hyenas. The girl lifted her head. Her earrings – delicate crucifixes – flashed in the light. The men conferred briefly, then decided who was going to get the first, the freshest meat. Then the first one fell upon her. The others helped – subduing a leg here, there an arm. That was only necessary at first. It did not take very long for her frail, bloodied body to go limp and then jerk unsatisfyingly. A rag doll broken by the sea of rage that battered her. By now, the men were bored. It was over. They straightened themselves up, wiped themselves clean. One lit a cigarette, flipping the match onto the girl, where it died on her skin. Theresa's flesh crawled when she saw the man kneel over the girl, unzip his pants, and place

297

his penis in her unresisting mouth. His movements were rhythmic, swift, and then he stepped back, satisfied. The girl twitched onto her side and did not choke. Then the screen went black. The first part was over.

The tape whirred on, but Theresa could not bear to watch more.

'You're a powerful director.' Her voice clattered into the silence, startling him, breaking the spell. He pressed 'pause': her comment had interrupted his mad flow. The image that hung on the screen looked familiar. She saw the time code on his camera flash rhythmically – she had as much time as was left on the tape: ninety minutes. She would not accept, though, that she had as little power as the girl she had just watched being brutalised. Theresa would fight. But her only weapon was to be quicker than the man on the other side of the camera.

'We could work well together,' she said. There was no mercy in him, she knew, but perhaps if she was useful she might survive a little longer. She summoned the actress in herself and imagined herself walking on stage, the audience obscured by the lights shining in her eyes. Theresa imagined her mother out there. The thought calmed her. It gave her the strength to improvise.

'We could try something new.' She prayed that he wouldn't hit her again.

'How old are you?' the man asked.

'I'm sixteen.' replied Theresa Angelo. 'I'm old enough.'

'Perfect,' he said. 'Perfect. It's time to get you ready, then.'

'Do you want to make love to me?' Theresa asked again, with a forced note of invitation.

'Oh, I will, my dear. I will. But not in the vulgar way you are offering in order to save your worthless little skin,' he spat at her. 'Now let's get you ready for your final act.' He had a hairbrush in his hand. 'Make yourself look decent,' he ordered.

Theresa took the brush and pulled it through her hair, trying to avoid the parts that were caked with dried blood. She made herself talk to him. It delayed him, broke into his fantasy. He had to start again after each answer.

'What kind of directing have you done?' she asked. 'Where did you learn?'

'I did some work for the Isis Club. Adult movies.' He turned back to the rope he was plaiting and twisting.

'That market is so saturated, isn't it?' said Theresa, chattily. 'I've done voice-overs for a few. Tell me about your market. These films you make here. Do you sell them? On the Internet? Mail order? That first one we saw was a good simulation. That girl was good.'

He looked at her, flustered. 'That was not a simulation. You'll see. These are the real thing.'

Theresa kept her attention on him. Hope flared in her again: she heard a sound – a single sound that stood out from the boom of the surf on the walls and the bleak moan of the foghorn at Green Point. She held her breath, but he seemed not to have heard it.

'Snuff movies?' Her voice was cheerful. She could have been asking for apple juice.

He laughed. 'You could call them that, I suppose. You could call them educational films. They teach a lesson.'

'Alice? Was she filth?' His hand froze. 'Your wife? A girlfriend? Your mother?'

'Why are you so interested in Alice?' He walked very slowly towards her. He had picked up a whip, was flicking it rhythmically across his left palm.

'That was the name on the first tape. I imagine they go in order? I thought that if I knew her I could get into character better.' The sound again. Closer this time. Louder. 'Tell me about her, the first one. Was she your mother?' The whip licked painfully at her ankle. Theresa had touched a raw spot.

'No, she wasn't my mother. That bitch died, as she should have, when I was very young.'

'So, who was she? A girlfriend? Someone who let you down?' The whip flicked again, ripping through the fabric of Theresa's blouse, leaving a red welt on her exposed belly.

'Alice was my big sister. Did she do her duty?' He pushed his face, purpled with congested blood, into hers. His breath was hot, rank on her face.

'What did she do to you? It must have been terrible.' Theresa's voice was cajoling, enticing.

'She was a slut, like you. Like all of you. Liked to know, liked to watch. Pretending to be so innocent, so "I couldn't help it" – when you know very well it's you yourself who is the cause.' He twisted her nipple viciously, pinching it, savouring the pain he saw in her eyes. Her fresh flow of involuntary tears seemed to calm him again, and he recovered himself. He turned and switched on the camera. Theresa hoped fervently that she had not been imagining the sounds beyond the room, beyond its darkness.

'Tell me about the others. What did they do for you?' The questions were a mistake. She would have given anything to snatch her words back: she had reminded the man of his purpose.

'They were a lot more docile than you. Better behaved. Just did what they were told, stupid little bitches. They thought, I suppose, that if they made me happy it would be easier for them. Like you think that if you distract me it will be easier for you.' He came towards her with the rope. 'It won't. You are going to watch them all now. You'll see what happened to them. Before and after. So you turn that slutty

little mind of yours to your performance. Give me your hand,'
he ordered.

He made two swift, deep cuts on the palm – across the
lifeline, through the heartline. He picked up the key and folded
her bleeding hand around it. Then he began to intricately
bind her hand. She watched in fascinated horror as her hand
– so familiar, the nails bitten down slightly – was transformed
into a bound obscenity.

He knelt in front of her and smiled. 'What lovely eyes, my
lamb. I'm afraid they will be next. As soon as I've fixed your
feet.'

It had been a while since she'd heard the sounds that had
sustained her. She felt the fierce resilience of her body – blindly
wanting to keep itself alive – ebb away. The fog of terror almost
overwhelmed her. She put her free hand down to steady
herself, unexpectedly feeling the smooth touch of the stone
she'd tripped over earlier. There the sound was again. This
time, though, he heard it too. He looked up, alert, listening.
But he returned to his task: as soon as he'd bound her feet,
it would be over.

Theresa lifted the stone as high as she could and smashed
it down on his skull. He pitched forward with a moan of
rage. She hit him again, marvelling at the smoothness of the
object in her hands. He lay still at her feet, blood oozing from
the back of his head. And once again, Theresa lifted the stone
high, at the ready, but this time she did not hit him.

A bunch of keys lay on the table. She fumbled for a moment
and fitted a large one snugly in the lock, barely aware of the
rust inside the mechanism as she turned it. Then she pulled
the door open and hurtled through, slamming it behind her.
She stood still in the dank tunnel, trying to orientate herself
in the dim light filtering from the stone chamber behind her.
From her left, she could hear someone calling. She turned

towards the voice and made her way as fast as she could, feeling her way down the dark tunnel. The voice was getting louder. Theresa paused to listen. It was a woman, calling her name.

'I'm here,' she meant to shout, but her voice was just above a whisper. She felt her way along the tunnel. The walls were rough and covered with slime. In places, the stone gave way and Theresa could feel a cold rush of air that seemed to indicate a smaller, subsidiary passageway. She kept her mind on the voice calling from up ahead, and felt rather than saw the bend in the tunnel wall. But as she rounded it, her heart leapt.

A woman holding a torch was running towards her. Theresa collapsed into Clare Hart's arms.

'Please, please take these off.' She was scrabbling pointlessly at the tight boots. Clare had a knife in her other hand.

'Hold still,' she said, inserting it into the top of one boot, and then the other. She made deft incisions, slicing through the suede, nicking Theresa only once. 'Where is he?'

Theresa pointed to the door. 'In there. I hit him.' Her voice was very faint. The adrenaline that had kept her going had ebbed away. She was on the verge of collapse. Clare called Riedwaan.

'Where the fuck are you?' he shouted into the phone.

'I've got her, Riedwaan, Theresa Angelo. She's safe. We need an ambulance.' Her words came out in a rush.

'Where are you, Clare? How can I send anything if I don't know where you are?'

'I'm in the storm-water drains. There's a tunnel behind the boathouse at Three Anchor Bay – the one on the far side of the slipway, where the elephant seal is. We need an ambulance for this girl. And I think one for Tohar. She's wounded him.'

'I'm at your flat. I'll be with you in a minute. Just get out of there. Get yourselves above ground.' Panic pulsed through Riedwaan's voice, galvanising Clare.

'Up you get, Theresa.' She gripped her arm firmly and pulled her up. The girl winced as Clare's fingers dug into the bruises on her arms. But she managed to get to her feet, leaning heavily on Clare's shoulder.

'We must lock him in. He won't let me go if he comes after us,' Theresa pleaded. Clare hesitated, the urgency of getting Theresa out and onto the promenade impelling her forward. 'Please,' said Theresa. 'We must.'

'Okay.' Clare capitulated. She turned back into the darkness, holding Theresa's hand to steady her. The door that Theresa had appeared from was slightly ajar. Clare pushed it open and looked inside. She took in the coil of rope, the table, the television, the camera. There was an overturned chair and a blood smear. But he was gone. Tohar was nowhere to be seen in the claustrophobic space. Her stomach lurched in horror. She turned towards Theresa, who was leaning against the tunnel wall where Clare had left her.

'Come, Theresa.' She grabbed hold of her hand, panic clutching at her throat as she pulled her in the direction of the boathouse. 'Come now.'

Theresa did not need to ask why. Fury welled up in her throat. Fury at herself for not striking that final blow. She should have known: third time lucky. She followed Clare. Her ears strained for sounds beyond the clatter of their feet – but she could make nothing out. She imagined the holes in the wall, the dark places where he might be hiding, waiting for her.

Clare had come in from the storm-water drain on the other side of the lighthouse, making her way through the subterranean passages. Clare gripped Theresa's hand painfully tight – as much to keep herself together as to keep Theresa with her. Her foot caught painfully on a rock and Clare dropped her torch, the sharp crack instantly snuffing its comforting light. Theresa's heart felt as if it would burst as the darkness enveloped her, sharpening her terrible sense that they were not alone in those tunnels.

Clare pushed herself back onto her feet and pulled Theresa up with her. She waited a moment for her eyes to adjust, and then headed towards the gleam of light coming from where she hoped the boathouses were. Twenty paces brought them up against a heavy door. Clare pushed hard, and it swung reluctantly inwards, every joint and bolt groaning. She stumbled through, with Theresa right behind her. Tohar's car gleamed in the faint light.

'There's the exit,' said Theresa, her whisper ghostly in the dark. They made their way around the car.

'Ssh,' whispered Clare, her hand stopping Theresa. It came again from the passage. A sibilant noise, as if something heavy was being dragged. Clare pushed the door closed and moved a heavy coil of rope in front of it. Fear squeezed at her throat, making it difficult to breathe. Theresa Angelo had no colour left in her face. She shook convulsively. But her voice was calm when she spoke. Clare was beginning to understand how she had managed to survive that far.

'The door's over there,' Theresa pointed. 'But there are two padlocks.' They heard the dragging sound again, closer this time, right near the door. And they heard a curse – though the voice had been rendered unrecognisable by pain and rage.

Once again, Clare took Theresa's hand. Her eyes had accustomed themselves to the dimness. Light filtered through chinks in the double door. She could make out bolts held in place with the huge padlocks. 'Hide behind the car. Keep behind me.' Theresa crumpled next to the rear wheel of the Jaguar. Clare had drawn her gun from its hiding place. There was a thud on the inner door. It shifted slightly. She aimed at the bottom lock of the boathouse door. The sound of the shot deafened her, but she steadied her hands and again took aim. The second lock exploded off the padlock just as the inner door burst open. Theresa screamed, scrambling to her feet. She pulled Clare after her, shoving the door open. The cool air welcomed them as they stumbled onto the filthy slipway.

'Clare,' said Riedwaan. Then he caught Theresa and held her against his chest. 'Theresa?' he asked. She nodded, beyond speech.

'Riedwaan,' Clare was hoarse. 'He's in there. He followed us.'

'Here's our back-up.' Clare looked up to see Rita Mkhize and three uniformed men from the hostage unit. 'You go up, Clare. The ambulance is on its way.' Riedwaan stepped back from her, holding back tears of relief at seeing her safe. From inside the boathouse there was the sound of a door closing. 'Let's get him.' The men followed him as he pushed the boathouse door open.

Clare led Theresa Angelo back to street level. 'Can I call my mom?' Clare handed over her cellphone. 'You dial, please.' Clare keyed in the number and waited for it to ring. A woman's frantic voice answered immediately. Clare handed the phone to Theresa.

'Mom? Mommy, it's me.'

Taking the phone from the sobbing girl, Clare gave Mrs Angelo directions. Then they went to wait for the ambulance, which would soon join the steadily increasing number of vehicles flashing their emergency lights.

Joe Zulu came over with two blankets. He wrapped one around Theresa. '*Eish, sisi*, I am very happy to see you.' The other he handed to Clare. 'And you, Clare.' He had ordered coffee at the petrol station. He heaped sugar into the cups, which he gave to the two of them. Theresa's hands were shaking so much that he held the paper cup for her to sip.

305

The ambulance pulled up just as Theresa's mother arrived. The car she was in had barely stopped before she was hurtling across the lawn. Mrs Angelo wrapped her arms around her child and held her as if she wanted to absorb her back into her body. Clare watched as mother and daughter turned and together collapsed into the arms of the man who had driven Mrs Angelo there. 'My baby,' he breathed into Theresa's blood-matted hair.

'I'll follow you to the hospital,' Mr Angelo said to the paramedics, helping his wife and daughter inside. Then he turned to Joe Zulu. 'Thank you.' His voice was hoarse with emotion.

Joe shrugged. 'She's the one who found Theresa,' he said, pointing to Clare. Mr Angelo turned to her.

'Thank you,' he said again. There was nothing else to be said. Clare simply nodded. Her thoughts were with Riedwaan now, deep inside the snaking underground tunnels below their feet.

53

Tohar forced himself up from the floor after the little bitch had dared to assault him. She would pay for that – as well as for everything else. He had followed her down the passage, towards the car. He smirked when he realised that she would be trapped in the boathouse. The keys for those locks were snug in his pocket. It might be fun to have a little bit of a game first. The other little tarts had been so tame in the end, acquiescing without any fight. Not as much fun as he had imagined. The Rohypnol had its uses, but it made them all so limp. This one hadn't had a dose yet, so there must still be quite a bit of fight in her.

The explosion of the first shot knocked Tohar off his feet. The second sent him scuttling back down the tunnel. The girl was not alone. Who had found her? He went into his studio, as he called it, and hid behind the bed of coiled rope. He traced a pattern there that one of his lovely girls had made with the blood that had drip, drip, dripped from her neatly cut throat. So much blood, even after being dead for a full half-hour. He had been surprised at that. And chagrined that it had spoilt the blouse he had specially bought. He had had to change her top. That had been difficult because her head had flopped annoyingly backwards. Her outfit had been spoiled. So he had been pleased when he got the next one. He had enjoyed her. They had been so baffled, the first ones, so uncompre-hending. Had pleaded so nicely. Not like this stupid little bitch, who had just criticised and asked questions. He was doing some poor man a favour by getting rid of her.

The sound at the door made Tohar freeze.

'Come out,' somebody called. There seemed to be several people at the door – all looking for him.

Tohar felt his bowels loosen. There was a boat in the room, and he quickly crouched behind it. The rasp of his breath sawed through the damp air. He tried to steady its rhythm, and also the hammer blows of his heart against his ribs. He listened. Nothing but the boom of the surf against the sea wall. The taste of fear was sour in his mouth. Fear and rage had formed into a small hard stone that had lodged behind his breastbone – like a tumour, he thought. A tumour just like the little bitches he had excised so neatly, so skilfully. He was like a surgeon: a better surgeon than his father had ever been.

The sudden thought of his father caused the fear he had contained to surge. His crouching here, the dark, the cold air – all this wiped out the years, and delivered him back into the pitiful boy's body he had worked so hard to escape. Hiding, waiting for the blows that inevitably came, no matter how well or how long he might hide. Tohar's father – great doctor that he was – had had the experience, skill and patience needed to lure contagion. For that was what he knew Otis to be. He would wait until hunger or fatigue or a full bladder – any weakness of the body – drove Otis from his hiding place. His father would be there, waiting for him. He would then shake his head resignedly and – his elegant fingers a vice around the boy's arm – take Otis to his sister's room. The thought of his sister now unleashed in Tohar a hot flow of rage that drove the ice of fear ahead of it. His pale sister was always seated in the same place, bound to be still for as long as Otis – hungry, exhausted, racked with the pain of not being able to relieve himself – hid away. Placed by their father in the window seat, she waited to witness his entertainment, Otis's humiliation. There she would sit, forced to watch as their father beat Otis. When he had finished – usually at the point where the boy lost control of his bladder or bowels – their father, the great surgeon, would lift his daughter's skirt and make a precise incision alongside each of the others that marked the boy's beatings. Then he would leave the girl, a mute witness now marked by what she had seen, to clean up the room and her brother as best she could.

The footsteps so close to him yanked Otis Tohar back to the present. The feel of the cold metal pressed against the back of his neck was unpleasant. The rough voice in his ear was laced with menace.

'Stand up, Mr Tohar,' it said. 'You are under arrest.' Tohar rose slowly. His head throbbed where Theresa had hit him. Surely that would count against her when he explained how she had assaulted him.

'Of course, Officer.' Tohar turned round to see a man whose face was unshaven, whose eyes were bloodshot, and whose clothes were cheap, ill-fitting. 'Who might you be?' he asked with cool politeness.

'Riedwaan Faizal,' answered the man. He kept the gun trained on Tohar. He had a pair of handcuffs which, to Tohar's surprise, he seemed intent on using. Then he turned Tohar around and pulled his arms sharply behind his back, snapping the cuffs around his wrists.

The uniformed policeman with Faizal turned Tohar around again and, to his amazement, spat at him. *'Kom, vuilgoed,'* he ordered, twisting his arms painfully upwards.

Riedwaan led him away, but as they passed the flickering television, Tohar pulled back. The final scenes of the film were playing out. Tohar tried to get a clearer look at the image of the girl jerking pathetically as he held his powerful hand over her mouth. It was hard to make out who she was, as her face was covered. He thought it might be the previous one. The one before this little cunt, who'd got away. He felt a delicious tightening in the groin as the girl gave a final spasm and then lay still.

Riedwaan Faizal shoved him forward. Tohar felt a blinding flash of pain as Faizal pushed his cuffed arms up even higher.

'You've dislocated my shoulder,' Tohar gasped indignantly.

'Oh, shit,' said Faizal, his voice a malignant hiss in Tohar's ear. 'But that'll be the least of your worries, where you're going. A handsome fellow like you is going to have lots of fun.'

Tohar stared helplessly, impassively, as the meaning of Faizal's words sank in.

'A slow puncture is what you'll get, I'd imagine,' said Faizal, his voice so low that only Tohar could hear. 'That's something that can be easily arranged.'

Riedwaan Faizal took the film from the camera and put it into his pocket. 'This will be interesting viewing, I'm sure. As good as a confession.'

'I have nothing to say without my lawyer,' said Tohar. 'And I'm sure he will be most interested in your threats.'

As he led Tohar to the police van, Riedwaan sneered, 'Okay, but let's see how you feel in the morning.' Then he handed him over to the uniformed police. 'Get Phiri to book him. I'm sure it'll give him a kick to do the honours.'

Riedwaan turned away, lit a cigarette, and dragged on it as if his life depended on it. He watched Clare talking to Joe Zulu, uncomfortable about breaking into their easy chat. But he forced himself to go over to her.

'Well done, Clare,' he said. Riedwaan put his arms around her. She leaned into his embrace.

'Don't you need to do all the formalities?'

'Superintendent Phiri will. He loves things like that. Let him have something to keep himself busy. In any case, there are the tapes, so a confession will hardly be necessary.' Riedwaan had seen the tapes stacked on the shelf. 'Each one was padlocked into a heart-shaped box. Wedding videos.'

'The keys,' whispered Clare. 'The flowers.' She looked over at Tohar. He was arguing with Rita Mhkize about being put in the back of the van. Rita turned to Joe Zulu who had gone over to help. The two of them bundled Tohar in. Rita slammed the doors shut. Clare heard Tohar yelp as the heavy doors hit his legs.

'So sorry, sir,' said Rita, dragging the keys across the mesh. She jumped in and started the car.

Clare sat down on the pavement. She wanted to go home, but she was unable to move. She watched Riedwaan filling in forms and talking to Joe Zulu. He had bagged the tapes and handed them to Phiri. Clare hoped that there would be enough other evidence to convict Tohar so that the parents of the murdered girls would never see the records of their daughters' deaths. Riedwaan patted his pockets. She knew that he was looking for his keys. Clare told herself that it was for the best that he was going home. She would not have to tiptoe around another person's heart. Life was just easier on your own. She would strip her bed when she got home and sleep in clean sheets.

'Are you all right?' Riedwaan helped Clare up onto her feet.

'I'm fine,' she said. 'Just drained, now that it's over.'

Riedwaan stroked her cheek, then moved his hand surely down the side of her neck. 'Shall I take you home now?' he asked.

Clare was too tired to resist. She nodded and followed him

towards her flat, ignoring the whistles from the uniforms. She needed a man's body in her bed tonight.

Once home, she drifted into sleep, waking very briefly to feel his hands warm on her skin. The fragment of a dream – a car trailing a plume of dust behind it – was already fading. She leaned over to kiss the sleeping man. Riedwaan smiled and pulled her towards him, holding her fast against his chest.

EPILOGUE

Landman is back at his desk. It is very late and the only sound above the distant roar of the surf is the mournful blast of the foghorn. His ears, lulled by the near silence, fail to alert him to the tiny click-click of a key turned deep inside the house. Neither does he sense the silent shadow as it moves down the stairs. He is absorbed in the columns of numbers in front of him. They do not add up, will not add up. He gets up, paces, then sits down in a leather wingback chair. The slow burn of anger in the pit of his stomach ignites into rage at Otis Tohar. The roar of his own blood distracts him so that when the voice – steady, clear – says, 'Look at me,' he turns instinctively.

A girl is standing in the doorway. She looks familiar. Cradled in her hand is a revolver. It gleams dully. The blind, round eye looks unblinkingly at him. He laughs, amused. When he stops laughing the silence is stifling. She moves the steady eye of the gun slowly downwards from his face to the arrogant splay of his thighs. She fires once. He laughs again in surprise, clutching at his groin. His manicured hands are drenched with the rhythmic spurt of arterial blood.

She smiles, lowers the gun and steps back. She closes the door. He stays calm, staunching the blood with one hand. With the other he scrabbles for his phone. Panic overwhelms him as he realises that this is the other thing that she has taken from him.

'Bitch.' His voice is already fading.

There is nothing to do but drag on the cigarette in his ashtray and hope that someone will come.

Whitney lets herself out of the front door. The car is waiting, its engine idling. The door slams shut behind her. She leans over to the woman at the steering-wheel and lifts the curtain of hair. Whitney kisses the scarred cheek and lets the hair swing back. The woman traces the healed brand under Whitney's T-shirt.

They drive north. An hour later the city is behind them. They turn off the tar road. The dust rises and hovers above them. It hides them – though there is nobody watching. Constance Hart is heading home. To a house she has not returned to in the twenty years since Kelvin Landman began his career by carving his mark on her back. Whitney sits besides her, cleaning her stolen gun calmly and efficiently. She hums. It is not a tune that Constance knows yet, but she joins her anyway.